Dubious about the Duke

Second Sons of London
Book Five

Alexa Aston

ARE YOU SIGNED UP FOR DRAGONBLADE'S BLOG?

You'll get the latest news and information on exclusive giveaways, exclusive excerpts, coming releases, sales, free books, cover reveals and more.

Check out our complete list of authors, too!

No spam, no junk. That's a promise!

Sign Up Here

www.dragonbladepublishing.com

>>>><<<<

Dearest Reader;

Thank you for your support of a small press. At Dragonblade Publishing, we strive to bring you the highest quality Historical Romance from some of the best authors in the business. Without your support, there is no 'us', so we sincerely hope you adore these stories and find some new favorite authors along the way.

Happy Reading!

CEO, Dragonblade Publishing

Additional Dragonblade books by Author Alexa Aston

Second Sons of London Series
Educated By The Earl
Debating With The Duke
Empowered By The Earl
Made for the Marquess
Dubious about the Duke

Dukes Done Wrong Series
Discouraging the Duke
Deflecting the Duke
Disrupting the Duke
Delighting the Duke
Destiny with a Duke

Dukes of Distinction Series
Duke of Renown
Duke of Charm
Duke of Disrepute
Duke of Arrogance
Duke of Honor

The St. Clairs Series
Devoted to the Duke
Midnight with the Marquess
Embracing the Earl
Defending the Duke
Suddenly a St. Clair
Starlight Night
The Twelve Days of Love (Novella)

Soldiers & Soulmates Series
To Heal an Earl
To Tame a Rogue

To Trust a Duke
To Save a Love
To Win a Widow
Yuletide at Gillingham (Novella)

The Lyon's Den Connected World
The Lyon's Lady Love

King's Cousins Series
The Pawn
The Heir
The Bastard

Medieval Runaway Wives
Song of the Heart
A Promise of Tomorrow
Destined for Love

Knights of Honor Series
Word of Honor
Marked by Honor
Code of Honor
Journey to Honor
Heart of Honor
Bold in Honor
Love and Honor
Gift of Honor
Path to Honor
Return to Honor

Pirates of Britannia Series
God of the Seas

De Wolfe Pack: The Series
Rise of de Wolfe

The de Wolfes of Esterley Castle
Diana
Derek
Thea

PROLOGUE

Ontario, Upper Canada—September 1812

SERAPHINA NICHOLLS BRUSHED her long, auburn hair as she gazed into the mirror. Tonight was another assembly and she would get to see Captain Edward Marsh. The thought of the handsome English officer caused her to smile.

For the first time, someone was interested in her more than her twin.

Sera loved Minta more than anyone on this earth. Her sister, however, was far more outgoing than Sera. Because of that, even though they favored one another, people always noticed Minta first and were drawn to her vivacity. Sera sometimes felt she observed life from the shadow of her twin, who had been born seven minutes before Sera had made her arrival in the world.

Captain Marsh had proven different from everyone in that he had greeted Minta that first time and then immediately turned his attentions to Sera. She had a hard time with people she did not know and found it difficult to open up to strangers. Sometimes, in a large group, she found her throat paralyzed, nothing coming out. Minta always looked after her on these occasions, fiercely protective of her barely younger sister.

Captain Marsh seemed to see something in Sera that she didn't even see in herself. She had discovered he also was shy with others and that they had a love of animals and nature. He hailed from the north of England and had been in His Majesty's army for seven years. England had been at war with Bonaparte since Sera was a young girl and now war had also come to North America, thanks to the Americans hoping to capitalize on England's attention being on the Little Corporal in Europe. She dreaded the day when Captain Marsh would have to leave Ontario.

Minta burst into the room, a whirlwind as usual, and smiled brightly. "Oh, good. You chose the yellow. I think it is prettier on you. Let me fasten you up and then you can help me to dress."

Sera helped her twin don a blue gown, which brought out the blue in Minta's eyes. They shared a wardrobe since both were the identical size, curvy and a few inches over five feet. Where Sera had auburn hair, Minta's was more copper in color. They also served as one another's lady's maid since they only had a handful of servants. Their father, Sir Radford Nicholls, had been appointed by the British government as the chief assistant to the Administrator of Upper Canada. Though the position was prestigious, a government salary did not stretch far and she and Minta had decorated their home in Ontario on a tight budget. They did have a cook and one maid, as well as a washerwoman who came in twice a week to do their household's laundry, but Sera and Minta handled many of the household responsibilities in place of their mother.

As she buttoned Minta's gown, Sera swallowed her sadness. She missed Mama terribly. When her father had been named to this new post in Canada, he had taken his girls with him, leaving his wife behind in England. Their maternal grandfather was quite ill and the doctor had said he only had a couple of weeks to live. Papa had urged Mama to stay with him in his final days and then she could sail to Ontario after the funeral.

That had not occurred, thanks to the Americans declaring war upon England. All passenger traffic between England and Canada had stopped, with only warships sailing the Atlantic recently. Mama was stuck in London and separated from her family though a letter had gotten through, revealing she was living with her sister, Lady Westlake, and her husband in town.

Sera loved Aunt Phyllis and Uncle West, who had never been blessed with children. They spent a majority of their year in London and so Sera and Minta had seen the pair frequently since they, too, lived in town year-round with Papa's post in the government. It comforted her some, knowing Mama was with them, but it did nothing to fill the emptiness inside Sera's heart. Of the twins, she was much closer to Mama than Minta was. Minta and Papa were peas in a pod and cut from the same cloth, both lively and outgoing, drawing others to them. Mama and Sera were much more reserved and understood one another when no one else did, no words necessary. Although Sera knew her twin had missed their mother, it was Sera who suffered more from Mama's absence in their lives.

She finished dressing Minta and said, "Let me do your hair now."

Her twin sat at their shared dressing table as Sera brushed the long locks, braiding them and pinning them up. They traded places and Minta styled Sera's hair, placing it in a low chignon as Sera requested. Captain Marsh had complimented the style on her only last week and she wanted to wear it in the same fashion to please him.

"Are you looking forward to tonight's assembly?" Minta asked, smiling. "Especially since a certain army captain is to be in attendance?"

Heat filled her cheeks and she nodded. "I hope Captain Marsh will ask me to dance tonight."

Minta chuckled. "He always asks you to dance, Sera. He is most taken with you." She wrapped her arms about Sera and hugged her tightly. "I hope he will have the good sense to offer for you."

Sera had the same hopes. Though she and Minta had been promised a Season in London, courtesy of their uncle and aunt, she had never had the desire to attend all the social affairs. Unlike Minta, who talked about the Season all the time, Sera had dreaded the thought of attending events with dozens—up to hundreds—of people, strangers she did not know. She had no desire to marry a title, which is what most girls making their come-outs wished for. Captain Marsh would do quite nicely.

If he offered marriage, that is.

She thought to how her parents had been a love match. Mama and Aunt Phyllis had made their come-outs together, with Aunt Phyllis wedding an earl at the end of their Season. Mama, on the other hand, had sorely disappointed her parents when she married a man they considered far below her socially. Though they may have lacked in some material possession, Sera saw her parents were deeply in love and that love was the food that fed their family.

"Do you love Captain Marsh?" Minta asked out of the blue.

Startled, Sera struggled to reply. Finally, she said, "I don't know. I like him. I enjoy being in his company. As for love, I don't know if it will blossom between us or not before he must go to the front."

Minta gazed upon her with sympathy. "That will be soon, I'm afraid."

Tears stung her eyes. "I know. I will merely live in the moment tonight and enjoy what time I can spend with him."

They went downstairs, where Papa awaited them, complimenting how they both looked. The assembly hall was a mere four blocks away. Linking arms with their father in the center, the three made their way there.

Once they arrived, Sera immediately searched the room, seeing several officers already present. These Canadian assemblies were fairly informal and no dance cards were ever issued to the ladies in attendance. Instead, a gentleman would ask for the upcoming dance.

A thrill shot through her as she saw Captain Marsh making his way toward them. She smiled widely, not bothering to disguise her growing feelings for the handsome young officer.

He reached them and bowed, saying, "Miss Nicholls. Miss Nicholls. It is good to see the both of you this evening."

His gaze remained upon Sera as two other officers joined them, obviously wishing to speak with Minta. Her sister winked at her and led the men away in order for Sera to have private time with the captain.

"Are you engaged for this first dance, Miss Nicholls?" he asked.

"I am if you ask me," she replied saucily, which was very out of character for her.

He looked taken aback for a moment and then smiled sunnily. "Then I am doing the asking, Miss Nicholls."

"And I am accepting, Captain Marsh."

They danced the first set and then Sera danced the second with a friend of Captain Marsh. No one asked to partner with her during the third set but she found Captain Marsh at her elbow.

"Would you care for some punch, Miss Nicholls? Then perhaps we might stroll outside."

Her pulse quickened and she said, "That would be agreeable, Captain."

He led her to the punchbowl and handed her a cup before offering his arm. They took a turn about the room, watching the dancers and sipping their punch. Once she had finished it, he took their cups and set them on a nearby table and walked her through the doors to the outside.

There were gardens behind the assembly hall and several benches scattered about. He led her to one and seated himself close to her, so close that their hips and thighs brushed. Then he slipped his hand around hers and squeezed it gently, causing her heart to skip a beat.

"I have two things to say to you tonight, Miss Nicholls. One is how much I have enjoyed your company since I met you."

"The feeling is mutual, Captain Marsh. I find that it is easier to talk with you than just about anyone else of my acquaintance."

He squeezed her fingers again and smiled. Then his smile faded and he said, "We will be shipping out in two days' time."

Though Sera had known this day was coming, it was like a punch to her gut. She sat wordlessly, not knowing how to reply.

"I do not wish to ask you to make any type of commitment to me. It would be unfair to you in case you met someone else during my absence. I do want you to know, however, that I hold you in great esteem and when this war with the Americans ends, I would like to come back and be allowed to court you if you are still free."

Sera knew what he was saying. The possibility he might be killed in battle hung over them and he did not wish for them to be officially linked by a betrothal.

"I will wait for you, Captain Marsh," she said softly. "I do not need a formal declaration or understanding between us. I will write to you as I hope you will to me when you can and when this war is done, we can see what the future holds for us."

He continued to hold her hand but his free one cradled her cheek, his thumb stroking it, bringing a delightful chill that ran along her spine. "I care for you, Sera," he said, using her Christian name for the first time. "I will do my bloody best not to be killed in this conflict and come back to you."

Then he bent, his lips brushing her softly for the briefest of moments.

When he raised his head, she saw love for her in his eyes. While she cared for him a great deal, she really couldn't say she was in love with him. It relieved her that he did not bring up the word and they sat for another quarter-hour, holding hands, a comfortable silence between them.

"We should return inside," he suggested. "I would like the opportunity to dance with you a final time."

She gazed at him, a lone tear cascading down her cheek. "I would like that very much, Edward."

They returned to the assembly room and as they danced, Sera tried to emblazon this moment in her memory. The sound of the music. The scent of his shaving soap. The feel of his hand in hers.

When the assembly ended, he bowed formally to her. "Until we meet again, Miss Nicholls."

Sera watched him walk away, carrying a piece of her heart with him.

CHAPTER ONE

London—April 1816

WIN CUTLER, THE Duke of Woodmont, looked on as his cousin spoke his wedding vows. Percy had always been not only his cousin but his closest friend. The pair had gone to school together, followed by university, and then as second sons were destined to do, they entered the military together.

He glanced about, seeing his other fellow Second Sons, the small society he had formed with his dearest friends, a group he had been a part of for many years. He looked at Ev, who was now the Duke of Camden. Ev had grown up next door to Owen, now the Earl of Danbury. Their third friend, Spence, was the Earl of Middlefield. When he and Percy had met this trio at Cambridge and the five had bonded together, they had even referred to themselves as the Second Sons of London, since all planned to go into military service after their university days.

They had spent most of their twenties together on the battlefield since England was at war with Bonaparte. Through a unique set of circumstances, however, one by one, the Second Sons sold their commissions and returned from the Continent to take up titles which they had not been raised to assume. Some, like Owen, had claimed a title from a brother he loved dearly. Others, such as Win, took the mantle from a sibling he couldn't stand and had never been close to.

Win had been the last of the Second Sons to inherit a peerage. His older brother, Terrance, had died in a den of iniquity, lost in a ghastly fire at a gaming hell which also catered to the darker side of men's desires. The fire and Terrance's subsequent death had allowed Win to join his fellow Second Sons in England. Since he had been ignored by his father in favor of the heir apparent and knew absolutely nothing of ducal responsibilities, three of the Second Sons had stepped up before the Season began, each one of them coming to Essex and guiding him through what he needed to learn in order to help Woodbridge, his country estate, to thrive. Win also had four other estates scattered about England and would be visiting them over the next year.

He turned his attention back to the ceremony as Percy and Minta spoke their vows to one another. He had worried for a long time about Percy, whom he had shared a tent with at war, and the nightmares which had plagued his cousin. Win hoped by leaving the army that Percy had put all of that behind him. It was exciting to see his shy, retiring cousin with such a huge grin upon his face as he gazed at his lovely, copper-haired bride. The Season was only two weeks old and already here was Percy joining the ranks of the other Second Sons with a wife.

Win knew one of his responsibilities would be to provide an heir for the dukedom. Ev's wife, Adalyn, had a reputation as a bit of a matchmaker and wanted to help Win in this endeavor. He had skipped this current Season in favor of learning more about his estates and working on them but he had promised Owen's wife, Louisa, that he would attend a house party she was giving at the end of the Season in late August. Whether he found a bride there or not remained to be seen. Win enjoyed a good romp in bed with a pretty woman but he doubted the cold fish of the *ton* would enjoy sex as much as he did. He supposed he would have a marriage much like his parents did, one where they barely could stand the sight of one another, but still did their duty and provided an heir and a spare to the dukedom.

His parents were long gone now. Terrance, who had been a good eight years older than his younger brother and pushing forty, hadn't acquired a wife. It would now fall to Win to see that the dukedom remained intact with an heir.

He studied his fellow Second Sons, all who had made love matches, despite that being rare among Polite Society. Spence held Tessa's hand in his. Ev had his arm wrapped about Adalyn's shoulders. Owen whispered something into Louisa's ear and she bestowed a radiant smile upon him as he took her hand and kissed her fingers. Win was unused to any public display of affection and was pleased for his friends—and Percy—who seemed happy in his choice of a marchioness.

Win decided love had already struck four times among the Second Sons and doubted it could happen a fifth time. He would trust in Adalyn and agree to offer for the woman she chose for him. But he would keep his feelings intact. Marriage, in his opinion, should be conducted as a business, while a mistress would be for his pleasure.

The ceremony concluded and Percy kissed his bride for much longer than was suitable, causing all the Second Sons to chuckle. Percy broke the kiss and looked out sheepishly at those gathered, which included Minta's aunt and uncle, Lord and Lady Westlake.

The clergyman announced the couple by their titles and Adalyn, as hostess, invited everyone to leave the drawing room and move to where the wedding breakfast would be held. Win found himself seated with Owen and Louisa, who caught him up on the particulars of Percy's and Minta's romance.

He finished eating and sat back, satisfied to be in the company of his closest friends, men he trusted with his life, both on the battlefield and even now as civilians. The first three wives, who were cousins and affectionately known as the Three Cousins, had taken Minta under their wings. He believed he would grow close to all these wives and, one day, consider them as sisters.

Percy and Minta began circulating in order to speak to their guests. He found himself with Minta.

"I am delighted to make your acquaintance, Your Grace," she said.

"No," he said, shaking his head. "There will be none of that *Your Grace-ing*. I know in this close circle that we are as family and so you should call me Win. It is short for Winston, a name I loathe, though Win will do nicely."

The red-headed beauty gave him a sweet smile. "Then Win it shall be," she proclaimed.

He asked her a few questions about her background and learned she had a twin who would be arriving sometime in June from Canada.

"Once your sister arrives, please send word to Woodbridge. I would be happy to come to town for a couple of days and meet her. Will she come to Kingwood once you and Percy leave town or will she live with your aunt and uncle until your parents arrive from Ontario?"

"Although Aunt Phyllis and Uncle West have assumed that Sera will stay with them, I am hoping she will make an extended visit to the country. My aunt and uncle choose to remain in London a good portion of the year. Sera loves nature and animals. I believe she would be happier at Kingwood with me."

He smiled. "It must have been hard to have been separated from her," he noted.

The new marchioness nodded solemnly. "Yes, we had never spent a night apart from one another but Sera wanted to spend more time with our mother, who had only recently arrived in Canada. She had been stuck in London during the war with the Americans."

A shadow crossed Minta's face. "Sera also had a sweetheart, an English army captain, who perished during the Battle of Lundy's Lane, one of the fiercest of the war. I think she needed a little time to grieve over his death."

"Were they betrothed?" he asked, sympathy for Minta's twin filling him.

"No, there was no formal understanding between them but

he had made his intentions clear that he wished to court her upon his return. Though Sera is arriving in the middle of the Season, she does not wish to jump into any events. She will, however, attend the house party which Louisa and Owen are giving. I hope that you will also be in attendance, Win. I would like the opportunity to get to know you better as I have the other Second Sons. I have come to look upon the Three Cousins as my sisters and the Second Sons as the brothers I never had."

"I do plan to be at the house party," he informed her. "Adalyn said she will be working on my behalf to find me a wife now that Percy is taken care of."

He smiled. "Who knows? Perhaps your sister and I will be matched together," and he chuckled.

Percy joined them and Minta excused herself.

"What do you think of my bride?" his cousin asked.

"I think Minta will make an admirable marchioness and that you will be just as much in love as the other Second Sons are."

Percy winced and Win found that interesting.

"Do you love Minta?" he pressed.

"Unfortunately, I do. But I don't feel I deserve her."

Win frowned. "I had the impression that you were a love match as the other Second Sons and their wives are."

Percy shook his head vehemently. "No words of love have been spoken and none will ever be spoken on my part."

Win's eyebrows rose and he said. "So, you intend to have a typical *ton* marriage?"

His cousin looked uncomfortable but nodded. Win didn't think it would last long. His cousin already loved his new wife and from what he could tell, Minta returned those feelings. Perhaps she had been wise to keep those words to herself, knowing how withdrawn her new husband could be. Still, Win thought by the next time he saw them, come June when Sera Nicholls arrived in London, that it would be a different story.

He introduced himself to Lord and Lady Westlake and had a pleasant conversation with the pair. Then it was time to wish the happy couple goodbye. He walked out with them and returned inside just as the Westlakes were also taking their leave.

Win had something on his mind and he told Ev he needed to speak to the Second Sons for advice.

Ev grinned. "You think a conversation will go on in which our wives are left out? Think again, old friend."

Ev's words startled Win. He was used to women being ornamental, left in the background. His mother had an almost nonexistent role in her two sons' lives and he'd had no sisters. He had spent his entire adult life in the army, sampling the wares of the traveling whores and, every now and then, coupling with a pretty widow in a village the army passed.

"I am not certain they wish to be included in this conversation, Ev."

Ev laughed aloud. "Then you don't know my Addie, much less Tessa or Louisa. They are a part of us, Win. The three of us—and now Percy—have married strong, independent, intelligent women. None of us would ever shut them out from an important conversation."

Ev's words were clear and so Win nodded in acquiescence. "Then let us join them and I will tell you about my dilemma."

They went to the drawing room and Ev told the others that Win had something he wished to share with them.

"I am seeking your advice on whether to pursue a matter and if I do choose to do so, how to go about it."

He glanced about the circle. "I assume everyone present knows how my brother died. Violently, in a fire." He watched them nod and continued. "Terrance was a horrible man and I have heard rumors that Terrance has a few bastards which he did nothing for. I think the right thing to do is to find them and provide for them," he stated.

"I think that is admirable, Win," Tessa said. "You are displaying honor and concern, which speaks highly of your character. You will bring luster back to the Woodmont name."

"I agree," Louisa added. "Who knows where these poor

children are living and how they are being provided for, if at all. You taking responsible for your brother's issue is admirable."

"I suggest that you hire a Bow Street Runner," Adalyn said. "They have connections everywhere and have a good success rate in matters such as these."

He found it interesting that all comments and advice were coming from the women and not his friends. He glanced about and saw the three men nodding their approval.

"I am not familiar with what a Bow Street Runner does, I'm afraid. I thought they were some type of police force here in town. Would you explain it to me and tell me how I might go about hiring one?"

"It is true in the past that Bow Street and their magistrates worked more to round up criminals," Owen said. "They still have a Day Patrol, which does not wear a uniform. These men walk the streets in various jurisdictions and the Foot Patrol takes over for them during the evenings until midnight. These men who walk the streets make certain connections with those citizens as they are out and about."

"There is also a Horse Patrol," Ev noted. "Although they might not be as helpful in this instance."

"Where Bow Street used to focus on crime, they now investigate other matters," Spence said. "From national security to social disorder."

"Yet they still take on cases for members of the *ton*," Adalyn emphasized. "Finding the by-blows the previous Woodmont sired would be something they would be likely to investigate. Their offices are on Bow Street, Win. You should speak to the chief magistrate and see if he believes this is an issue the runners might pursue."

He nodded slowly. "Yes, I believe a private investigator is what is called for in these circumstances. I have spoken to several of the servants, both here and at Woodbridge. From the little they know, it seems they believe there are two children out there with Terrance's blood running through their veins. I think it is the right thing to find them and see to their needs. Their mothers, as well."

"The runners will use the information you have and take to the streets. They have sources in every walk of life and at every level of society," Owen confirmed. "They most likely will look into foundling homes since the children might have been placed there." He paused. "There is the possibility that they did not survive their births, though. Life is harsh for unmarried women."

Determination filled him. "I think I will go to Bow Street now and talk to this chief magistrate." He stood. "Thank you for listening to my quandary. Your advice will help me take the next step in finding these children."

"If you do find them, Win, remember they are not merely children. They are your nephews and nieces," Louisa reminded.

He hadn't given the matter that much thought beyond wanting to right whatever wrongs Terrance had perpetrated and seeing that his bastards had roofs over their heads and clothes on their backs, as well as food on their tables.

"Do you think I should bring them to Woodbridge?" he asked, shocked by the idea.

Tessa, who sat nearby, placed a hand on Win's sleeve. "You will know the best thing to do when the time comes." She squeezed his arm reassuringly.

Win hoped she was right.

CHAPTER TWO

London—June 1816

EXCITEMENT RIPPLED THROUGH Sera as the ship moved closer to the dock. She scanned the crowd below and found Minta. They began waving wildly at one another. Her twin then turned to two men standing behind her, gesturing and pointing.

Who could they be?

She supposed they might be suitors of Minta's, gentlemen her sister had met during this current Season, and wondered if Minta had brought them to the docks so that Sera might meet them and pass judgment. She glanced at the one on the left. He was tall, with dark blond hair and an athletic frame and quite pleasing to the eye. The other was slightly taller, his shoulders broad and his frame more muscular.

He was also devastatingly handsome.

She swallowed, her gaze connecting with his for a moment even from a distance. He nodded to her and she did the same. She supposed this was the one Minta would prefer because of his looks and size. Sera would be intimidated by a man so large.

She glanced back to the other one and then noticed her aunt and uncle now stood next to him. Her smile widened and she waved again. Aunt Phyllis began blowing her kisses and Uncle West beamed at her. Oh, how she had missed the two of them!

It took several minutes for the ship to dock. During that time, Sera made her way to the gangplank. She wanted to be the first off the ship.

Finally, a crew member removed the barrier and nodded at her. She went flying down the gangplank and saw Minta charging up it. The twins met halfway and fell into one another's arms, laughing and crying at the same time.

"I have missed you so much," Minta said, pulling back and looking Sera in the eyes. "We can never be separated like this again." Her twin embraced her once more, hugging her tightly.

"Can we get by?" a voice called.

Turning, Sera saw they were blocking the way of other passengers who wished to disembark. Slipping her arm through Minta's, they moved quickly down the rest of the gangplank and moved toward their aunt and uncle.

"You look beautiful," Sera told her sister as they walked. "You are glowing."

Minta paused and faced her. "It is because I am in love," she declared.

Sera wondered if that were the case, why had Minta brought two suitors to meet her? Then she swallowed, worried that her twin meant one of the gentlemen for her. Panic filled her. She wasn't ready to meet strangers, much less be paired off with a gentleman.

"I feel the tension pouring through you," her twin observed and stopped their movement. "What's wrong? Are you upset that I have found my soulmate?"

"Of course not," she protested weakly.

Being separated from Minta had been bad enough—but marriage would separate them for good. Minta would wed and her new husband would want his wife all to himself, not wanting a sister to be hanging about.

"You will adore Percy," Minta said. "I do believe he is at least as shy as—if not more so—than you."

"Truly?"

Minta nodded. "It is one of the things that drew me to him, oddly enough. You know how outgoing I am. Yet Percy called out to me in a way I cannot explain." She paused. "We are already wed, Sera. I am now the Marchioness of Kingston."

Shock rippled through her. "You . . . are already wed? But . . . the Season has yet to end."

It worried her that Minta had wed so quickly. Her twin had a tendency to be impulsive. Oh, why hadn't she waited to hear what Sera thought of this marquess?

But Minta had said she was in love. Her headstrong sister's emotions ran strong. If Minta truly loved this man, then nothing would have stopped her.

"He deliberately compromised me at a garden party," Minta revealed, mischief lighting her eyes.

"He . . . ruined you? And yet you love him?" Confusion filled Sera. "But you said he was reserved. This makes no sense at all, Minta."

Her sister hugged her. "Oh, I have so much to tell you, Sera. Just know that Percy loved me and wanted me so much that he acted totally out of character. He was afraid some other gentleman would dazzle me. And then there was that wicked Lady Vickers who tried to tarnish my name and blackmail Percy."

"What?"

Minta laughed. "You'll hear it all. I am sorry I am speaking in riddles. Come meet Percy. He's here with Aunt Phyllis and Uncle West. Percy's cousin, the Duke of Woodmont, also came to welcome you back to England."

So, it was a duke who was the other man beside Minta's handsome new husband. Well, Sera wasn't in any mood to meet new people. All she wanted was to be with her family. Besides, a duke would be intimidating. That was the last person Sera wished to be around. Of course, he was the marquess' cousin and had been gracious enough to be a party to those greeting her. She would do her best to look him in the eyes and be polite. Then she hoped he would be gone.

Minta took her arm again and they started toward those who had come to meet her ship. When they reached her aunt and uncle, Sera broke away and fell into Aunt Phyllis' arms.

"Oh, my dear," her aunt cooed. "My wonderful Sera. How you have been missed."

Tears sprang to her eyes as she hugged Aunt Phyllis. Her aunt and uncle were childless and had been like a second set of parents to Minta and her. In fact, it was Uncle West who had paid for Minta's new wardrobe for this Season and he was to do the same next spring for Sera when she made her come-out into Polite Society.

"I love you," she told her aunt.

"Come here," Uncle West said gruffly, pulling her into a bear hug. "That's my girl."

She felt as if she had come home, being with her twin and these family members. Not that she wouldn't miss her parents, but Sera knew they would be traveling back to England next spring. It had been several years since she had seen Aunt Phyllis and Uncle West. She supposed she would live with them since Minta was now a married woman.

Her sister pulled on her arm. "Let her go, Uncle West. I must introduce her to Percy."

Her uncle relaxed his hold on her and kissed her cheek. "It is good to have you in our fold again, Sera."

"I feel the same," she said, misty-eyed.

Turning, she faced the two gentlemen and swallowed hard, trying not to be bashful. After all, one was her brother-in-law and she would be seeing him frequently in the decades to come. The other was his cousin and that gentleman might come to feel like family in the future.

Much to her surprise, Minta slipped her arm through the arm of the man Sera had assumed to be the cousin.

"Sera, this is Percy, the Marquess of Kingston," her sister said, pride in her voice and her obvious love for the marquess evident on her face. "Percy, this is my better half." She chuckled. "At least the better behaved half of the Nicholls' girls.'"

The marquess gave her a shy smile and they looked at one another for a moment. In that brief space of time, Sera believed she had found a kindred spirit.

She curtseyed. "It is lovely to meet you, Lord Kingston. Minta would not easily have been swayed into marriage so I know that you are someone who is very special."

He grinned unabashedly. "The sun rises and sets on Minta as far as I am concerned. Fortunately, she took a liking to me." He glanced down at his wife. "And I love her with all my heart."

The marquess then lightly kissed Minta, shocking Sera. People simply didn't go about kissing one another in public, especially members of the *ton*.

Her twin laughed and, in that laughter, Sera saw how happy her sister was. To think a shy marquess had won Minta over spoke a great deal on Lord Kingston's behalf.

"You must call me Percy," he told her. "I insist. I wasn't supposed to be a marquess. My brother, Rupert, held the title. Unfortunately, I lost him far too soon." He looked wistful. "I will admit I am still getting used to being a peer of the realm. But I know how close you and Minta are and I refuse to stand upon any formality. You are my sister. I am your brother."

Turning, the marquess indicated the duke. "And this is my dearest friend in the world and also my cousin, the Duke of Woodmont."

Sera forced her eyes up in order to meet the duke's. She swallowed hard. This man was like a god come to life, more handsome than any she had ever seen. His size dwarfed her and she thought he must be almost a foot taller than she was. His dark brown hair had highlights of gold in it and warm, brown eyes gazed at her intently.

Quickly dropping her gaze to her feet, she curtseyed again. "Your Grace," she managed to squeak out.

Suddenly, he captured her hand in his and started away with it. She glanced up and saw he raised it to his sensual lips. Heat filled her cheeks as he kissed it.

And kept holding it.

Sera looked down. Then back up. Then down again, her heart racing violently.

"It is a great pleasure to meet you, Miss Nicholls," he said, his voice as deep and smooth as velvet.

She forced herself to meet his gaze. And couldn't think of a thing to say.

The duke released her hand. "Your sister will find complete happiness now that you have returned to England."

She bit her lip, her throat constricted. She hated this about herself. Although this man was a stranger, he seemed kind. Why couldn't she ever relax around others?

Minta, sensing Sera's distress, came and slipped her arm through Sera's. "We need to go home and have tea. Can a footman see to Sera's luggage?"

"I already sent two on that errand, my love," Percy said.

Sera could sense her sister soften at the endearment, which was so unlike her. Minta had always been practical. Even though their parents were still in love after many years of marriage, Minta had shared with Sera that she wasn't interested in seeking love for herself. That she only wanted a man of good character who would provide well for her and give her children.

Things had certainly changed in the time the twins had been apart.

"Then we should return to the carriage," Minta declared, taking charge of the situation as Sera was used to seeing occur. "Are you coming to tea with us?" she asked her aunt.

"I am afraid we can't," Aunt Phyllis said. "We committed to an event this afternoon. In fact, we should head to it now, else we will be late."

"Then dinner?" Sera suggested.

"Yes, we can do that," Uncle West said.

She said goodbye to her aunt and uncle and they parted. Minta pulled Sera along, chattering away. They arrived at a carriage so grand, she stopped in her tracks.

"This is yours?" she asked.

"I didn't plan on wedding a marquess." Her sister grinned. "But it does have its advantages."

A footman placed stairs down and Percy immediately stepped up, taking his wife's hand and helping her into the carriage. He did the same for Sera.

Inside, Minta said, "Sit there. I know how you dislike riding backward."

She sat, her heart beginning to thump wildly again. If Minta sat across from her, that meant Percy would sit next to his wife.

And that would leave her sitting beside the Duke of Woodmont.

CHAPTER THREE

P ERCY INDICATED FOR Win to climb inside the carriage and he
did so, situating himself next to Sera Nicholls. The faint scent
of jasmine tickled his nose and he realized it came from her.

His cousin joined them. "They are loading your trunks now,
Sera. We should be off soon."

Win didn't mind any extra time spent in the carriage.

Because he was intrigued by his seatmate. More than he
should have been.

He wouldn't disguise the fact that a pretty girl could turn his
head. His friends joked about it, in fact. But Miss Nicholls was
more than a pretty face.

She was breathtaking.

He glanced across at Minta, whom he found rather attractive.
She had sparkling blue eyes and hair which was the shade of
copper. Her sister, on the other hand, had incredibly vivid green
eyes. He'd had to look quickly to note their color because she
gazed at her feet so much. He remembered something said about
her being quite shy and decided that was why she had looked
away so much as they were introduced. He liked her hair's color
better. It was auburn, more brown than red inside the coach, but
on the London docks with the summer sun shining down on it, it
had seemed to catch fire. Win longed to loosen her chignon and
stream his fingers through it.

No, he told himself. Sera Nicholls was not some fancy piece he could play with for a bit and then discard. She was a lady, one who would join their circle of friends. He could already see the Three Cousins stepping in and sheltering Sera, drawing her to them as they offered their friendship to her. Minta would also be a fierce protector of her twin. Win would never wish to be an object of wrath of the wives of the Second Sons.

That meant Sera would be off-limits.

He must think of her as Miss Nicholls. While it was all well and good for Percy to ask his sister-in-law to address him informally, Win was a duke. Even a duke's family members rarely called him by his given name. Instead, they would use his title, while others who fawned over him would always call him "Your Grace". Other than the Second Sons and their wives, no one referred to him as Win. Even his own wife would most likely call him Woodmont.

The thought saddened him. Perhaps he would come to an understanding with the new duchess and at least in private have her call him Win. Then he thought better of it. He knew he wanted a true *ton* marriage—and that meant keeping his distance from the woman who wed him. Yes, he would go to her bed and get children off her, but he did not wish to be particularly close to her.

He breathed in jasmine again and a yearning filled him.

He wanted to kiss Sera Nicholls.

Win swore under his breath.

"I beg your pardon, Your Grace?"

Turning, he saw Miss Nicholls look up at him before her eyes darted away nervously.

"Nothing," he told her. "I just thought of something that I needed to do."

"If you cannot take tea with us, I understand. After all, I am not your relative, am I?"

"Well, we are in a circular way," he said, wishing she would look at him. He glanced and saw Percy and Minta in conversation and decided he needed to draw out this woman with the quiet beauty.

"How did you find Canada, Miss Nicholls?"

He glanced down and saw she twisted her hands in her lap. Then obviously aware she was doing so, she forced them to still.

"It had a rugged beauty," she said softly. "I liked how it was untamed."

"Your sister says you enjoy being out in nature."

Her gaze flew to his and then lowered again. "You have discussed me?"

"Minta was very eager for you to arrive. She missed you tremendously. She spoke of how you prefer the country and nature and hopes you will go to Essex with her and Percy instead of stay in town with Lord and Lady Westlake."

She sighed. "I cannot do that, much as I would like to."

"Why not?" he asked, his curiosity about her growing.

"Minta and Percy are newlyweds. They should have time to be alone and not have me around."

Win cleared his throat and she looked up, those emerald eyes piercing him. "They have been wed over two months now. Besides, Minta truly wants you at Kingwood. So does Percy. He told me so himself."

He didn't think a small, white lie would hurt. It was true Minta did want her twin to stay in the country. And Percy was so besotted with his marchioness that he would agree to anything. Win was actually glad his cousin had told his new wife how he felt about her. Percy had written to Win of it and how Minta returned his love. He couldn't be happier for the pair. Percy had always been so reserved, unless he was around the Second Sons. It pleased him how Minta was bringing Percy out of his shell.

Win wondered how Miss Nicholls' launch into Polite Society would go. Her shyness would lead many to ignore her—even mark her as a wallflower. Of course, he could make a difference. If he danced with her next Season, that would garner plenty of attention. Merely being a duke and seeking her out to partner in a dance would draw interest from others to her. He would have to remember to do so when she made her come-out next spring.

Hope filled her eyes. "You truly don't think Percy would mind hosting me?"

He chuckled. "Kingwood is an enormous estate. You will be given an entire suite of rooms. Why, you could even be given your own wing if you so desired. I know it would make your sister happy to have you with her. She mentioned you will not make your debut until next year."

Miss Nicholls grimaced. "Oh, that."

"You are not eager to join the members of the *ton*?" he pressed, still wanting to learn about her.

She winced. "Not a bit. Minta was always the one talking about having a Season. Aunt Phyllis promised both of us one but we were stuck in Ontario when that time came. I would prefer not to move among the *ton*."

"You are bashful. Retiring."

She nodded. "Very. In case you haven't noticed."

He noticed she smiled now, albeit one that was hard to catch since she kept her eyes focused on her hands in her lap.

"I haven't been out in society myself," he shared.

Her head snapped up. "Why not?"

"I am the last of the Second Sons to return to England."

When she frowned, he realized she did not know the term.

"There are five of us. Percy and I grew up on neighboring estates and knew each other from the cradle. Ev, Owen, and Spence went to school together. We all met up at Cambridge and became fast friends, dubbing ourselves the Second Sons of London because our older brothers were the first sons and heirs apparent."

"Go on," she encouraged, for once looking him in the eyes for more than a few seconds.

"We five had commissions purchased for us and went off to war together. Fortune smiled upon us, as we were all placed in the same or neighboring regiments."

"As officers?"

"Yes. Then, one by one, odd circumstances touched each of our lives, and we returned to England to claim a title never meant to be ours. Spence was the first, followed by Ev, then Owen, and finally Percy. I brought up the rear." He smiled. "I preferred to learn about my estates instead of gallivanting about during the Season. My friends each spent time at Woodbridge, tutoring me regarding my responsibilities and position in Polite Society. I have spent the entire Season on my estates, learning."

Her brows knit together, puzzled. "Then why are you here today?"

"Because Percy means the world to me. I told him and Minta I would come to town to welcome you back to England."

What Win didn't mention was that he already had plans to come to London since he had received word from Jack Blumer. The Bow Street Runner told him he had located Terrance's two bastards and that it was important for Win to hurry to London. They were to meet tomorrow morning, where he hoped the detective would be able to give him information about Terrance's by-blows.

"That was most kind of you, Your Grace. You must care for your cousin a great deal."

"Percy is more brother to me than cousin," he shared. "My own brother cared little for me. He was over eight years my senior and had nothing to do with me. He was a terrible man. A blight on the Cutler name."

Miss Nicholls looked taken aback by his vehemence.

"Forgive me. I am still angry at many things my brother did. When I returned from overseas after I resigned my commission, I found Terrance had neglected his tenants and country estates, spending most of his time in town, deep in his cups. Fortunately, the Woodbridge steward, Kepler, and the stewards on my other estates kept things running smoothly."

Her jaw dropped. "You have . . .more than one estate?" She blinked rapidly several times. "I suppose . . .-well, you are a duke.

I knew they were wealthy but …" Her voice trailed off.

He smiled. "It has taken a little getting used to on my part. After all, I was destined to spend my entire adult life in the army. An officer, even one of high rank, is not paid handsomely. To come back to so much has made my head reel at times, never thinking any of it would be mine."

"What rank did you attain, Your Grace?"

"I was a colonel," he told her, a bit of pride soaring within him.

"I was friendly with a captain," she said softly. "He . . . was killed in battle."

Win kicked himself mentally. He recalled Minta mentioning that her twin had a sweetheart who perished in the war with the Americans.

"Were you close to this friend?" he asked.

She nodded. "We had only known each other a short while when he left for the front." She shook her head. "He died almost two years ago."

"You still miss him."

Her head tilted and she pursed her lips. "I think I miss the idea of him."

"What do you mean?"

Her cheeks flushed with color, making her beauty glow. "We had danced together at a few assemblies. He noticed me. Everyone always noticed Minta first. But Captain Marsh saw *me*. It was the first time that had ever occurred and I will admit, a heady feeling. He promised to court me when he returned. Obviously, he never did. I can only wonder if we might have suited and if things would have worked out between us."

Win studied her, drawn in by her words, as well as her loveliness. "Did you love him?"

"No," she said, shaking her head. "I did like him, though. I suppose my lingering sadness is for what might have been. I hate that he was cut down in the prime of his life."

He hated that only one man had seen her. He could understand why other gentlemen—or even women—had always been drawn to Minta. She was vivacious and friendly and would attract attention easily. On the other hand, her sister was reserved and quiet and others would miss how deep she truly was. It was a shame that only one person outside her family had recognized her worth—and that he had been cut down by the enemy.

It had been the same with Percy and him their entire lives. Win was the one who drew attention because he was full of life and demanded others pay attention to him. Percy had always held back and lurked in Win's shadow. He had always brought his friend and cousin along everywhere with him but he could see now how Percy might have resented Win or even been jealous of him.

Percy had Minta now. He was coming into his own, happiness filling his life.

Sera Nicholls deserved the same.

Win vowed then to help this woman rise to her potential.

The carriage slowed and he looked to Percy and Minta. He realized he had been so wrapped up in his conversation with Miss Nicholls that he had forgotten they were even inside the carriage.

"Oh, it looks as if we are almost home," Minta declared.

"I have told your sister that you desire her company when you and Percy retreat to the country later this week," he said.

Minta looked hopefully at her twin. "Would you come with us, Sera? Please?"

Win glanced at the woman next to him and saw her hesitate.

"I told Miss Nicholls that Percy wouldn't mind in the least having his new sister-in-law at Kingwood," he said firmly, his gaze connecting with his cousin's.

As always, they could speak volumes without words and Percy immediately understood.

"I won't take no for an answer, Sera," Percy said. "In fact, I *expect* you to come to Kingwood. Besides the fact that Minta and I will both enjoy your company, there would be no point in you staying in town. Lord and Lady Westlake will continue to attend

Season affairs. You would be left at home with nothing to do—unless you want to make your come-out this late."

"No," Miss Nicholls said, biting her lip. "Next Season will be plenty fine with me."

"Then it is settled," Minta said. "We get you all to ourselves. I am going to need you to stay with us until next Season." She glanced to Percy and he nodded eagerly.

"You see, we are going to have a baby," Minta announced.

The carriage stopped as Miss Nicholls squealed with delight. Both sisters leaned forward and embraced, then they drew apart and began babbling quickly. Win saw Percy smile indulgently at his wife and then his cousin looked to him.

"What do you think of our news?"

Win thrust out a hand. "Congratulations, Percy. I hope you'll have your heir."

His cousin shrugged. "Frankly, I would prefer a redheaded female who would twist me about her smallest finger."

The words shocked Win. Didn't every peer of the realm want an heir first and foremost?

Then he looked to the twins, still chattering away as the door opened and a footman set down the steps.

Win suddenly found himself wishing he had a wife of his own who was carrying his heir.

Then Sera Nicholls turned, her flushed face full of happiness. "Isn't it the most marvelous news?"

He nodded, his gut tightening. His heart had never uttered one word to him—but now, after thirty years of silence, it screamed at him.

It told Win that he wanted Sera Nicholls as his duchess.

CHAPTER FOUR

SERA WATCHED AS the Duke of Woodmont left the carriage, his broad back covered by the snug coat. His even snugger breeches, tucked into polished Wellingtons, showed off his muscular legs, causing her mouth to grow dry.

It had surprised her how easily she had conversed with him on the way home. Yes, she had a hard time looking at him at first but then the more they spoke, the more it seemed as if he were someone she had known forever.

Percy followed, then Minta went next, and she brought up the rear. Her brother-in-law lifted Minta by the waist to the ground, gently resting her there, looking at his wife as if she were a rare treasure. It was obvious the pair was hopelessly in love and Sera couldn't be happier. With a baby on the way, their family would continue to grow.

She held out her hand, expecting a footman to take it. Instead, the duke's fingers clasped hers, causing her heart to slam against her ribs. She moved down the stairs gingerly, afraid she would miss a step and tumble to the ground, which might cause her to die of embarrassment.

Once on the ground, Sera pulled on her hand, trying to break the contact between them. His touch had shivers racing along her spine and made her breathing shallow. He didn't release it however, tucking it into the crook of his arm instead.

"I shall escort you to the drawing room," he announced in a very ducal way.

Something told her that even though this man had not been a duke for very long, he had always gotten his way. Edward had told her that officers who achieved higher ranks, such as Woodmont becoming a colonel, were born leaders who muscled their way to the top of the ladder.

Sera pictured Woodmont on a ladder, knocking others aside as he climbed it in those oh-so-tight breeches.

And she giggled.

The duke looked down at her. "Do you find something amusing, Miss Nicholls?"

Her face flamed at his attention directed at her. In fact, it looked as if he was studying her mouth, causing a wave of heat to ripple through her. Surely, he couldn't know what she was thinking? She had never had wicked thoughts such as these.

Until this man came along.

In a way, it made her feel disloyal to Edward. She had dutifully written the army captain and received a few letters from him in return. As time passed, she thought the kiss they had shared had proven that there was no spark existing between them. She had written less frequently, hoping a little emotional distance might be better.

Unfortunately, Edward's parents seem to be everywhere she turned. He must have spoken to them of his plans to woo her because Mrs. Marsh sought her out on every occasion and dominated her time. Avoiding the Marshes wasn't possible, since Mr. Marsh worked in the government alongside her father. The more Mrs. Marsh cozied up to Sera, the more she felt trapped.

It was almost a relief to receive news of his death. She regretted feeling that way and did mourn him for a year, wearing black as if they truly had been betrothed. Her heart told her she was only going through the motions, though. That things never would have worked out between them. When Mrs. Marsh began to cling to Sera at public events, treating her like a widowed daughter-in-law, Sera had known it was time to leave Ontario. She had only stayed behind when Minta returned to England because she wanted more time with Mama. But even her mother knew how unhappy Sera was—and that Mrs. Marsh's behavior was a large part of it.

That's why she had left Upper Canada when she did instead of waiting and returning next spring with her parents. Part of her wished to escape Ontario and the memories of Edward, as well as no longer making herself available to the Marshes. The other part yearned to stretch her wings as Minta did and try for a Season. She wondered if there truly might be a gentleman present in Polite Society who would make for a good husband and partner to her.

For that is what Sera longed for. She wanted to be the equal of a man. She wanted to love him even more than he loved her. She wanted exactly what her parents had, a lasting love that transcended place and time.

Would she find it next Season? Even if she dreaded going through it?

She inhaled the bergamot cologne that the duke wore, thinking how she was attracted to him and wanting to dispel that notion. A powerful duke would not give the time of day to someone of her station. Woodmont was only being polite because he was so attached to his cousin. Besides, she would never make for a duchess. They were the women who led Polite Society and set the tone and fashion each Season. A duchess would not wish to have the floor swallow her up. Sera was not the kind of woman a duke would ever notice, much less one as dashing as Woodmont. He would never think a woman his equal. He was rich, powerful, and totally out of her atmosphere.

But she wondered how he kissed. How his kiss might compare to the one Edward had bestowed upon her so long ago.

"Balderdash," she murmured.

"I beg your pardon?"

Sera glanced up at the handsome duke and bit her lip. "Nothing, Your Grace. I am merely overwhelmed by the trappings of the marquess' townhouse."

He chuckled as they followed Minta and Percy down the corridor to the drawing room. "You should see my townhouse."

"I am certain it is most beautiful," she said graciously.

He laughed. "It's opulent, I will give you that. I had never laid eyes upon it until I inherited it."

His words confused her. "I'm sorry?"

"Oh, I was never allowed to come to town when my parents did for the Season. I stayed home at Woodbridge with my tutor and, later, I was away at school. Now, Terrance did come to town. Once he reached university age, he spent summers in London between his academic terms."

"While you remained in the country?" she asked, as he led her inside the drawing room.

"Terrance was the heir apparent. My parents barely acknowledged my existence. In fact," he said, leaning close as if sharing a confidence, "they would be horrified to learn I actually inherited the ducal title."

He seated her as Percy spoke to his butler and Minta rang for tea.

"It was very different for Minta and me growing up," she admitted to him. "We were the center of our parents' world. Though Papa has worked hard for the crown, he always made time for us when he came home from his office. And Mama spent much of her days with the two of us." She paused. "They were a love match and still are deeply in love. Papa didn't seem to mind at all that we were girls although I understand it is different since he had no title or entailed lands to pass down."

A maid appeared with a teacart and Minta began pouring out, handing over the cups and saucers.

"Our cook is a good one," she bragged. "I have shared a few recipes with her that you and I used to make, Sera."

"You . . . cook?" the duke asked, looking from her to Minta and back.

When Sera ignored his comment and sipped her tea, Minta said, "We did have a cook but not many servants. Sera and I grew up doing many of the household tasks. Mama thought it important that we learn something about the kitchens and Sera and I have spent many happy hours in it. We both learned to cook several dishes. Sera is a better baker than I am, though. Sweets are her specialty."

The duke smiled engagingly at her. "I do love a good sweet myself. Perhaps you could pass along your recipes to my cook, Miss Nicholls."

"I would be happy to do so, Your Grace. I could even make biscuits or your favorite cake for you."

She realized that was actually far too personal and found herself blushing.

"I will hold you to that, Miss Nicholls," he said, his even, white teeth gleaming in a smile directed at her.

Her cheeks burned even more and she busied herself rear-ranging items on her plate.

"You do know you are supposed to eat what's there," the duke teased.

Sera looked up, appealing wordlessly to Minta to intervene.

Her sister only smiled smugly and said, "Can I get anyone more tea?"

Frustrated, she jammed a tart into her mouth. The entire tart. It fit—but she couldn't say a word. She could barely chew. She tried sipping tea to moisten the lump in her mouth.

And the Duke of Woodmont laughed aloud.

He took pity on her, handing his handkerchief to her. "Spit it out, Miss Nicholls. You'll never successfully get it down."

Mortified, she took it and turned away, spitting the mangled tart into the cloth and wadding the handkerchief up.

"That reminds me of the time we had that contest at university, Percy."

Her brother-in-law smiled. "That's right. Someone bet us— the Second Sons—that they could eat more scones than we could." He paused. "Was it a quarter-hour? Or half?"

"Half," the duke confirmed. "Naturally, the entire tavern began placing bets on who the victor would be. I didn't mind losing to a Second Son but I would have hated losing to anyone else."

"Who won?" asked Minta.

"Owen," said Percy and the duke at the same time.

"Actually, Owen tied with Spence if I recall correctly," Percy said.

"And then the tavern's owner extended it another five minutes. That's when Owen claimed victory," Woodmont said, wiping a tear from his eyes. "Owen had to be carried home by the rest of us. It was worse than any time he ever drank too much."

"The Second Sons are Percy's and Win's good friends from their university days," Minta said to Sera.

"Yes, His Grace mentioned them in the carriage," she said.

Her sister smiled. "That doesn't surprise me. They are very close. I have grown close to their wives, who all happen to be cousins. You are going to adore the Three Cousins, which is how they are affectionately known."

"Does everyone in London have nicknames?" she asked.

The duke's gaze met hers. "Only the fun ones." Then he burst out laughing again.

Sera's blush spread down her neck and up to her roots. "I don't suppose I will ever be given a nickname then. I am not someone others enjoy being around."

"Don't say that," Minta said fiercely, sticking up for her twin as she had many times over the years. "You are fun around me. And you will laugh with the Three Cousins. They all should be at the house party."

"What is a house party?" she asked.

"Oh, you don't know, do you?" her sister said. "I wrote you a few letters but I suppose they arrived too late for you to see them. Owen and Louisa—Lord and Lady Danbury—are giving a house party at the end of the Season. I thought it would be the perfect way to introduce you to our friends and have you mingle in Polite Society a bit without being overwhelmed at the first ball next Season."

"It is a time when a group of people come together at a country estate for a week or two," Percy added. "There are all kinds of games and entertainment. This way, you can meet our friends and grow comfortable being with them. By the time you enter the *ton* next spring, you will have a group of friends to help launch you. They are some of the most powerful women in Polite Society."

Panic filled her at the thought of attending an event such as this.

"Who will be there?" she asked, her voice going hoarse.

"The Second Sons and their wives. They will gather in advance so we can have time together. Then a small group of ladies and gentlemen will arrive." Minta looked at her worriedly. "Perhaps we can have you meet each couple separately so that you will be acquainted with them before the house party begins."

"You can go without me," Sera said shakily, knowing going to an event such as this would be painful and awkward. "I will return to town and spend that time with Uncle West and Aunt Phyllis while you are there."

"Sera, this will be good for you," her twin said cautiously. "It is the ideal way to meet others in a more intimate gathering so that you won't be overwhelmed when the Season begins next year."

Stubbornness set in. "You cannot make me go, Minta. I am a grown woman of two and twenty."

"I know how old you are. I am several minutes your elder," snapped her sister. Then Minta's tone softened. "Please come, Sera. It will be so much fun. You will like the Three Cousins. They are eager to meet you because I have spoken of you so often to them."

Hating to admit this, especially since she felt the duke's intense gaze upon her, she said, "I am not fun, especially in large groups, and you know this, Minta. You know I prefer solitary activities. Gardening. Reading. Walking. Playing my violin. I would rather not go to a party which runs for so long. Perhaps I can meet your friends another time."

"If Miss Nicholls isn't going, then neither I am," stated the duke.

She turned to face him. "What?"

"I told you I haven't attended a single *ton* event, Miss Nicholls. Owen and Louisa talked me into going to this house party. Adalyn, Ev's wife, is a bit of a matchmaker and has plans to pair me with someone during it. She says house parties are a wonderful way to get to know others since you are around one another for an extended amount of time and can actually have a conversation. I gather *ton* events are loud and many of them involve dancing, which is not conducive for learning much about anyone."

His brows arched. "I hate to disappoint my friends but I was hoping we could attend this party together since neither of us knows anyone else in the *ton*. I could use a friendly face."

"But you will have all the Second Sons and their wives there. You know them," she protested.

"None of them are in the unique position that you and I are, however, in that we know no one else. I would rather do this together, Miss Nicholls, but if you are refusing to go, I will bow out myself. Adalyn can find a wife for me next year. Or the next."

Exasperation filled her. "Your attendance should not hinge upon mine, Your Grace."

"It does," he said, stubbornness settling in his eyes. "And I am in need of a duchess. I thought finding one at this house party would be easier. Then I wouldn't even have to attend the Season next year if I chose not to."

He eyed her steadily. "So, what do you say, Miss Nicholls? Shall we storm this house party together—or will you force me to wait until next spring to find my duchess?"

Guilt filled her. She didn't want him to skip the event simply because she wanted to do so. And in truth, it would be a decent way to meet a handful of people and not be dazed when she entered a ballroom next year.

Minta gave her an encouraging smile. "Just think, Sera. You also might find someone you care for at this party. Many people leave a house party betrothed. Please, say you'll come."

She glanced toward Percy, the only one who had remained silent during this exchange. "Do you have anything to add?"

"Only that the only time I am truly relaxed in the company of others, it is when I am with the Second Sons and their wives. They are a wonderful, loyal, steadfast group. It would do you good to befriend them, Sera. Besides, Adalyn is a genius at pairing couples together. Why not give her—and this house party—a chance?"

Sera looked at her sister and then to the duke, her heart pounding.

"All right. I will attend. But I don't want to be forced into making a match with anyone."

CHAPTER FIVE

W IN WAITED IN his study for Jack Blumer to arrive the following morning. The Bow Street Runner had sent word to Woodbridge that he had found two children Terrance had sired. Blumer had indicated the situation was dire and that Win should come to London immediately to see it resolved.

He drummed his fingers on the desktop, too antsy to concentrate on anything. He wondered about these bastards the Bow Street Runner had located and the women who had produced the pair. He would have to see his solicitor once he had a better grasp of the situation because he wished to set up funds for them. He didn't think it would be wise to have a large amount the mothers could draw from. Perhaps, instead, he would award them a quarterly allowance for the care of the children. It would take care of clothing and feeding them. Even schooling if they were boys.

He sat back in his chair, closing his eyes, marveling at how his life had changed so rapidly, as it had for his fellow Second Sons. Who would have thought the group of five steadfast friends would one day leave the battlefields and take their places in the House of Lords and Polite Society?

Of course, Win wasn't participating in this Season, as he had shared with Sera Nicholls. He had enjoyed avoiding Polite Society even as he rolled up his sleeves and got to work at Woodbridge.

Fortunately, Kepler, his steward on the estate, had proven to be a fount of knowledge. He had walked Win through things, as had three of the Second Sons. Spence, Ev, and Owen had all taken a week to come to Essex and help their friend adjust to his new role as Win immersed himself in being the Duke of Woodmont.

Trusting Kepler to keep things in hand, Win had actually visited two of his other estates, seeing they were well managed. He had two others to inspect but wanted to settle this matter of Terrance's by-blows before he did so.

Then there was the upcoming house party to attend. Adalyn had written to him, telling him she and Louisa were preparing the guest list even as they kept an eye on which young women made matches and which ones would still be eligible—and suitable—to attend Louisa's party and possibly be considered as a match for him. Win didn't truly care whom he wed. Marriage was an obligation in that it would provide him the way to have a legitimate heir. He did see how his friends' marriages were different from those of the *ton* in that the four men had all made love matches.

He had absolutely no interest in love.

His parents' marriage had been arranged and they tolerated one another enough to have produced an heir and a spare. He rarely had been around them, he and Terrance being left in the country while they were in town for the Season, and later he and his brother had been away at school for much of the year. While he was happy for his fellow Second Sons finding love, he thought the concept did not apply to him. He enjoyed the favors of women too much to ever truly settle down with one of them. He would do his ducal duty and find the appropriate woman Polite Society would approve of to be his wife. He would sire an heir and a spare and perhaps a female child or two, but he had no intention of spending any amount of time with a wife, much less giving her his heart as he saw with his friends.

He actually looked forward to having children and being more involved in their lives than his parents ever had been in his.

The Second Sons were a shining example of what good fathers should be, even if he felt some of them went slightly overboard in their affections. He would allow Adalyn to make the entire process simple. She would choose a wife for him. It would be just one of many things on a list he checked off, completing an important and necessary task.

A brisk knock at the door brought him back to the present. "Come," he said, and the door was opened by his butler.

"Mr. Blumer has arrived, Your Grace."

"Show him in, please."

Moments later, the Bow Street Runner appeared in the doorway and strode into the room.

"Your Grace. Good morning. May I sit?"

"Of course," Win said, indicating a chair directly in front of his desk.

The detective took it and Win waited expectantly for what would be revealed.

"No beating about the bush, Your Grace. You are the uncle to two boys," Blumer informed him. "Freddie is six. Charlie is also six."

Freddie and Charlie . . .

"Tell me everything you can about them, Mr. Blumer," he encouraged. "Who their mothers are. The circumstances in which they were conceived. Their current home situations."

Blumer nodded brusquely. "Freddie—Frederick on his birth record—is the by-blow of the previous Duke of Woodmont and Sandra Sawyer, a stage actress. She served as your brother's mistress for three years until she became with child."

"I am assuming he absolved himself from all responsibility once he learned about that."

The detective nodded. "Miss Sawyer was well known in theatre circles, perhaps the most talented actress in London. In fact, I saw her in two different productions myself. She was a natural on the stage, extremely talented, and quite beautiful." He paused and then added, "Not anymore."

"She is no longer on the stage—or she is no longer beautiful after birthing my brother's bastard? I know many women lose their figures but I had not heard of one losing her face before."

A grim expression crossed the runner's face. "Miss Sawyer has consumption, Your Grace. She hasn't long to live."

Win frowned. "Where is she? And is there anyone in her family who could take the boy?"

"I have located the boardinghouse she has been staying at for the past year. She lives in a room with Freddie and his half-brother, Charlie. Charles, on his birth certificate. Neither one named His Grace as the father, though."

"Why is this Charlie living with Miss Sawyer and her son?"

"Apparently, His Grace impregnated not only Miss Sawyer but her dresser in the theater, the woman who maintained Miss Sawyer's costumes and helped her change during performances. Her name was Sally. I have no last name for her. The dresser died in childbirth and her employer, Miss Sawyer, took on the babe to raise with her own."

Win saw the shadows darken the detective's face and he continued. "Miss Sawyer had a bit of a nest egg, not only because she was the highest paid actress on the London stage, but she had served as the mistress for two other lords previously, a marquess and an earl. Apparently—unlike your brother—both men were quite generous in their gifts to her. Among them were a small townhouse and numerous jewels."

Puzzled, Win asked, "Then why is she living in a room at a boardinghouse with two small children?"

"Miss Sawyer had to take time off during her confinement and after giving birth to Freddie. She couldn't traipse about the stage, big as a barrel. By the time the next Season rolled around, younger women with fairer faces had taken her place. The London stage is a fickle one, Your Grace. Miss Sawyer lived off selling the various jewels in her possession and did so for five years. Then the townhouse was repossessed. It seems the marquess, though he had moved on from Miss Sawyer, never actually put the deed in her name and had left it in his own. His heir claimed the title, begging your pardon, a righteous prick, as is his wife. They discovered ownership and booted Miss Sawyer and the two boys from the residence. By this time, from what I can surmise, she was down to the last bauble, a diamond bracelet which she sold for a fraction of its worth."

The runner's gaze met Win's. "Jewelers and pawnbrokers know when they have a client in a tight position and they took advantage of her circumstances. Consequently, Miss Sawyer is down to her last farthing. She has not paid her rent in two months and she is not going to last two days."

"What?"

Blumer leaned forward. "She has consumption, as I said, Your Grace. I think the landlady, Mrs. Bridges, has a kind heart and was merely allowing her to stay on in order that she did not die on the streets."

This news took Win aback. "She has no other relatives who could take in these boys? Or the dresser had no relatives step forward to claim little Charlie?"

The runner sadly shook his head. "No, Your Grace. I will tell you now, the foundling home will not take boys at six. They are too old."

Confusion filled him. "Then what is to happen to them?" he asked.

"They will be turned out from the boardinghouse to the streets, Your Grace. It's a common enough story in London."

Win slammed a hand on the desk. "That will not happen under my watch. I will take them in."

It surprised him hearing the vehemence in his voice—and the fact he was willing to take on two young boys. Though the thought of his brother's bastards living in his home sickened him. He thought of an alternative.

"I suppose I can bring them to Woodbridge with me. I can hire someone and provide them a cottage on the estate. Even see to their education when they come of age."

"That is most generous of you, Your Grace. I doubt many men in your position would take on his brother's by-blows."

Win rose. "Take me to them now. I want to meet Miss Sawyer and assure her both boys will have a home and be looked after."

Admiration flickered in Blumer's eyes and he nodded. "Then let's have at it, Your Grace."

Win rang for his butler and asked that the carriage be readied. While they waited, he asked Blumer about the boys themselves.

"I have yet to see either one of them, Your Grace. They were not present when I interviewed Miss Sawyer."

"You truly believe she has a limited time?"

Nodding, the detective said, "I do."

"Then we should fetch a doctor and have him accompany us to Miss Sawyer's, as well." He rang again and asked his butler the name of the physician his family had used when in London.

"Why, that would be Dr. Cook, Your Grace."

The butler supplied the doctor's address and a footman notified him the carriage was ready to leave. He and the Bow Street Runner went outside to the vehicle and Win instructed the coachman to stop first at Dr. Cook's office.

When they arrived at the address, Blumer said, "Wait here, Your Grace. I will go inside and explain the situation to Dr. Cook."

"Very well," Win agreed. He supposed it wasn't like a duke to go about such tasks. He couldn't help but wonder if this physician would come with them but then realized that he *was* a duke and that the man would have little reason to turn down his request.

Sure enough, less than ten minutes later, Blumer and Dr. Cook climbed inside the carriage.

"Your Grace, it is a pleasure to meet you. I have cared for your family for several years now."

"You understand the circumstances?"

The doctor nodded grimly. "I do. if Miss Sawyer is as bad off as Mr. Blumer here says she is, there will be little I can do for her, other than to make her comfortable."

"Do whatever you must, Doctor," he said. "I will also want you to check the boys over before I take them back to Woodbridge."

"I would be happy to do so, Your Grace."

They rode the rest of the way in silence, Win going through a list of tenants in his head, thinking whom he might place these two boys with. He would be willing to pay monthly for their care. There were a few tenants who were childless, not by choice from what he gathered. Perhaps they'd be willing to take on the two by-blows and raise them as their own. He would, naturally, provide for them behind the scenes. Anger simmered through him, knowing that Terrance had walked away from his responsibilities once Sandra Sawyer had been found with child. To then turn his attentions to her dresser must have been a slap in the face to the actress.

They arrived at the boardinghouse and once again, Blumer said, "Wait here, Your Grace. Let Dr. Cook and I go inside and smooth the way."

Patience had never been one of Win's virtues but he understood the situation was delicate and he nodded in agreement.

A quarter of an hour later, the runner returned to the coach.

"Miss Sawyer is ready to see you now, Your Grace. Dr. Cook has examined her and he agreed with my assessment. She won't last long so you must see her now and learn what you can before she expires."

Win accompanied the detective into the building, where a woman greeted them, anxiously wringing her hands together.

"This is Mrs. Bridges. She runs the boardinghouse."

He took in the woman's shabby gown and pinched features. "I understand that Miss Sawyer has been unable to pay her rent for a few months now."

"Yes, Your Grace," the woman replied. "I hadn't the heart to turn her out. Miss Sawyer is so very kind."

"Do not worry, Mrs. Bridges. I will speak to my solicitor and see that you receive the monies owed to you. In fact, for your generosity, I will make certain that you are paid triple what you are owed."

"You mustn't do that, Your Grace," Mrs. Bridges protested.

He took her hands in his and found that she trembled. "You showed a great kindness to a stranger, Mrs. Bridges. I want to repay that same kindness to you."

Tears ran down the woman's cheeks as she thanked him. Win squeezed her hands and released them. "Show me to Miss Sawyer's room."

CHAPTER SIX

J ACK BLUMER LED Win up the rickety stairs, which creaked and groaned under the weight of the two men. He stopped in front of a door.

"Would you like to go in and see Miss Sawyer on your own?"

"Please accompany me," he said after giving it a moment of thought. "It is always better to have two people listening in case one forgets some small detail which could prove to be important."

"Very well, Your Grace."

Blumer pushed open the door and the two men stepped inside. Dr. Cook stood by the bed, his medical bag sitting at the foot of it. He released Miss Sawyer's hand.

"Speak to His Grace now and then I will give you something to help you sleep," he said gently. To Win, the doctor said, "I will be waiting outside." He exited the room.

Blumer kept close to the door as Win approached the bed. He saw now what the detective had meant. Laying in the bed was a woman so gaunt, she looked as if someone had locked her away and starved her for weeks. Her dark hair was greasy and matted, falling about her shoulders. Yet he could see that once she had been a great beauty from her bone structure and the vibrant green eyes that shone in her hollow face.

"Your Grace," she said hoarsely and moved to sit up.

Immediately, he went and plumped the two pillows, stained and worn, and eased her back onto them.

"You have questions. I have answers."

She paused, grasping a handkerchief that sat next to her and bringing it to her mouth as she coughed weakly. As she withdrew it from her lips, Win saw the blood-filled sputum on the cloth.

"I am the Duke of Woodmont, brother to . . . Freddie's father. And Charlie's."

At the mention of the boys, she smiled. For a moment, Miss Sawyer was once more a beautiful woman.

"I was the daughter of a clergyman and longed to go on the stage," she said, her voice raspy. "I ran away with a traveling actors' troupe and eventually found my way to London. I had looks and an hourglass figure, Your Grace. And plenty of talent."

"Mr. Blumer said he had seen you on the stage and sang your praises," Win told her.

"Looks fade, so I knew I wouldn't have leading roles but for a handful of years. I assumed I would take on character parts as I aged."

She paused again and coughed for a full minute. Once more, the handkerchief came away stained with her fluids.

"I chose my lovers carefully. The two before your brother were much older men. They gifted me with presents which I knew I could sell someday in the future and live off that." She smiled sadly. "And then I fell in love. With Terrance."

Miss Sawyer fell silent and Win did not press her. Finally, she said, "He was so handsome that he stole my breath. I immediately ended my affair with a marquess." Her mouth turned down. "Terrance treated me poorly. He never gave me the gifts the other two did. The more shabbily he treated me, I am ashamed to admit, the more I wanted him. He knew it. He used me. And I didn't care. I lost all self-respect and groveled at his feet.

"Then I turned up with child."

She looked so small and forlorn that Win took a step toward the bed and perched upon it. Taking her hand, he squeezed it.

"Go on," he urged.

"My courses flowed regularly. Though we had taken precautions, I knew something had changed. My body didn't seem my own. My breasts ached and began to grow fuller. The week my courses did not arrive, I told Terrance I would bear his child."

He brushed her hair away from her face. "How did he respond?"

A harsh, guttural sound came from her. "He shouted obscenities at me. Slapped me. Threw me to the ground. Threatened to kill me." She sighed. "He told me he never wanted to see me again."

Another coughing fit occurred and he waited until she could speak again, even giving her a sip from a cup of water that sat on a nearby table.

"On his way out the door, he came across Sally, my dresser."

Miss Sawyer closed her eyes and Win saw the pain etched into her face, both it and disease aging her.

"He was so angry with me." She shook her head. "He took it out on Sally. Violated her. The poor girl had never even been kissed."

Rage poured through Win. "He raped her?"

The former actress nodded. "Yes. And soon, Sally found she also was with child." Her voice was now a whisper as she took another sip of water.

"I continued onstage until I could no longer hide my condition. By then, all of Polite Society knew what had occurred. Sally and I retreated to the townhouse my marquess had gifted to me."

Tears brimmed in her eyes. "My child came two weeks late. The midwife said that wasn't unusual with a first child. Sally's labor pains started the same day, only hours after mine did. We lay in the same bed together in order to make it easier on the midwife. I gave birth to Freddie first." Her mouth trembled. "Charlie arrived almost twenty minutes later. And Sally died with my arm around her as I nursed my newborn son."

Shock filled Win. His eyes flew to Blumer, who shrugged,

obviously taken aback by the actress' revelations.

More coughing occurred and he patiently waited for Miss Sawyer to recover.

When she did, she said, "I've let Charlie think he was mine all these years. That he and Freddie are brothers. I thought it would be easier."

"What have you told them of their father?"

"Nothing. Other than his name was Sawyer and he died before they were born. They have only turned six a week ago. They haven't known to ask many questions." She paused, her gaze meeting his. "They do know I am dying."

"Where are they now?"

Miss Sawyer shook her head. "I don't know. The past two months, I have gotten worse and worse. They have come and gone. I haven't been able to mother them. I don't know what they've been up to."

She tightened her fingers on his. "Please, Your Grace. Look for them. Promise that you will help find them a home."

Determination filled Win. "They will come to live on my country estate, Miss Sawyer. I shall find a childless couple to take them on and care for them. I will see that they learn to read and write. If they want an education, it is theirs. If they choose to learn a trade, I will see they have the proper instruction."

Her tears flowed freely now and she kissed his hand. "Thank you, Your Grace. You . . . are similar in coloring and looks to your brother. But you . . . are nothing like him." She winced. "He is the true bastard. Not my boys."

A violent shudder seized her and she began coughing up blood. It poured from her nose and mouth.

"Get Dr. Cook," Win shouted and Blumer opened the door.

Miss Sawyer clutched at her throat as if she couldn't breathe. He patted her on the back like a fool, thinking it might do some good. More blood spewed from her, landing upon his coat and trousers.

Dr. Cook said, "Move, Your Grace. Wait outside."

He stepped away from the bed and found he couldn't leave, watching as she trembled and coughed. Then she gasped and fell back onto the pillows.

And was still.

Win saw her large green eyes staring out vacantly. The physician brushed his palm across them, closing them.

"She's gone," Cook said.

"I will see to the burial costs," he said.

"You don't have to do that," Your Grace," the runner said.

"I know. I want to do it for her. It is the least I can do after my brother treated her so abominably and abandoned her." He swallowed, his heart heavy, seeing the once-beautiful actress lying in all the blood and filth.

"Blumer, do you have any idea where her boys might be?"

"Somewhere on the streets," the detective said. "I'll find them now."

Win gazed steadily at the runner. "We'll find them. Together."

CHAPTER SEVEN

J ACK BLUMER WENT out in search of Freddie and Charlie, agreeing to meet up with Win at the boardinghouse in two hours, with or without the boys. Dr. Cook returned to his office since the boys weren't available for him to examine.

Win told Mrs. Bridges to leave Miss Sawyer in her room and sent his coachman to retrieve his solicitor.

"I don't care what he is doing. He is to come with you immediately. Is that understood?"

"Aye, Your Grace," the driver said. "I'll use your name and he'll drop everything."

He stopped a boy on the streets and asked who the nearest undertaker was. When the boy replied, Win tossed him a coin.

"Bring him here at once and there will be another coin in it for you."

The boy's eyes lit in surprise. "Yes, my lord." He took off running down the street.

Less than ten minutes later, a somber man dressed in black appeared with the boy. Win paid the lad, giving him two additional coins simply because he wanted to see joy shine in the child's face.

"Thank you, my lord!" he cried, pocketing his newfound gain and racing away.

"I am the Duke of Woodmont," he told the undertaker. "Upstairs in Mrs. Bridges' boardinghouse you will find a Miss Sawyer, who recently expired. You are to handle everything, including the burial."

The undertaker's eyes widened. "Yes, Your Grace. Where would you like Miss Sawyer to be buried?"

"It doesn't matter," he said dismissively. "Just handle the entire affair and report your expenses to my solicitor."

He provided Cottrell's address and then paced in front of the boardinghouse, anxiously awaiting Cottrell's appearance. As he waited, he stopped two people who went to enter the boardinghouse, asking them about the boys and where they might be. One man had only seen the children in passing and had no information to give him.

The second was far more revealing.

"Them two are trouble," the red-faced boarder shared. "They weren't when they first got here but their mother is sick. Too sick to discipline them. They're always into mischief in the neighborhood. I say it'd do them good to be caught and transported to Botany Bay."

The thought of two young children being charged as criminals and sent halfway around the world sickened Win. He gave the man his haughtiest ducal look and the boarder rushed into the boardinghouse, slamming the door.

His carriage pulled up soon after and Win climbed inside it, finding Cottrell and one of his associates within.

Quickly, he explained about how he had located the previous duke's two bastards and how he wanted to provide for them.

"The mother expired an hour ago," he told the pair, not wanting to go into detail about how the boys had separate mothers. Terrance dumping his pregnant mistress was bad enough. Brutalizing her dresser was far worse.

"I will pay for the burial expenses," he continued. "I will also place the boys with one of my tenants. I wish to provide them with proper clothing and I believe I owe them an education or help in training them in some trade. Draw up whatever papers are necessary on your end."

"That is most generous of you, Your Grace," Cottrell said. "But quite unnecessary. His Grace did not claim these by-blows. Surely, you are under no obligation to provide for them."

He glared at the solicitor until the man cowered. "They have Cutler blood in them. I will see they are taken care of. Don't ever question me again, Cottrell. Else you'll find yourself no longer in my employ."

"Yes, Your Grace," the solicitor said, bobbing his head up and down several times. "It will be taken care of immediately."

Win exited the vehicle and instructed his coachman to return the pair to Cottrell's offices and then return to the boardinghouse. He hoped by then Freddie and Charlie would have been found.

"Very good, Your Grace." The driver flicked his wrists and the horses set out.

By now, the undertaker had returned with his wagon and another man. They entered the boardinghouse and, several minutes later, they returned, carrying Miss Sawyer's body wrapped in some kind of sheeting. They placed it in the bed of the wagon and both men tipped their hats to him.

Blumer rounded the corner as the wagon started up and Win looked at the detective expectantly. "Well?"

Frowning, Blumer said, "I found them. But there's been a bit of trouble. They filched an apple apiece and the grocer wanted them taken away. Transported, Your Grace."

Win recalled the boarder saying the boys deserved to be sent to Australia. "Would such a petty crime call for such a severe action?"

The Bow Street Runner nodded his head. "It isn't just arson or murder that can earn a place on a ship bound to Botany Bay, Your Grace. Theft is most likely the most frequent crime. I've known some who have been sent from England's shores for stealing a hairbrush. Beans. A case of tea."

Dread filled Win, thinking of the two orphans being placed on a ship with criminals. He doubted they would survive such a long journey or if they did, how they would be abused by the more hardened criminals aboard.

"Have they been taken away yet?"

"No," Blumer informed him. "I gave the grocer a few notes and told him to hold off reporting anything. That someone wanted to talk to the two boys first. Someone of great importance."

"Take me to them," he ordered.

His carriage wasn't back yet and so he and Blumer walked several blocks. The entered the grocer's shop and a small, thin man with sparse white hair rushed to greet them.

"I am the Duke of Woodmont," Win said, standing tall as he used his officer's posture and ducal authority. "I am here to see the two boys."

"Stole an apple each, they did, Your Grace. And it wasn't the first time. This is merely the first I've been able to catch them."

He glared down at the smaller man. "Did you ever think they were hungry—and that's why they took something?"

The grocer trembled under Win's gaze. "But they stole, Your Grace. They should be punished."

Pushing his hand into his pocket, he retrieved a ten-pound note and handed it to the grocer. "This is to cover your cost for previous losses—and to let me take the boys into my custody."

"Ten pounds," the grocer said, wonder in his voice as he gazed upon the note. "Ten pounds," he repeated.

"I hope that is sufficient," he said, knowing it was more than generous.

"You can take them, Your Grace. Just see that they don't come back."

"Where are they?" he asked, looking about the shop.

"I locked them in a closet," the grocer said smugly.

Anger flared in him. "Give me the key. Now," he barked.

The man ran behind the counter and retrieved it, telling him where the closet was.

"Stay here," he commanded both the grocer and runner.

Win parted the curtains and stepped into the back of the store, finding the closet. He paused before it, collecting himself. He did not want to frighten the newly-orphaned boys.

He knocked on the door. "Freddie, Charlie, are you in there?"

A knock from within sounded. "Who wants to know?" a small voice asked.

"The Duke of Woodmont."

Silence.

"I am going to unlock the door and let you out. I need to speak to you."

Again, silence.

Win inserted the key into the lock and turned it, opening the door.

The pair blew by him so fast, he spun around.

"Stop!" he cried and then ran after them when they didn't obey him. He thought everyone obeyed a duke.

Fortunately, the two ran into the grocer's shop and by the time Win parted the curtains he saw Blumer had each one by the scruff of the neck.

"Got 'em, Your Grace," the runner said, a grim expression on his face.

He moved forward quickly and took Freddie by the elbow, surmising who he was since he had the same jade eyes and dark hair as the deceased Sandra Sawyer.

Kneeling, still grasping the boy's elbow, he said, "Hello, Freddie. I am the Duke of Woodmont. Dukes are very powerful men. You are to obey me. Is that understood?" His tone was firm and just short of menacing.

"Yes," Freddie squeaked.

"Yes, Your Grace," he said, waiting, staring at the boy.

"Yes, Your Grace," Freddie finally said.

Win turned to Charlie and clasped his elbow. "Charlie, will you obey me?"

Charlie's eyes flew to Freddie, who nodded. It was interesting to see that Freddie was the leader between the two.

"Yes. Your Grace," Charlie said, looking back at Win.

"You are a fast learner, Charlie. That is good. I am going to let go of Freddie and you. The two of you are going to walk with Mr. Blumer and me back to Mrs. Bridges' boardinghouse. Can you be trusted to do so?"

Both boys nodded solemnly.

Win and Blumer released their holds—and the boys took off, no hesitation on their part.

"Bloody hell," he muttered, thinking this was going to be much harder than he had anticipated.

They raced outside, seeing the boys round the corner.

"We needn't give chase, Your Grace," Blumer said. "They'll go back to their mother. When they do, we can collect them then."

The men returned to the boardinghouse. By now, Win's carriage had returned. He instructed the driver to park a couple of blocks away, not wanting Freddie or Charlie to know of his presence within the building.

They entered the boardinghouse and got Mrs. Bridges' permission to wait for the orphans in Miss Sawyer's room.

"Do you have any idea how long it will take them to return?" he asked.

"No, Your Grace. They're good boys but they've run a bit wild ever since Miss Sawyer fell so ill. Now with their mother, they're as sweet as the day is long."

"Do not let them know we are here," he warned.

Blumer accompanied him upstairs. They searched the room, finding no extra clothes for any of the three occupants of the room. That would be something the boys would need.

He sat on the bed, which Mrs. Bridges had already stripped, while Blumer stood in the corner, leaning against the wall, looking out the window in order to see the boys when they approached.

Win wondered how awful their lives must have been, seeing their only parent waste away. How desperate they would have to be to steal an apple because their bellies ached. It confirmed his decision to locate the pair in the first place and do right by them.

Close to two hours later, Blumer cleared his throat. "They just entered the building."

No other words were exchanged since neither man wanted to give away the room was occupied. Win did move close to the door so he could grab one or both children as they entered.

The door opened slowly and Freddie poked his head in.

"Mum?" he said softly, frowning at the empty bed.

Win latched on to Freddie's arm and jerked him inside.

"Run!" Freddie shouted to Charlie, who hesitated in the corridor.

Win moved to where the boy could see him. "I have your brother. If you run, you will never see him again."

Knowing Charlie was the follower, he hoped his threat would work.

"Run, I said," Freddie demanded, jerking back and forth, trying to free himself and seeing it was impossible.

"No," Charlie said. "We stay together. Mum said."

Both boys' gazes turned to the empty bed and Win said, "Come in, Charlie."

Charlie shuffled into the room and Win closed the door. Releasing Freddie, he stepped so his back was against the door, blocking their escape. Blumer moved in front of the window for the same reason.

"Sit," Win said.

The boys went to the bed and sat.

"Where's Mum?" Freddie asked, defiance in his voice.

He moved away from the door and knelt in front of them. "Your mother isn't suffering any longer."

"She's dead?" Charlie asked, his eyes wide.

Win nodded. "She asked me to care for you before she passed," he said gently.

"Why?" asked Freddie, suspicion in his eyes. "Who are you?"

He didn't want to reveal his relationship to these young boys but he said, "I knew your father."

"You knew him?" Charlie asked in wonder. "He died before Freddie and me were born."

"I knew him," Win repeated. "He would want me to help look after you since your mother can't anymore."

"Were you here when she died?" asked Freddie, his voice trembling.

"I was. I had brought a doctor. I did not know she was suffering so." With another white lie, he said, "The doctor gave her something to help the pain and coughing. She fell asleep—and didn't wake up."

"Where is she?" Charlie asked, looking lost.

"The undertaker came and took her body away. She will be buried," he explained. "You and your brother will come with me to the country. I live in Essex at an estate called Woodbridge. I will find one of my tenants for you to live with. I can even see that you go to school to learn to read and write."

"We can read," Freddie said belligerently. "A little. Mum was teaching us."

"That's very good," he praised. "We can talk about your education and what you might wish to do when you grow up on the way to Essex."

"She's really dead?" Freddie asked, his voice cracking.

Win placed a hand on the boy's shoulder. "She really is. But she loved the two of you very much. She wanted you to learn as much as you could and grow up to be big and strong."

He thought how very thin these two were and how they had stolen food to survive.

"Come. We shall go to my carriage. We'll buy some meat pies along the way. You can eat them as we travel to Essex."

"Meat pies?" Charlie asked, his eyes widening.

"Yes. You may have as many as you would like," he promised.

In the end, Win thought it was that promise of meat pies that convinced the hungry orphans to come with him and climb inside the carriage.

CHAPTER EIGHT

Kingwood—July

S ERA AWOKE AND immediately felt the warmth next to her. She smiled and looked down to see Lady Analise Haddock nestled against her. The little girl, almost two-and-a-half, had made her way to Sera's bed again. She slept peacefully, her thumb in her mouth.

She stroked the girl's hair, golden and curly like her mother's, and Analise yawned. Her eyes slowly opened and she grinned.

Removing her thumb, she said, "Sera."

"Good morning, Analise. We should return you to the nursery. Your nanny will be frantic, wondering where you are."

Analise giggled.

Sera slipped from the bed and reached for her dressing gown. Once she had it on, she lifted Analise from the bed.

"We go see Mama?"

"Nanny first. Then your mama," she promised.

As they left the chamber, she thought how much she would miss Analise. Adam, too. He was just beginning to crawl and was a delight to watch. They were the children of Lord and Lady Middlefield, now Spencer and Tessa to Sera. The earl and his countess had spent the past week at Kingwood and, already, they seemed as family. She suspected her twin had written to each of the Three Cousins, sharing Sera's trepidation about the upcoming house party and her crippling shyness, because each of the women had written to Minta, asking if they might come and meet her sister before the party in late August.

It hadn't taken long for Sera to warm up to the earl and countess. Tessa was kind and compassionate, while Spencer was a little solemn. He opened up more as the visit went on and she now counted the married pair as new friends. Playing with their children had been a true, unexpected treat.

Just as they reached the Middlefield bedchamber, the door opened and Tessa stepped out.

"Mama!" cried Analise, reaching out her arms toward her mother.

Tessa took her. "She crawled into your bed again?"

"Yes. I was just returning her to the nursery."

Tessa kissed her daughter's head. "She's a slippery one. Nanny has her hands full with this one. And Adam crawling everywhere." She glanced down at her daughter. "We shouldn't worry Nanny, Analise. You are supposed to stay in the nursery with her and Adam."

The girl's bottom lip thrust out in a pout. "But I wanted Sera. I love Sera."

Sera laughed. "I love you, too, Analise."

The two women went to the nursery, depositing Analise with her nanny, who apologized to the countess.

"I am sorry she got by me again, Lady Middlefield."

"Don't worry, Nanny," Tessa said. "These things happen. I had told Analise that we were leaving for home this morning."

"That's why I wanted Sera," the little girl piped up. She reached out and Sera took her, kissing her cheek.

"You need to stay with Nanny and Adam now. You can get dressed and have your breakfast, just like I am going to do with your mama and papa and Uncle Percy and Aunt Minta."

Analise nodded and Sera set her down. She ran to her doll, which sat on a chair in the corner of the room, and picked it up, hugging it.

"Let's slip out," Tessa said quietly.

They returned downstairs and each went to her bedchamber. Sera rang for a maid to help dress her and then she made her way to the breakfast room, where she found Percy and Spencer chatting.

"Good morning," she told the pair and then went through the buffet, selecting a few items to eat as a footman poured her a cup of tea and left it at her seat.

It was certainly nice to be waited upon. Percy had an army of servants, both here and in London. She had help in dressing and never had to think about lighting a fire or cooking a meal. It hadn't taken long for her to get used to having things done for her and she felt quite spoiled.

Sera also felt freer than she had before. The country air in Essex did her good. Meeting Tessa and Spencer and getting to know them over the past week had seemed almost liberating—and she had never made friends or warmed up to others easily. If Adalyn and Louisa were half as nice as Tessa, Sera could see how she would have an entire circle of friends by the time the house party began.

Her thoughts turned again to the Duke of Woodmont. His estate, Woodbridge, was six miles from Kingwood. Though they had been back in Essex for over a week now and Minta had sent invitations twice for His Grace to come and dine since his friends were visiting, the duke had regretfully declined both times.

Sera hoped it wasn't because of her.

She had felt something spark between her and Woodmont. At the same time, he had put her totally at ease. Usually, she was reticent around any stranger but she had chattered like a magpie as they conversed in the carriage on her way to Minta's London home. When he had come inside for tea, she had worried she would clam up but, again, their conversation had proven natural, adding Minta and Percy to the mix. The duke had even boldly proclaimed he would not attend the Danburys' house party unless Sera came, too.

She had agreed to do so. Because he intrigued her.

Oh, she didn't think the duke had any kind of romantic interest in her. He was simply a gentleman who wanted to put his cousin's sister-in-law at ease. Though Woodmont had not been the heir apparent, no one would guess that when they met him. To Sera, he seemed every inch what a duke should be—tall, handsome, powerful, wealthy.

It did bother her, though, that he hadn't come to Kingwood. She didn't sense any kind of estrangement between him and the Middlefields. They were a lovely couple and part of Minta's and Percy's close social circle.

Then why hadn't he bothered to visit?

"Are you ready for your journey back to Stoneridge?" she asked Spencer.

"It will be good to return home," he admitted. "We had only been there a short while since we had been in town for several months. I do love the country, however. You must come and visit us at Stoneridge, Sera. I know as much as Tessa and I would enjoy having you visit, Analise and Adam would like it even more."

Tessa and Minta entered the room and Tessa said, "Analise crawled from her bed and wound up in Sera's again."

"Again?" the earl said. "I apologize for my daughter's behavior." He grinned shamelessly. "Yet I cannot help admire her cleverness. At two, Analise is a brave girl to leave her bed, sneak past her nanny, find the right bedchamber, and enter as quiet as a thief."

Everyone laughed. Sera already knew how indulgent Spencer was to his two children, spoiling them with love and attention, which she didn't consider spoiling at all.

"Do you have everything ready?" Minta asked and then she flung a hand across her mouth, leaping to her feet and fleeing the room.

Percy hurried after her though Sera knew there was nothing

her kind brother-in-law could do. Minta had regularly left the room several times a day since Sera's arrival. It had worried her at first because she had never truly been around a woman increasing but Tessa had informed her this was commonplace. Although Sera did look forward to having children, she did not wish to rush to a chamber pot numerous times a day.

And she also wondered what it was like to get with child. Mama had never spoken about the process to the twins. She wondered how much—if anything—Aunt Phyllis had told Minta before she wed the marquess.

She decided she would ask once the Middlefields left today. It would be better to allay her curiosity now than wait until the eve of her wedding and learn things she might have a hard time processing.

"Do Percy and Minta have any other visitors coming?" Spencer asked her.

"You know they do," she teased. "It did not take me long to figure out that just as the Second Sons came and helped the Duke of Woodmont ease into his new role after he left the military, the Three Cousins are also doing their best to assuage my fears regarding my launch into Polite Society when I attend the house party."

"Were we that obvious?" Tessa asked. "Minta shared with us how shy you can be, Sera, but I haven't found you overly shy at all."

"That is because from the moment you and Spencer set foot upon Kingwood, you made me feel a part of you," Sera replied. "I felt from the beginning as if I had known the two of you for a long time. I hope it will be that way when I meet the other two couples. As to answering your question, Lord and Lady Danbury will be the next to arrive in three days' time. I believe she wanted to come next so she would be able to spend more time at home as the date for her house party draws near."

"You will adore Louisa," Tessa assured her. "And Owen, rascal that he is, is ever so much fun. Spencer, Ev, and Percy are the more sedate ones of the bunch, while Owen and Win are the fun-loving rogues."

Hearing that about the Duke of Woodmont forced her once again to see how very unsuitable she would be for him. Not that he had any interest in her.

"But that is the yin and yang of things, my love," Spencer said, taking his wife's hand and kissing her fingers.

Sera was already growing used to such small, intimate gestures because she saw them often with both Percy and Minta and Spencer and Tessa.

"What is yin and yang?" she asked, curious about the phrase she had never heard before.

"It is an ancient Chinese philosophy I learned about at Cambridge," Spencer told her. "It describes two halves that together complete wholeness. How opposite forces can complement one another and become connected, strengthening the other until a new balance is created."

Tessa chuckled. "Spencer enjoys philosophy. What he is saying is that the Second Sons have each wed a woman that is different from them, almost an opposite. Your sister and Percy are prime examples. Percy is the most reserved man I have ever met. When around the Second Sons, he is comfortable and more himself but when he is out and about among the *ton*, he is withdrawn and aloof. Minta, as you know, is spirted and ebullient, full of good cheer. She helps balance Percy and brings out the best in him."

"I do agree they are well-matched," Sera said. "Though I never would have chosen Percy for my twin, I can see how they are suited for another."

"I think you are like Percy in many respects, Sera," Spencer said. "You are thoughtful and reserved, observing the world and its inhabitants. When you are comfortable with others, such as close friends and family, you aren't shy in the least bit." He paused. "I know this house party might prove difficult for you at first but by then you will know all five of the Second Sons and the four wives. Adalyn may think your perfect match lies with a man who can bring out your best qualities. One who is more outgoing than you are."

"Would you be opposed to a match with such a man?" Tessa asked.

Sera felt herself blushing profusely. "I had not thought of trying to make a match at the house party. Minta told me this affair would merely be a way for me to meet others and grow more comfortable among members of Polite Society."

"That is true," Tessa mused, "but I have yet to attend a house party where some couple did not announce their engagement. House parties lend themselves to getting to know others rapidly. I think it is an ideal way to meet a future husband. I know Adalyn has mentioned that she will be trying to find Win his duchess." She frowned. "He seems disinterested in doing so on his own and says he eschews love."

Tessa brightened. "Perhaps you might find your match in Win, Sera."

Her face now flamed with those words. "I do not think His Grace would be interested in a shy mouse such as me."

"If he doesn't recognize your worth, then it would be his loss," Spencer stated. "I know Louisa will be inviting several eligible bachelors to the house party. Be open, Sera. Give every gentleman his chance."

"I will," she promised quietly, thinking that no one present would be interested in romancing her.

Especially not the Duke of Woodmont.

Minta and Percy rejoined them and Minta apologized for suddenly rushing out.

"Do not worry about that," Tessa said. "You are among friends. Besides, you will spend the entire time until the baby's birth at Kingwood. The only exception will be Louisa's house party, which we were just discussing"

"I hope I am finished with all this annoying nausea by late August," Minta said, wrinkling her nose.

A sudden panic filled Sera.

What if Minta grew so ill that she was not up to attending the house party?

"I know what you are thinking," her twin said. "I will be going to Louisa's party. You are not getting off that easy. Besides, you promised Win you would attend." Minta turned to the others. "Win was adamant. If Sera skipped the party, so would he. He would only attend if she did, as well."

"Win said that?" Tessa asked, sitting up, obviously interested. She gazed upon Sera, who felt herself growing warm. "Do you truly think you might suit with Win? I know you did not spend much time with him but, sometimes, an attraction is instant."

Sera now blushed to her roots, uncomfortable by all the attention she was receiving.

"The duke is in no way interested in me as his wife," she said flatly. "A duchess is a leader in society. I am not even a follower, Tessa. I am more someone who sits in the corner and observes all that happens around me."

"Still, you were comfortable with Win," Minta said. "I have never seen you warm up to a stranger as you did Win on the day you arrived. Why, the two of you kept up a constant conversation in the carriage and throughout teatime. Not even Captain Marsh had you jabbering so."

"Captain Marsh?" Spencer asked.

Sera dug her nails into her palms. "He was an English officer I met while we were living in Ontario. We were . . . friendly."

She dropped her gaze and felt all eyes in the room were upon her.

"I am sorry I brought up Captain Marsh," Minta said gently.

Forcing her head up, she turned to her twin. "No, do not be sorry. He has been gone two years now. I am a bit wistful—even sad—but the melancholy has passed." She looked at their guests. "Captain Marsh had asked if he might court me when he returned from war. Unfortunately, he was lost on the battlefield."

"I am sorry for your loss, Sera," Tessa said, tears welling in her eyes.

"Thank you. I lost a friend. We had yet to see if we might have a future together." She swallowed. "But that is in the past. I am happy to be here in England now with my sister. And my new friends."

Bailey announced that the Middlefield carriages were ready and waiting and that all the luggage had been stored and the children brought downstairs. They left the breakfast room and Sera found Analise rushing toward her. She lifted the girl in her arms.

"I'll miss you, Aunt Sera."

"I will miss you and Adam."

"Will you come see us?"

Sera nodded. "I will do so."

She returned Analise to her nanny and kissed a sleeping Adam on his brow. Then Spencer wrapped her in a bear hug.

"I will hold you to your promise to come to us," he said.

Sera and Tessa embraced, with her new friend saying, "Write to me, Sera. I shall do the same and let Analise draw on the pages I send. I will see you at Louisa's next month."

Tessa kissed her cheek and then said her goodbyes to Minta and Percy. The three of them stood and waved as the carriages rolled down the lane.

Percy slipped an arm about Minta's waist and they turned toward the house.

"Coming?" Percy asked, looking over his shoulder.

"I think I will go spend some time in the gardens," she replied.

Sera made her way there. The gardens were by far her favorite place at Kingwood and she went deep into them, finding her favorite bench and sitting upon it.

The upcoming house party worried her. For once, it was not the strangers she would have to be introduced to. She knew she would have numerous friends there, knowing she would claim the other cousins and husbands among them during the next six weeks.

No, what worried her was those very friends might push her toward the Duke of Woodmont. A man who didn't seem all that interested in whom he married. A man who didn't believe in love.

Sera felt the exact opposite. She had lived with the shining example of her parents, a couple deeply in love after more than two decades of marriage. She also saw how happy Minta was with Percy.

Her mind was made up. She would not wed for any reason other than love. It would take a special man to love someone with her shy nature but she would settle for nothing less. She deserved love. She needed a special man who would love her completely and love her just as she was.

That man would never be the Duke of Woodmont.

CHAPTER NINE

THEY WERE UNRULY. Uncontrollable. Incorrigible.

What the bloody hell was Win going to do with these boys?

He had brought them to Essex, first stopping in the nearby village in order for the local tailor to measure them. The man refused, citing the boys' overall filth.

"Sorry, Your Grace, but you must get them cleaned up before I'll touch them." The tailor had frowned. "Might I suggest that you check them for lice?"

Win hadn't even thought of that. Much less the idea of his fancy carriage being infested with parasites.

He had ordered his driver to head for Woodbridge and turned the boys over to his butler and housekeeper, the Farmwells. Larson, his valet, was also pressed into service. He had told them to scrub Freddie and Charlie until every bit of grime was gone.

It had taken all three servants, along with three footmen, to hold them down.

Larson had been sent into the attics to scour trunks for any clothing that might fit the pair, while Win had visited with his steward. Kepler had told him of a childless couple in their early thirties who had always longed for children. Win immediately went to see the Birdwells, telling them he wished to place two boys into their care and guaranteeing them he would award them the monies to help clothe, house, and feed Freddie and Charlie. He mentioned seeing to their education and possible apprenticeship at some craft if the two weren't interested in farming. The Birdwells blubbered like babes, thanking Win for this opportunity to finally become parents.

He did not disclose his relationship with the boys. Win didn't know if he ever would. Though he felt an obligation to rectify Terrance's mistakes, he didn't really view his brother's bastards as relations of his. They were strangers, caught up in a long-ago scandal, and really had little to do with him. He would do his ducal duty and see they were placed in a good home and given opportunities they wouldn't have had access to. He saw no need to ever disclose they were related.

Freddie and Charlie had looked presentable by the time he returned to the house. He saw little of Terrance in them and figured both favored their mothers in looks—and hopefully their dispositions, as well. Larson had found old clothes of his and Terrance's which fit them. The quality of the material was good and men's fashions rarely changed. He did not think a return trip to the village tailor was needed at this time.

Win explained to Freddie and Charlie how they were going to live with the Birdwells now that their mama had passed. He would check on them periodically. At least he would have Larson or Kepler do so. Feeling his duty to his brother's by-blows would soon be fulfilled, he personally escorted the boys to the Birdwells' cottage and left them.

Two days passed, busy ones for Win, and when Larson told him he was going to deliver a few more sets of clothing to the cottage, Win decided he would complete the task himself. It wouldn't hurt to see the boys with their new guardians and observe how the Birdwells were treating them.

When he arrived, he found Mrs. Birdwell in tears. Win had never been able to handle tears and since he couldn't understand a word the woman said as she blubbered, he turned to her husband.

Birdwell broke the news. "We can't do it anymore, Your Grace."

"Can't do what?" he asked, puzzled by the statement.

"Care for them little devils," the farmer whispered, looking around the cottage as if someone might overhear him.

"I don't understand."

"They . . . are . . . well, Your Grace, there's no polite way to put this. I wouldn't wish that pair on anyone. Sorry, Your Grace. You're going to have to take them back."

"Take them . . . back?" The notion hadn't occurred to him. "That's simply not possible."

Birdwell nodded. "We don't want them. They're evil little bastards. I won't go into what they have done but you must take them off our hands now else Mrs. Birdwell might suffer a breakdown."

Win stiffened and then realized Birdwell used the term generically. The farmer had no idea Freddie and Charlie *were* bastards—of the former Duke of Woodmont.

Frowning, he asked, "Do you know who else might take them on?"

Birdwell vehemently shook his head. "No one at Woodbridge, Your Grace. I wouldn't wish them on anyone here. I would warn others against it. They're evil little buggers." Then looking sheepish, he had added, "Sorry, Your Grace."

When he pressed the farmer further, Birdwell—and his wife—clammed up. They wouldn't give Win any specific example of what had occurred during the past two days. They merely demanded that he take the boys back.

Realizing he had no choice, especially since he didn't want to alienate such good tenants, he agreed to take charge of Freddie and Charlie.

Finding them, however, was another matter. Win and his coachman searched for the better part of the day until they returned to the cottage, hoping the boys would do so, as well.

Sure enough, they were sitting outside the door, cross-legged, drawing with sticks in the dirt. They leaped to their feet when they spied him.

"Your Grace!" they cried in unison.

"You came to save us!" Freddie added. "Them Birdwells didn't want us, Your Grace. Made us wait out here for you."

That bothered him. But what troubled him more was whatever these two had done to make the childless couple give up on their dream of having children. Especially since Win would have paid them quite a bit extra for the boys' care.

He nodded to his coachman, who returned to the carriage, and Win took each boy by the hand. He walked them to the vehicle and helped them inside before joining them.

On the way home, he had spoken to them in serious tones, saying they had done a disservice to the Birdwells, who had been willing to take them on, telling them how disappointed their parents would have been. Both boys appeared visibly contrite.

He decided they must be hurting and perhaps he should keep them with him. He could make them his wards. It wasn't as if they could inherit since they were bastards but he could educate them and they could be trained to work on the estate and make themselves useful.

Truth be told, Win saw much of himself in the two orphans. They never knew their father. His had ignored him to the point where Win didn't truly know a single thing about his father. Their mother had grown too ill to see to their needs. His mother had barely acknowledged him. In some ways, he was almost an orphan himself. That sealed his decision. He would keep Freddie and Charlie at Woodbridge and do what he could to make them feel special.

Of course, that meant finding someone to care for them. They were too old for a nursery governess and neither knew how to read or write, which a tutor would expect. Win decided the best course of action would be to hire a governess, who could see to their educational and physical needs and be a companion to them. Once the governess caught them up, they could be sent to school at a later date.

He had now been through two governesses in two weeks.

Farmwell had suggested writing to the agency which had represented him and Mrs. Farmwell. They could fill any number of positions, from butlers to cooks to governesses. Knowing the situation was dire, Win had gone into London the next morning, bringing the boys along with him because he was too afraid of what they might do in his absence. They were thrilled to travel with him, having enjoyed the carriage ride from London to Essex earlier that week. Charlie asked if they would be able to have more meat pies. He promised them they could.

Win had met with the head of the agency, briefing him on the boys' background in rather vague terms. He simply said the boys were distant relatives who had grown up in abject poverty and had no schooling. Both parents were dead and they were to become his wards. He needed a governess with a firm hand to take them under her wing and care for them since they had a propensity for getting into trouble.

The agency's owner had sung the praises of a particular governess, who had recently completed an assignment and was free to take up a new position. While the man sent word to her, Win took the boys to a bookstore, allowing them to pick out several books filled with pictures. Both Freddie and Charlie had been well-behaved. They stopped for meat pies at a stall and also drank a cup of lemonade before returning to the agency. He couldn't for the life of him see what the Birdwells had to complain about because the boys were the picture of sweetness. They continued to be little angels the entire ride back to Essex, the new governess in tow.

She came to him three days later, looking a good ten years older, and announced she was returning to London due to her frayed nerves. Once again, she refused to give any specific instances of what was driving her away. Win accompanied her to town, leaving the boys in Larson's hands. His valet was a man never ruffled and Win assumed watching two six year olds for an entire day would not trouble the servant.

He deposited the governess at the agency and demanded another one be sent immediately. He specifically asked for one capable of disciplining unruly children. The new governess, sour-faced and in her mid-forties, accompanied him back to London. She asked a few questions about her charges and then fell silent the rest of the day.

She lasted a little more than a week.

When she came to Win, he was already expecting it. Actually, dreading it. Larson had begged him never to force him to watch the children again. When he passed whispering servants, they immediately fell silent. No one would tell him what was going on in his own household. By God, he was a duke!

This time, the governess described in great detail what she found wrong with the boys. In his mind, he viewed what she revealed as mere pranks. Of course, that many in a row for a good week would be hard to bear. She told Win of toads placed in her shoes and spiders in her bed. Salt poured into her tea. Honey matted in her hair while she slept. She demanded to be conveyed to London that very minute, saying Freddie and Charlie were hellions of the worst kind and she wouldn't remain under this roof a minute longer.

He acquiesced to her demand and, this time, did not journey with her to the employment agency. Instead, he called Freddie and Charlie to his study.

Both boys entered with solemn looks on their faces, knowing they were in trouble. He came from behind his desk and sat in a chair across from the settee he ordered them to sit upon.

In his sternest voice, Win asked, "Why were you so mean and spiteful to your governess?"

Freddie harumphed as well as any duke. "Well, she was mean and spiteful to us first."

Win lectured them but saw they quickly grew bored. Frustration filled him. No one wanted these two. He couldn't cut them loose. They carried his family's blood.

He decided to consult Percy. His cousin had a unique way of viewing situations, perhaps because he was so quiet and observed others with interest. If anyone might know what to do about Freddie and Charlie, it would be Percy.

Besides, he had been thinking about Sera Nicholls ever since he had left London. This would give him an excuse to see her, as well. Perhaps the auburn-haired beauty might even have a suggestion to help make the boys behave.

Ringing for Farmwell, Mrs. Farmwell, and Larson, he left Freddie and Charlie in his study so he could speak to the servants in private. Win told the trio he would be gone to his cousin's for several hours and that they needed to manage the boys. He ignored the looks they exchanged with one another.

"Do whatever it takes. Assign every servant in the house to watch them if you must. Ply them with cake if that will keep them quiet. Let them run outside until exhaustion sets in. Just see that they don't trouble any of my tenants and don't burn the house down while I am gone. Is that understood?"

The three nodded glumly and he ordered, "Follow me," before opening the door and stepping inside the study again.

Win looked at the boys, who actually had remained sitting on the settee. "I must visit my cousin, Lord Kingston. He lives on the next estate over. I will be gone several hours. You are to behave and not be destructive in any way. No pranks will be tolerated. Is that understood?" he thundered.

"Yes, Your Grace," the pair meekly said in unison.

Looking at them, he saw two forlorn orphans. But he had learned over the course of the past two weeks that looks were terribly deceiving.

He went to the stables and realized his carriage was on the road, conveying the mean, spiteful governess back to town. He really didn't want to ride by horseback the six miles to Kingwood and arrive hot and sweaty. Thank goodness he recalled seeing another carriage when he first arrived at Woodbridge several months ago. It had been the one his father had used. The head groom had mentioned that the former duke had found it lacking, ordering the present coach.

Win had the second carriage readied and the head groom himself volunteered to drive the team to Kingwood.

Climbing inside the vehicle, he leaned his head against the velvet cushion and closed his eyes. Weariness filled him. Yet the closer he came to Kingwood, anticipation began building within him. He wondered if he would be as taken with Sera Nicholls this time as he was at their first meeting. He had longed to kiss her. Had even thought about making her his duchess, which was a foolish idea. He decided it was pure lust he had felt for her. He hadn't been with a woman in a good while and she was a remarkable beauty. She was Minta's sister, for goodness' sake, not a woman to be dallied with.

Win resolved to seek out Percy and speak only to him regarding his problems. Seeing Miss Nicholls was a poor idea. He would see enough of her at that blasted house party coming up in late August. By then, he better have found a solution to the little terrors under his roof.

Else he'd have to break his promise to Miss Nicholls and skip the party altogether.

CHAPTER TEN

WIN'S CARRIAGE PULLED up at the front door of Kingwood. From the moment the vehicle had crossed onto Percy's lands, a calm had settled over him. He had spent many a happy time here as a boy. Percy's parents had been kind to him and Lady Kingston had always made certain her cook baked treats that Win enjoyed. Rupert, who had been three years older than Percy and Win, was willing to spend time with the younger boys, showing them the best places to fish and how to bait their hooks. He also took the pair riding. Win had looked upon Rupert as more of a brother than Terrance, who had never paid the slightest mind to his younger brother.

When word had reached the front that Rupert had drowned in a sailing accident, Win had worried about Percy's state of mind. Though the brothers had not seen each other in years, thanks to the war with Bonaparte preventing officers from returning home for even short leaves of absence, Rupert and Percy had corresponded regularly. Win had hated that Percy had to go home to an empty house and only memories of his family and loving brother.

At least he had found Minta. It still surprised him that the sparkling, outgoing beauty had taken the time to learn of the true Percy, the kind, quick-witted, loyal friend who only opened up around the Second Sons. Thank goodness she had. When Percy had confessed to Win of loving his wife, he had hoped his cousin would share that with his bride. Thank goodness Percy had. Win had witnessed the newlyweds being very affectionate when he had seen them in London the day Sera arrived. The looks exchanged between them spoke of a deep, abiding affection and bond that would only grow over the years. He knew his cousin and wife would be excellent parents.

It caused him to think once again of having children of his own. His and Percy's children would grow up together, much as they had. Their families would celebrate holidays. The boys would go off to the same school. Possibly even fight alongside one another in war one day though Win hoped that would not be the case.

Thoughts of children led him back to Sera Nicholls. He really needed to stop thinking about her. She was far too shy for his tastes. That alone would make her a poor duchess. Besides, he truly liked her—and he really didn't wish to like his wife. Especially if they were going to live separate lives. He needed to simply put himself in Adalyn's hands and let her choose a suitable woman. If she got along with the wives of the Second Sons, that would make him feel moderately better, as if he hadn't totally abandoned her.

But after all he had seen in the war, coupled with the appalling example of marriage he had witnessed from his parents, Win didn't feel he was capable of the kind of marriage his friends had made. He would do his duty and sire the needed heir and spare but he wanted to be able to go his own way, pursuing the activities—and women—that came across his path. That alone was reason enough to avoid Sera. He wouldn't want to hurt her and face the wrath of Minta. Probably Percy, as well.

He climbed from the carriage and knocked on the door, being greeted by Bailey.

"Ah, it is so good to see you, Your Grace," the butler said.

"And you, as well. How is Mrs. Bailey?"

"She is doing well. Thank you for asking, Your Grace. Lord

Kingston did not tell me you would be calling today."

"It was a spur of the moment decision, Bailey. Is he out on the estate?"

"Yes, Your Grace. Both he and Lady Kingston are visiting tenants." Bailey glanced at the grandfather clock standing in the foyer. "They are to return by teatime. Since it is only an hour away, would you care to wait for them?"

Win thought he should be productive and go see Rowell, the former steward to the Earl of Newcombe, who was now Percy's estate manager. Since Win's own steward, Kepler, would be retiring in the next few months, he should go and find Rowell and see if he knew of anyone who might be looking for a new position.

Instead, he said, "I will wait. Is Miss Nicholls available?"

Bailey smiled. "She is in the drawing room, Your Grace. Practicing her violin."

"She plays?"

"Quite well. In fact, I have never heard a more talented musician. Mrs. Bailey has to stay on the maids because they linger as they dust, wanting to hear Miss Nicholls play. The compromise has been for the door to remain open as Miss Nicholls practices so the servants may enjoy the music if they are nearby."

"Very good. I shall go up and hear her myself. No need to announce me, Bailey."

Win excused himself and headed up the stairs, intrigued by the idea that Sera played an instrument other than the pianoforte, as all young ladies in England seemed to do.

As he reached the top of the stairs, he heard the strains of the music and paused, listening to the piece.

Sera Nicholls was more than talented. She was a virtuosa.

Making his way along the corridor, he saw a maid dusting a statue, a wistful smile on her face. Then she saw him and straightened, moving down the hall in the opposite direction.

Win entered the drawing room and saw Sera at the far end. She perched in a wing chair that faced the large bay window looking out on the gardens. He moved deeper into the room but did not want to disturb her play, slipping into a chair without making a sound.

He wished he could see the expression on her face as she played. The beautiful music almost moved him to tears, which shocked him.

Because Win had never shed any before.

As a boy, tears had been frowned upon. As a man, he had tamped down his emotions every time he lost a soldier in battle. Any grief he felt was bottled up inside him. The letters that reached him on the Continent that informed him of his parents' deaths hadn't affected him in the slightest. Only hearing of Rupert's death had brought a tightening to his throat and chest, which he immediately disregarded, wanting to be strong for Percy.

Sera finished the haunting piece. Her bow stilled and she lowered both it and the violin.

"That was remarkable," he said quietly.

She startled at hearing his voice, whipping around. Her eyes went wide and he saw the deep green of them.

He rose and came toward her, taking a chair near hers. "I didn't wish to disturb you as you played. I am sorry if I upset you. Your playing . . . it was . . . as if it told a story. I can't quite explain my reaction."

Her radiant smile lit both her face and the room. "That is a lovely compliment, Your Grace. Music does tell a story. Different ones for different people. That is what I love about it. You can hear a piece and create images in your mind. Write your own story. Feel a multitude of emotions. Another person will interpret it entirely different."

"Win," he reminded her. "His Grace is for others. Not family and close friends."

She blushed at his words, making her look like a rose he wished to pluck.

"I know you asked me to do so, Your Grace, but I am not

truly family. Besides, men and women are never close friends."

"I beg to differ," he said, leaning forward, his elbows resting on his thighs. "Though I haven't known my friends' wives for long, I already look upon them as sisters. I believe over the years, friendship between us will grow. The same will be true with us, Sera."

He deliberately used her first name, liking the sound of it on his lips.

"Only in private, however," he continued. "Polite Society would be scandalized if we addressed one another in an intimate fashion at one of their gatherings."

Her blush deepened and he yearned to place his palm against her cheek and feel its heat.

She lowered her gaze. "I understand."

He didn't want her to turn shy and hoped she might open up as they talked. She had done so in the carriage, reminding him of how Percy would relax around those he was comfortable with and his shyness would disappear.

"Tell me about how you learned to play," he urged.

Sera glanced back up and then stood, taking her instrument to a case which was opened on a nearby table. She placed the violin and bow inside and closed it.

"Mama started Minta and me at pianoforte lessons when we were six. I fell in love with music then. Our teacher told our parents that while Minta was an excellent student and would make for a wonderful player, he saw I had a true gift. He urged them to allow me to try an instrument beyond the pianoforte."

Returning to her seat, she said, "Papa's government salary was stretched enough by our taking pianoforte lessons, making it impossible for me to have additional ones. Uncle West heard me play and when Mama told him what our instructor had shared, he volunteered to pay for any other lessons."

"That was quite generous of him."

"I refused," she said, surprising him. "I did not want Papa to feel bad about it. After a year of lessons on the pianoforte, I already knew enough to continue to teach myself on the instrument and I did so. Minta continued her lessons, while Uncle West helped find a violin instructor for me."

She smiled wistfully. "I feel in love with the violin. How it could sound almost human at times. How it felt as if I had magic in my fingers when I took up my bow. I decided to keep to it."

"You are remarkably talented, Sera."

"Thank you," she said softly. "It is something I turn to often. When I am sad, playing can cheer me. When I am excited, it can calm me. When I am lonely, my violin is my friend." She paused. "I played quite a bit after receiving news of Captain Marsh's death and again when Minta left for England and I remained in Canada."

Win's gut twisted. He didn't like hearing how the army captain's death had affected her. It made him angry. Then he realized he was jealous—of a dead man. That was utterly ridiculous. Sera had already told Win she did not love Marsh. That she merely wondered what might have been between them if he had lived and returned to her. Still, it troubled Win.

And that worried him.

He felt too much for this woman when he didn't want to feel anything for her. He feared if he attended his friends' house party, it would throw them together too often and his feelings for her would magnify. He couldn't allow that. He couldn't marry Sera Nicholls. He didn't want to marry Sera Nicholls. Win wanted to continue to divorce his feelings from himself and be neutral regarding his future wife.

It would be impossible to attend. For if he did, he would kiss her. Do more than kiss her.

And that would be disastrous.

But how could he tell her he wouldn't be in attendance? He assumed the party was being given for her as much as for him. With her retiring nature, it would be difficult to throw her into a London Season and ask her to find a husband. A house party would give her the opportunity to find a gentleman in a much different atmosphere. The small, intimate nature of the gathering would be conducive in showing all of Sera's good qualities. Why, if she merely played her violin once, she would probably have offers of marriage.

Suddenly, he realized he couldn't be at this house party with her and see her with other men. Watch as flirtation—and even romance—unfolded between her and others. The thought of someone besides him kissing Sera made his blood boil.

That was reason enough to skip the festivities.

He couldn't tell her now, though. She couldn't learn in advance of his withdrawal because she would do the same, ruining her opportunity. Win would have to wait and send word to Owen and Louisa the day of the party. Between now and then, surely he could come up with some complicated, acceptable excuse as to why he would have to absent himself from the affair.

Clearing his throat, he said, "I am glad music provided such comfort to you."

"Do you play an instrument?" she asked.

He shook his head. "No. The subject never came up in our household. If it had, no one would have thought to include me in the lessons. Everything revolved around Terrance, the heir apparent. I was an afterthought. If that."

Sera leaned over and placed her hand on his arm, causing a jolt. She must have felt it, too, because she quickly lifted it away.

"I am sorry you had the parents you did, Win. It was their loss that they didn't bother to see what an amazing child they had."

He chuckled, trying to lighten the mood since a sexual energy crackled the air. "I have never been amazing. Merely adequate. I was intelligent but did not apply myself to my studies, either at school or university. I was more interested in having fun. I did, I believe, live up to the high standards demanded of an officer of His Majesty's army, however."

Sighing, he added, "And now I am trying to do my best to address my ducal responsibilities."

She smiled shyly at him, causing his heart to turn over. "I think you could do anything you made your mind up to do, Win."

Before he could reply, Percy called out, "Bailey told us you were here. It is good to see you, Win."

His cousin and Minta crossed to where Win and Sera sat.

"It is about time you visited us," Minta scolded. "I sent you invitations twice to come to dinner while Tessa and Spencer were with us."

Win shook his head. "I was—actually, am—dealing with an impossible situation. It is the reason why I could not take advantage of your hospitality, Minta.

"And it is the reason I have come to you today for advice."

CHAPTER ELEVEN

S ERA WAS STILL trembling as Minta and Percy entered the drawing room.

She had merely wanted to comfort Win when she touched his arm. He was so large—and larger than life—yet she heard something in his tone. A touch of melancholy mixed with wistfulness. Even though he was an adult, somewhere inside of him was that little boy who had been ignored. Pushed aside in favor of the heir to the dukedom. It had to have hurt then. It seemed whether Win knew it or not, it still affected him today.

He had spoken briefly of his family on the carriage ride from the London docks to Percy's townhouse. His brother had been much older and paid no attention to his sibling. The same brother had sorely neglected his responsibilities when he had become the Duke of Woodmont. Now, Win was having to rectify those mistakes. All while hurting.

At least he had had Percy and his brother as cousins. From things Percy had said ever since Sera arrived, Win had spent a great deal of his time at Kingwood with the Perry brothers and Rupert had been an ideal older brother to them both.

She was glad her sister and brother-in-law arrived when they did, wanting to get in control of her feelings as much as her body. Why did she grow short of breath when Win was around? Why did merely brushing her fingers on his arm cause such a tidal wave to stir within her? Sera knew he had also felt something at the exchange for he quickly tried to make light of things.

But what advice might he be in need of?

For a moment, she thought it could be about his future duchess. That caused her belly to feel nauseated. She chastised herself mentally, knowing a future with a man such as the Duke of Woodmont was impossible. Adalyn would find a bright, charming, gracious woman whom Win would wed, not some shy little mouse such as herself. It would hurt, though, when she saw him matched with a woman at the house party. That was the purpose of the event. To find Win a bride. And most likely, a husband for her. Her timidity would not bode well as she entered the *ton* next Season. It would be better to find a husband now and be on his arm by the time spring came to England.

But to see Win with another woman already tore at her. She had never felt jealousy of any kind. Never thought to possess another.

Until she had met His Grace, the Duke of Woodmont.

Sera pushed such foolishness aside. Her hope now would be to find a gentleman she could respect. One who would make for a good husband and father. Hopefully, one who lived far from Essex and Kent, where all the Second Sons had their main country estates. If she were wed to a man who lived far to the north or west, then she wouldn't have to be in the company of the close-knit group.

And she wouldn't have to see Win doting on his duchess.

She didn't believe him when he said he wished for a loveless marriage. He would be influenced by his friends, the brothers of his heart, and be as affectionate and loving as those four men were to their wives. Sera herself hoped to find love and if she didn't, she prayed it would grow over time with the man she spoke her vows to at the altar.

"Tea is coming," Minta said, dragging Sera from her thoughts. "Bailey told us Win had arrived and I told them to send up the teacart immediately."

"Shall we move over to where there is more seating?" Percy suggested.

Before Sera could rise, Win was next to her chair, offering his hand. She took it, feeling the ripple of . . . something . . . run through her. He guided her to a settee and took the seat next to her. She didn't really want to be sitting next to him. He was too large and took up too much space. In fact, she could feel the heat coming from him because they were so close.

What would it feel like to have his warm body next to her in bed?

She half-groaned, half-sputtered, clearing her throat as if she had swallowed wrong. Win lightly thumped her on the back, his palm warm.

"Are you all right?" he asked in that deep voice that sent shivers up her spine.

"Yes," she said brusquely, wishing his attention would be anywhere except on her. She feared he might somehow read her lascivious thoughts, things she had never thought of until he came into her life.

That alone let her know that she and Edward Marsh never would have been right for one another. She had feared it after he kissed her and she hadn't felt much of anything. Sera had lied to herself, believing that he would come home and they would court and marry and everything would work out between them. It might have occurred that way. Because most likely, she never would have met Win. She would have lived a far different life as the wife of an army captain and never circulated in the social circle she did now with Minta's friends.

The teacart arrived and her twin poured out for everyone.

"Be sure and drink up," Win advised Sera. "Hot tea should soothe whatever is caught in your throat."

"Thank you," she murmured.

"I heard Sera playing her violin when I arrived," Win told the others. "She has a remarkable talent."

Percy smiled at her. "Yes, Sera's music is most soothing. Even if Minta had ten sisters, I know Sera would be my favorite, thanks to her sweet spirit and her violin playing."

"Sera and I often play duets together," Minta shared.

Win smiled broadly. "You must play for me then," he begged. "Just one number and then we can continue with tea."

"Now?" Sera squeaked. "We haven't practiced anything together in ages."

"This isn't a performance at a dinner party, Sera," Minta chided. "It is merely a song played for a friend."

Friend . . .

"All right," she wavered, rising. "Do you have any idea what you wish to play?" she asked her sister as Minta moved to the pianoforte and Sera retrieved her violin.

Minta told her and Sera nodded, agreeing with the choice. She took a seat and allowed her sister to begin playing before she joined in. Minta also sang as they played, her low alto rich.

Usually, Sera became lost in the music anytime she picked up her instrument. On this occasion, though, she sensed Win's gaze penetrating her. It didn't make her nervous, however. Instead, it emboldened her. Her fingers felt nimble. When the last note sounded, Sera believed she had played the best she ever had.

Win and Percy applauded enthusiastically, with Percy kissing his wife's cheek as they returned to their seats.

"That was fabulous, my love. The two of you together could go on the stage."

"Thank you, Percy. I must say that Sera always gently pushes me to new heights. I play and sing better when we perform together."

"That was exceptional," Win said. "I feel fortunate to have heard the two of you. I won't soon forget how your performance moved me."

He looked at her. She looked at her teacup.

As tea continued, though, she opened up. Despite her nerves being around Win, he also made her want to speak up more. Somehow, she felt more confident in his presence.

"What advice are you seeking?" Percy finally asked.

Win looked taken aback for a moment and then laughed heartily, the rich rumble in his chest causing her mouth to go dry.

"Sorry. It is not a laughing matter. I am at the end of my proverbial rope, however."

"What's wrong?" Percy asked, looking concerned.

"Thanks to the Bow Street Runner I hired, Terrance's by-blows have been located."

Sera frowned. She wasn't quite sure what a by-blow was but didn't want to volunteer that information.

Win must have sensed her discomfort and turned to her. "The day Percy and Minta wed, I shared with the others that my brother had sired a few children out of wedlock," he explained, making very clear the meaning of what a by-blow was to her. "I later shared this with Percy." He grinned. "Which means Minta most certainly knew."

"I most certainly did," her sister said saucily. "We tell each other everything." Minta grew serious. "So, you have found them. How many are there?"

"Jack Blumer is fairly certain there are only the two. That Terrance must have taken more precautions. There is also the possibility that my brother didn't even know about the second one." Win sighed. "Let me tell you everything."

Sera sat, spellbound, as Win told of his brother's mistress, an actress who had become with child, much to the duke's displeasure. Her nails dug into her palms as she heard not only how the duke had rejected Miss Sawyer—but how he had assaulted her dresser, who had also found herself carrying the duke's illegitimate babe.

"Sally died in childbirth shortly after Miss Sawyer had delivered Freddie. She took in Charlie as her own and the two boys believe they are brothers."

"Instead of half-brothers born on the same day," Percy commented.

"Thank God neither boy favors Terrance," Win said. "If I didn't know the story, I wouldn't think they were his. Freddie is dark-haired and green-eyed. Charlie has both brown hair and eyes. My brother was blond and blue-eyed," he explained for Sera's and Minta's benefit.

"Since you've discovered them and know their story, will you give Miss Sawyer a monthly stipend to help with their care and education?" she asked.

Win raked a hand through his hair. "That was my original plan. Unfortunately, Blumer took me to Miss Sawyer, who was dying of consumption. She barely got out her tale of woe when she died. I had brought a doctor with us and he said nothing could have been done to prolong her life. I paid for her burial expenses and brought the boys to Woodbridge. I thought to have a couple on my estate raise them. They have no children of their own and it seemed the right thing to do."

"When did this happen?" Minta asked. "And do you seek advice on their schooling?"

"Or are you wishing to keep quiet about their relationship to you?" Percy pressed.

"They have been in Essex almost two weeks. Unfortunately, the Birdwells decided not to parent the boys." Win's hand raked through his hair again and Sera thought that a telling gesture. "They . . . gave them back."

"They gave them back?" she echoed. "Did I hear you correctly?"

Win nodded. "You did. Freddie and Charlie spent two days with the couple. They were so incorrigible that the Birdwells told me they couldn't care for the pair. In fact, they wouldn't wish them upon anyone."

Sera drew in a quick breath, shocked by his words.

"I thought I might take them on as my wards," Win revealed, "still not disclosing the relationship between us. I have merely told them I knew their father."

He stood and began pacing. "It has been an unmitigated disaster."

Quickly, the words rushed from him. He spoke of how he

had gone to London and acquired a governess for the boys. How they had terrorized her and she demanded to be sent back to London. That he engaged a second governess from the same agency. She also had quit, describing the boys' many pranks and how she wasn't going to teach such hellions.

Win returned to his seat, picking up his teacup and draining the contents. "What am I to do with them?" he asked. "None of my servants can manage them. In fact, I had to play the haughty duke and demand they watch the boys while I came here for a few hours. None of my tenants will take them. I doubt anyone in the local village would. I cannot in good conscience return them to London. Blumer, the Bow Street Runner, said they were already too old to be placed at a foundling home. Even if one took them on, I already know the scheming pair. They would be out the door before my carriage pulled away from the establishment. The streets of London are no place for two six-year-old orphans."

He shook his head. "I am at my wit's end. That is why I have turned to you today."

Sera saw both Minta and Percy were speechless.

"I will help care for them," she said, her voice sounding faint as the blood rushed to her ears.

CHAPTER TWELVE

"WHAT?" ALL THREE cried, looking at her as if she had gone mad.

Sera stood her ground. "You have said it yourself, Minta. How good I am with children. Percy saw it when Tessa and Spencer were here."

"That is true," Percy confirmed. "You had Analise and Adam eating out of your hand." He looked at Win. "Sera is quite good. Especially since she has never had any children of her own."

"But these are two boys. Terrible boys. Six-year-old boys," Minta interjected. "It is one thing for a two-year-old and a baby to adore you. From what Win has said, Freddie and Charlie are incorrigible. Please, Sera, think how badly behaved they must be for the Birdwells to return them to Win. I don't want to see you run ragged by such hellions."

She ignored her twin's pleading and looked directly at Win. "You need me. You have admitted as much. You cannot do it alone. Your servants are baffled at how to handle them. You have nowhere else to turn. You might as well let me help. Let me see if I can get through to them."

He raked both hands through his hair, clearly frustrated. "I did not come here to drag you away from your sister, Sera. You have only been together a couple of weeks. Besides, aren't Owen and Louisa coming to visit? And then Ev and Adalyn? I cannot ask you to do this."

"You didn't ask me to. I volunteered," she pointed out. "This will save the others from coming to Kingwood when they have better things to do. I will meet them at the house party as it is."

When he didn't look as if he would budge, she added, "Look, Win. You have nowhere else to turn. No one else willing to come help out. I am not saying I will be successful but I would like to give it a try. I like to be useful and I am really of no use at Kingwood. Yes, I have spent some time with Minta but I know she would rather be with Percy."

"That's not so," her sister protested weakly.

"You are newlyweds, Minta. I felt odd about coming with you to Kingwood in the first place. Take this extra time with Percy. After all, the babe will be here before you know it and then there will be three of you. Enjoy your time alone together. You know I have always loved children and animals more than people. I can go to Woodbridge and help care for these boys until the house party. That is six weeks away." She smiled. "By then, I will either have broken them in and gotten them under control— or I will actually be eager to leave and attend a party."

Win frowned. "But what of clothing? I know how important that is to ladies. You'll want to be fitted for gowns for the house party."

"That won't be necessary. Minta and I have always shared our gowns since we are identical in size. It helped stretch Papa's salary farther by us sharing a wardrobe." She chuckled. "And in another six weeks, Minta may need to have new gowns of her own made up to wear because she will be increasing. I might have use of her entire wardrobe during the house party, most likely."

"That is true," her sister admitted. "And we weren't going to worry about a new wardrobe for Sera until next year at any rate. I wanted her to be bedecked in the latest of fashions."

"I may be lucky enough to snag a husband at this house party and keep Uncle West from having to buy me that new wardrobe."

She noticed Win frowned deeply at her words but pushed that aside. "What do you say?" May I accompany you home? Even for a few days—or a week? Let me see what I can do with the boys. If I am unsuccessful, then you may interview another governess. Surely these two can't run off every governess in England. And I might actually be able to handle them."

Reluctance shone in Win's eyes but he nodded. "All right. You can return to Kingwood with me."

"Why don't you let Sera come first thing tomorrow?" Minta suggested. "That way we will have time to pack for her and you can prepare Freddie and Charlie for her arrival."

"No," she said firmly, overriding Minta, something she rarely did. She noticed her twin's brows arch in surprise. "These boys are an immediate problem. What good will it do to put off my going to Woodbridge? In fact, I think the idea of preparing them for me would only set me up for failure with them."

She looked and saw Win smiling at her. "So, you plan to storm the castle in a surprise attack?"

Sera returned his smile. "Exactly. They will never know what hit them."

Minta sniffed. "Well, at least come upstairs with me so we can pack a few things for you. I'll gather everything else you will need for an extended stay and send them over tomorrow." She looked at her husband. "Perhaps Percy and I could bring Sera's things and visit."

"No," she said again. "Give me a few days with them before you make an appearance. I want to get them into a routine. Routine is important."

Her sister sighed. "Very well then." She rose. "Come along and let's get you ready for a few days then."

"We won't be long," she promised Win and then she followed Minta from the drawing room.

The moment they were alone in the corridor together, Minta asked, "What were you thinking?"

"I was thinking I could help."

"They are hellions, Sera. I doubt anyone can help them."

"Well, Win isn't going to abandon them," she pointed out. "That means they are in his life for good. I might as well try and help give him some peace and those boys stability."

"You are unlike yourself," Minta said as they went up the stairs. "You are . . . more assertive than I have ever seen you." She looked at Sera. "But I think this is a good thing. If helping these two orphans will bring you out of your shell, you will have more success at the house party."

"By success, you mean landing a husband," Sera said flatly.

"Well, yes. Isn't that the goal?"

Sera didn't respond but, suddenly, she wasn't so sure. All her life, she had been subtly nudged toward marriage, as every woman was. She did love children and always wanted ones of her own. But what if she were meant to teach and love other people's children instead of ones of her own? She had worried about what it took to get children. How you came together with a man. She wasn't certain that was something she was interested in doing. She had heard servants gossiping about men and women coupling and how it hurt. Sera had planned to ask Minta about it though since her sister was overly affectionate with Percy, it must be good between them physically.

She worried with her innate shyness that she would never find happiness in the bedroom, much less satisfy her husband. Her thoughts turned to the very large and physical Win. He would expect a wife to submit to who knows what in bed, as well as have a string of mistresses, if he truly followed the typical *ton* marriage. That alone told her to push aside any notion of him as a future husband. She merely had an infatuation regarding him. He was handsome beyond words, affable, and interesting. She would relegate him to a status of friend of the family, which is all he could ever be. Adalyn would find him a wife at the house party and Sera would do her best to always be pleasant to the new duchess since she supposed it was inevitable they would see each other frequently over the years.

Unless Sera chose not to wed and pursue the idea of gover-nessing.

"You seem to like Win," her sister pointed out. "You haven't been shy around him in the least." Minta paused, her eyes widening. "Are you interested in him, Sera? If you are, staying at Woodbridge—"

"No," she said quickly, hoping she would not blush. "He is just easy to talk with. I simply want to help him." She looked at her sister steadily. "Besides, do you see me as a duchess, Minta? The last thing I would be suited to be would be a duchess."

Her twin gave her a sympathetic look. "I understand."

They arrived at her bedchamber and Minta rang for a maid to help with the packing. Sera laid out her night rail and three gowns, with the accompanying undergarments, for the servant to pack.

"This should be enough until you and Percy bring me more to wear," she said.

Minta fingered one of the gowns. "Oh, Sera, these are hope-lessly out of date. Let me send a few of mine with you instead. I have been too wrapped up in Percy to even notice what you have been wearing since you arrived in England. I'm so sorry."

"No, you can send along the rest of my wardrobe and some of your gowns in a few days. I will be with boys and hope to spend a lot of time with them outdoors. I don't want to ruin any of your gowns. My old ones will suffice."

"But what about dinner each night? Surely, you will eat with Win."

She hadn't thought of that. "I doubt it," she said quickly. "I will most likely eat with Freddie and Charlie."

Her sister frowned. "That sounds as if you'll be a governess."

"Well, I will be caring for them around the clock, Minta. Sharing a meal with my charges would be expected. If I didn't, can you imagine what they might do in the nursery? Or perhaps the schoolroom. If there is one at Woodbridge, I believe that would be a good place for us to eat together."

Minta laughed. "Oh, there will be a schoolroom. And a room for everything else imaginable. Sera, Win is a duke! His estate will be far larger than Kingwood, as will his house."

"Larger than Percy's?"

The thought boggled Sera's mind. It had taken her a good three days to find her way around Kingwood's house. The grounds were large and she hadn't finished exploring those yet. She couldn't imagine Win's holding to be larger. But Minta was right. After all, Win was the Duke of Woodmont. A duke was just a step below a prince. She supposed Woodbridge would be enormous and the surrounding estate vast.

The maid arrived and quickly assembled Sera's things. Sera asked for her sturdy boots to be packed as well.

"If Win's estate is as large as you say, then I will be exploring quite a bit of it with the boys. I don't want any of my slippers to suffer the dust or mud we might encounter."

They returned to the drawing room and Win rose. "Are you set?"

"Yes, a footman is taking my things to your carriage now," she replied.

"Then I suppose we should be off. I've been gone longer than I expected as it is."

Minta and Percy walked them out. While the ducal carriage was large and very nice, it wasn't as grand as Percy's. Then she remembered that Win had sent the governess to London in it. To think this was his spare carriage allowed Sera a small idea of just how wealthy he must be. Her family had never owned a carriage. To maintain one in London, along with horses and a coachman, was prohibitively expensive. They had made do with walking or hailing a hansom cab when necessary. Often, Uncle West would send his carriage for them whenever they went to dinner at his townhouse. Sometimes, Aunt Phyllis would arrive in it and take them shopping or to a bookshop, as well.

Sera was happy for her sister, having married well. Not only did Percy provide for Minta financially, but she could see how happy the couple was together. The babe would only strengthen the bond between them. She thought how happy she would be to be an aunt and decided she needed to start knitting items soon in order for them to be ready by the time the baby came.

"We will come not tomorrow or the next day but the one following," Minta promised. "That should give you enough time to establish whatever routine you wish."

Her twin hugged her tightly and whispered, "Take care."

Percy also embraced her. "We will see you soon, Sera. I hope you enjoy your time with these boys. And remember, there is no shame in deciding you want to come home before the house party."

"And leave me stranded?" Win joked.

He gestured toward the carriage and handed her up. Sera tried to ignore the tingle that rippled through her at his touch as she entered the vehicle and sat facing forward. Win joined her, sitting beside her. She should have sat on the other bench and faced him but she despised riding backward. It did something to her belly and head.

But having Win seated so close to her, the spice of his cologne and the warmth of his body near, unsettled her.

As the carriage started up, Sera waved to her sister and brother-in-law and then sat back against the cushions.

"Thank you," Win said. "I don't know of any lady who would have volunteered as you have, especially hearing how unruly Freddie and Charlie can be."

"I haven't even met them—but I do not think they are badly behaved at all."

He frowned, the crease between his brows looking very appealing. "Why would you say that? I shared with you some of the trouble they have created. Sera, they have run off two governesses in less than two weeks."

"I think they have just been mischievous, Win. That they aren't bad. They are simply acting out. Think about it. Their world has turned upside down in the last year and now in the past fortnight. They went from living in a nice townhouse to being crammed into a single room at a boardinghouse. Their mother was having to sell anything of value to keep them going. From what you shared, it sounds as if they were down to their last farthing. Their mother was so ill she could no longer care for them and so they began to run wild and act out."

She shifted in the seat, trying to move slightly away from him as she faced him.

"Then their world was turned even more upside down when you arrived and announced that their mother, the only stable adult in their lives, had passed. They never got a chance to say goodbye to her. They were whisked away from London, the only place they had ever lived, to the country. For city boys, a move to the country would be a shock to their systems. Then they were placed with people who did not want them. Returned to you because supposedly they were so horrible. They've struck out because they are hurting. That is why they were unkind to their governesses."

"I hadn't thought of all that," he admitted. "I supposed they should be grateful they didn't have to live on the streets but you are right. I am a stranger to them. The country is a strange world. They only have each other to cling to." He smiled at her. "Thank you for opening my eyes, Sera. I am seeing things from their point of view instead of my own. I only hope you won't regret coming."

"They need stability. They need to see that the rug won't be pulled out from under them. Whether they know it or not, they need me."

Win's gaze penetrated her. "I think I need you, too," he said softly.

And then he kissed her.

CHAPTER THIRTEEN

T HE LAST THING Win wanted to do was kiss Sera.
But he did it anyway.

Actually, it was what he had wanted to do since he'd met her. The past few weeks, she had come to dominate his thoughts. He knew kissing her was absolutely the wrong action on his part. Even as he lowered his lips to hers, his mind was screaming at him to stop. That she was Minta's sister. Percy's sister-in-law. A sweet woman who undoubtedly had dreams of love in her heart.

Something he could never give her.

Instead, he took. Greedily. Oh, he started slowly at first, softly brushing his lips against her divine ones, so soft and full. His hand moved to cradle her cheek, wanting to feel her warmth and touch the satin skin. He grazed his thumb back and forth against her cheek as he inhaled the sweet scent of jasmine that perpetually clung to her. He supposed she poured the scent into her bath. The thought of a naked Sera caused his cock to stir.

Gradually, he increased the pressure of his lips against hers. Instead of the soft, sweet kiss that had started out, he wanted more. His hand moved from her cheek to her nape, holding her steady as his tongue teased the seam of her lips. He was glad he had hold of her because he was afraid the movement would cause her to withdraw. And if she did, he might perish.

Slowly, she opened to him, uncertainty oozing from her,

letting him know that if she had been kissed before, this was the first time tongues would be involved. When his plunged inside, he heard her gasp. His hand continued to cup her nape and his other moved to her waist. Win stroked her velvet softness, tasting the sweetness of the lemon cake she had eaten at tea and something more. Something that was Sera alone, a taste new to him, tempting him.

He pulled her toward him until her breasts grazed his chest. He longed to taste them, as well, the rounded globes so close, calling out to him. He thought that might shock her too much so he continued plundering the sweetness of her mouth, enjoying the little throaty sighs and moans that came from her.

Her hands had moved to his chest, her palms flat against it, her fingers beginning to knead him like a satisfied kitten. He smiled against her mouth and felt her do the same. Emboldened now, he continued kissing her, but his hand crept from her waist to her breast. He palmed it, kneading it, feeling its fullness swell with his touch. Brushing the pad of his thumb across her nipple, she whimpered, making him feel powerful—and possessive. Win knew he was the first man to have kissed her like this. Touched her like this.

By God, he wanted to be the last.

She leaned into him and he wanted her closer to him. Without breaking the kiss, he managed to lift her into his lap, setting her down gently, one arm bracing her back. His hand wandered to her breast again, teasing the nipple, grazing it with his fingernail, thrilling at the sound she made.

He deepened the kiss further, knowing he had never kissed a woman this long and yet feeling as if no time at all had passed. Her hands now tightened on his shoulders, her nails digging into him. If not for the coat he wore, she would be leaving her marks on him.

Breaking the kiss, he allowed his lips to hover just above hers. She whimpered again, her way of telling him she wanted more. Softly, he bit into her full, bottom lip, causing her to stiffen and then sigh. He sucked and nibbled on it, causing her to wriggle against him, which was not a good thing.

How much time had passed? Surely, they would pull up at Woodbridge soon.

Win had to stop this madness. Cast aside all thoughts of marking her as his. He was playing with fire and knew they both had already been singed.

He kissed her hard one more time, wanting a last taste of her. No, a final taste.

Breaking the kiss, he saw how flushed her face was. Her eyelids fluttered several times and then opened, the green orbs dark and dazed.

He lifted her, placing her on the seat next to him again. Much as he hated to, he would apologize.

"I am sorry, Sera. More sorry than I can convey," he began.

Win had expected her to meekly accept his apology. Even be embarrassed by what had happened between them.

Instead, she slapped him.

Quiet, shy, sweet Sera Nicholls slapped him.

It stunned him.

"Why the bloody hell would you go and ruin things?" she demanded, turning away from him to gaze out the window.

He swallowed, still tasting her. Still wanting her.

"Sera, I took advantage of you. It was wrong of me to do so."

Her back stiffened. She kept silent.

"Minta will explain the rules of Polite Society to you if she already hasn't. Unattached females are not to be alone with gentlemen, else they might have a tendency to behave in a very ungentlemanly way, as I just did."

Silence.

"I have wanted to kiss you for some time," he admitted, trying a different tactic. "You are a very beautiful woman."

"But not duchess material," she said softly.

He swallowed. "I have told you that I will not be as the Second Sons. I do not expect to love my wife. Or in truth, even be friends with her. I view marriage as a business arrangement." He paused. "I like you, Sera. I want to be your friend. If I made you my duchess, you would be very unhappy. You deserve a man who will love you. I can never do that."

She turned to him, tears glistening in her eyes. "I understand. And I do want love, as impossible as that seems. If I cannot have it, I will refuse to wed."

"You don't mean that."

"I do," she said, fire in her eyes. "Either I will marry on my terms or I will remain alone."

Win didn't want to see her that way. "I hope you do find love, Sera," he told her, though the thought of another man touching her made him grow ill. "Remember that you might find a kind gentleman and that after you wed, love may grow between you."

"Is there anything else you wish to tell me about the boys?" she asked, her tone wintry.

"No. In truth, I know very little about them."

A storm brewed in her eyes. "Then that is the first thing that you should remedy."

He frowned. "What do you mean?"

"They are your nephews, Win. Your flesh and blood. They are family. You should treat them as such."

"I haven't told them we are related," he protested.

Her eyes narrowed. "Then perhaps you should. If they knew they had a relative—someone who cared for them—they might not behave in such an atrocious manner."

He shook his head. "I will have to think on that, Sera."

"Perhaps you should address me as Miss Nicholls."

"Why?"

"It is how the boys and the staff will. I want you to do the same."

He realized her pride was wanting to put distance between them. It probably was a good idea. It was already going to be hard enough having her stay under his roof. The sooner he got it through his thick skull that he had made a mistake and Sera was forbidden fruit, the better.

"All right," he agreed. "Am I to tell Freddie and Charlie that you are their new governess?"

"Let me do the talking," she said succinctly and fell silent, once more staring out the window.

Less than a minute later, the carriage turned onto the drive that led up to the house.

Win didn't know what he was feeling. Or rather, he was feeling too much. Guilt. Lust. Sadness. Anger. Sera had turned him inside out. Or rather kissing her had done so. If he hadn't opened Pandora's box with a kiss, they would be speaking pleasantly toward one another. Instead, she was as cold as an icicle, while turmoil roiled within him.

The carriage arrived at the house and came to a halt. He waited a moment as the footman set the stairs in place and opened the coach's door, then he sprang outside. Farmwell stood on the gravel, ready to greet him. He nodded to the butler and then turned to help Sera down. His footman had already taken her hand and helped her from the vehicle. She smiled and thanked him.

Win cursed silently, jealous of a bloody footman.

He looked to the butler and said, "Farmwell, Miss Nicholls is the boys' new governess."

Relief flooded Farmwell's face. "It is wonderful to have you at Woodbridge, Miss Nicholls."

"Thank you, Farmwell. I am looking forward to meeting my charges."

The servant regained his composure. "I hope you will meet with success, Miss Nicholls."

"There is only a small valise for now," Win said. "The rest of Miss Nicholls' things will arrive in a few days."

"I took the liberty of preparing the governess' room, Your Grace. Just so that it would be ready for the next arrival."

He frowned, not wanting Sera to stay in the servants' quarters.

"Thank you for doing so, Farmwell. If my things could be taken there now, I would like to meet Freddie and Charlie."

"Of course, Miss Nicholls. If you will come with me."

"I'll come along, as well," Win said. "I should be the one to introduce you to them," he said stubbornly.

Sera didn't comment. She merely followed Farmwell into the house, where she was introduced to Mrs. Farmwell, a frantic look on her face. When the housekeeper heard Sera was a governess, tears sprang to her eyes.

"Oh, it is very good to have you at Woodbridge, Miss Nicholls. Let me take you to the schoolroom where the boys are."

"I can do that, Mrs. Farmwell," he said. "It is this way, Miss Nicholls."

He led her up three flights of stairs, wondering if she were ever going to speak to him again. They arrived at the door to the schoolroom and he paused, his hand on the door.

"I realize you are doing me a tremendous favor. Remember that if you are unhappy in any way, you do not have to stay."

"I understand, Your Grace," she said formally.

Win looked at her large eyes and sweet lips and wanted to kiss her again. Fighting the urge—and succeeding—he opened the door.

The boys sat at the table where he had learned his alphabet and done sums with a tutor before leaving Woodbridge for school. They looked guilty the moment they saw him. Standing in the room were both his steward and valet, both with stern looks on their faces.

"You may leave," he told the pair and they exited quickly.

Turning to the boys, he said, "This is Miss Nicholls. She is to be your new governess."

Freddie and Charlie exchanged a look which he couldn't read. Win knew something unspoken was said between them.

Sera came toward them. "It is polite to stand when a lady

enters the room, even if she is a governess. And you certainly want to always stand when you meet a new acquaintance, be it a butcher or the king." Her tone was firm but friendly.

The orphans came to their feet and studied her.

She moved to them and knelt so that she was eye level with them, a small but clever move on her part.

She smiled warmly at them and said, "I am Seraphina Nicholls and am very happy to be here with you. Would you introduce yourself to me?"

"I'm Freddie. Freddie Sawyer. This is my brother, Charlie."

Sera thrust out her hand and a startled Freddie merely looked at it.

"Shake hands with me, Freddie," she said easily.

The boy did so and she added, "I am pleased to meet you." Releasing his hand, she offered hers to Charlie. He eagerly took it and shook it, a little too hard, in Win's opinion.

"I'm Charlie. I'm six," he told her.

"I'm six, too," Freddie quickly said.

"Let's sit and become better acquainted, shall we?"

Sera took a seat at the table and the boys sat opposite her.

"Are you going to sit, Your Grace?" Freddie asked.

"I will stand, thank you."

He leaned against the doorframe and watched the magic unfold.

Sera never raised her voice. She never sounded like a governess. Instead, she asked the boys about themselves and told them about herself. Soon, the three were laughing like old friends. None of her habitual shyness was evident. Win supposed that only occurred around other adults.

As he listened to their conversation, he learned a great deal about Freddie and Charlie—and felt ashamed that he had not taken the time to get to know anything personal about them. He had stuffed them with meat pies and told them to stop bouncing about his carriage on the journey from London. It hadn't occurred to him to treat them as people.

But that is exactly what Sera did.

Besides learning about the boys, he found out a great deal about her, as well. She loved to read and told them about the books she would share with them. When Charlie pointed out that neither he nor Freddie could read but a few words and the last governess had told them they were too stupid to learn, Sera hadn't said a bad word about the woman and her unprofessional behavior. She mere told the pair she had a special way of teaching reading and sums and that she could already tell they would be splendid at both.

Sera told them they would spend a good deal of their time outdoors, learning to garden.

"That sounds like work we won't get paid for," Freddie said, his displeasure obvious.

"Digging in the dirt is great fun," she replied. "Yes, we will get dirty. There is such satisfaction, though, when you've planted something and watered it. We'll watch it grow."

Sera told them they would visit the tenants on the estate and learn all about the animals.

"Can we ride a horse?" Charlie asked, hope in his eyes.

"Of course, we will all ride. You will become very good at it. I know these things."

"You know a lot, Miss Nicholls," Freddie said, worship in his eyes.

"I do—but I will teach you what I can and then you will know a lot."

The orphans giggled, the first time Win had heard that. It warmed his heart.

"We will also fish. I am quite the fisherman."

"But you're not a man, Miss Nicholls," Charlie pointed out. "You'd be . . . a fisherwoman!" he cried.

"I suppose I am," she agreed, her laughter tinkling, filling the schoolroom with light.

Win fell in love with Sera at that moment.

CHAPTER FOURTEEN

S ERA FELL IN love with the boys from the moment she met them.

Freddie was obviously the leader of the two. He was slightly taller and an air of defiance blanketed him. She was certain he had been the protector of their little family. Charlie was smaller and even thinner than Freddie, which broke her heart. She wondered how much they'd had to eat, especially in those last days before their mother passed.

She disagreed with Win about keeping their relationship to him secret but she could see he wasn't ready to fully commit to his nephews. She doubted he even thought of the boys as nephews. Win only recently met them. Hadn't even known they existed all these years. Sera thought it criminal that Terrance Cutler had gotten two different women with child and walked away from his responsibilities to both mothers and his sons. From the little Win had said about his older brother, though, it was possible the boys had been better off without the duke in their lives.

Hopefully, she could change Win's views regarding the boys. It would take time. She had about six weeks before the house party started.

Sera planned to make the most of each day.

A maid appeared in the doorway, drawing Sera's attention.

She carried a tray.

"I brought the little ones their dinner," she said uncertainly, eyeing the boys with trepidation.

Win moved into the room from where he had leaned against the doorframe the entire time Sera had talked with the boys.

"Do you eat you meals in the schoolroom?" she asked.

"We have today," Freddie said. "We've bounced about a bit since we've been here."

The moment the maid set a plate in front of Freddie, she saw he was about to dig in.

"Wait," she cautioned gently.

"Why? I'm hungry."

"Because Charlie is also hungry and it is kind to wait for everyone who is sitting at the table to receive his or her dinner. Then you may start."

"Well, that's rubbish," Freddie declared.

When Sera gazed steadily at him, the young boy wilted.

"All right. I'll wait. But I don't like it."

"You don't have to like it. You just have to do it," she said. "You're going to live in this great house from now on. It will be a privilege to live here but there are rules you must follow."

"Freddie hates rules," Charlie said, his mouth already full.

"One rule I insist upon is that no one speaks when his mouth is full." Again, she stared at Charlie, who looked sheepish as he chewed and then swallowed.

"Why are there rules?" Freddie asked, taking a bite after he spoke.

"Mankind was put here to rule over everything. They brought order—rules—so that there wouldn't be chaos. I will slowly expose you to the rules, both here in the house and beyond."

"There are rules on the streets," Freddie noted. "They aren't written down in any book but you just learn them. If you don't?" He shrugged.

"Were you on the streets very long?"

"Pretty much since we moved to the boardinghouse," Freddie said. "Mum was sick and some bloke took our house away. Dunno why."

"Smaller bites, Freddie. Chew until you can swallow. If you wolf down your food, you don't taste it and cannot appreciate it."

"All right." He slowed a bit and his brother matched him, fork for fork.

"Mum sold her jewels," Charlie said matter-of-factly. "She had 'em a long time. From when she used to work on the stage." He frowned. "I'm not sure what she did but she stopped doing it when we was born."

"When we were born," Sera gently corrected and Charlie echoed her words. She smiled at him and he looked at her adoringly.

As they ate, she explained the stage. "Someone writes down words. Sometimes funny or sad or mysterious. The story they tell can be written in a book one can read or it can be performed. Acted out in front of an audience. That's what your mama did. She played a role—the part of someone."

"She was very talented," Win interjected, moving toward them and taking a seat next to her.

The chairs were meant for children. Sera knew how large she felt sitting in one and couldn't imagine how Win was even able to sit. But it pleased her mightily that he had taken a seat with them.

"Did you see her?" Charlie asked. "Watch her pretend to be someone else?"

"No, but remember Mr. Blumer? He was the man who came with me to find you. He saw her twice on stage and said she was the most talented actress he had ever seen. The most beautiful one, too."

Both boys beamed at Win's words.

"Maybe I'll be an actor," Freddie declared.

"And me," Charlie added, not wanting to be left out.

"You have many years to decide if you want to go on the stage and tell stories to audiences. London is the largest city in England and it has several playhouses. Sometimes, an acting troupe travels throughout England and they will perform in different cities for a set amount of time. Besides the actors, it takes many people to help pull off a performance," she revealed.

"Like what?" Freddie asked.

"They have people who sew the costumes the actors wear and dressers who help dress them. Often during a play, an actor will change clothes several times. That's one of the ways an audience knows time is passing. There are people who make and care for the props used on stage, as well."

"What's a prop?" Charlie asked, licking his fingers since he had finished.

"No licking. Wipe your hands and mouth with your napkin," Sera said, making light of it as she continued. "Props are objects people use in a play. They may carry a candle or give someone a book or flowers. They may sit in a chair. Someone has to place those things on the stage—and change them between scenes or acts, the ways a play is divided up. Then there is the background. Artists paint the backdrops. Another person places makeup on the actors' faces so the audience can see them better. There are people who direct the actors on what to do. How to move on a stage. How to say their lines."

"What do you mean?" Freddie asked, clearly puzzled.

She thought a moment. "Take this sentence, for example. I lost my dog." She made certain she said every word the same way in a neutral fashion. "Now listen to the differences. "*I* lost my dog. I *lost* my dog. I lost my *dog*."

"They were all different!" cried Charlie.

"Exactly. The director helps an actor interpret a line. Helps him decide which words to emphasize. He helps them decide how they should say a line. If they should move as they say it or stand still. If they should look sad or happy or lonely or afraid."

Sera watched Freddie use his napkin on his mouth and hands without being prompted and nodded at him in recognition.

"Then there are the people who clean the theater between performances. People who sell the tickets to the audience."

"And someone had to hire the actors in the first place," Win chimed in. "They have to decide who is right for each role."

"What does that mean?" Freddie asked.

"Maybe the director—the person who helps the actors decide how to play their role—envisions someone tall and handsome in a certain role. Or he'd rather see someone short and stout play the part instead. If it is a love story, he won't want an eighty-year-old man as the hero and a twenty-year-old girl as the heroine."

Both boys burst out laughing at that.

And Win laughed along with them.

Sera already saw progress. The boys were behaving beautifully. They had learned a few table manners. More importantly, Win was seeing his nephews as real people. They had revealed quite a bit about themselves and their lives as she had spoken with them. She also hoped Freddie and Charlie would start seeing Win as a person, too, and not just the duke.

Her stomach growled and both boys burst out laughing. She found herself—and Win—laughing along with them.

"You're hungry, Miss Nicholls," Charlie said, slapping his knee. "My belly ain't ever growled that loud."

"The maid did not know to bring dinner to me," she said. "I will eat all my meals with you from now on."

Win cleared his throat. "I think breakfast will be enough, Miss Nicholls. And you can sit with the boys when they have their milk and bread. But I would like you to dine with me each evening. That way, you can report on the progress the boys have made each day. I am very interested in hearing about it."

Freddie looked at Win suspiciously. "Why do you want to know about us?"

"Because you are going to be living in my house. I am interested in everyone who lives here."

"What about Miss Nicholls?" piped up Charlie. "Are you interested in her?"

Sera felt her cheeks burn as Win looked at her. "Oh, yes, Charlie. I most certainly am interested in Miss Nicholls."

She would save her protests for later. It wouldn't do for the boys to see her argue with Win. And argue they would. She had no intention of eating dinner with him each night.

Because it would make her want things she simply couldn't have.

⇥⟫⟨⇤

WIN DIDN'T KNOW how he would convince Sera to marry him— but he knew he had always achieved whatever he set his mind to. He might be known as fun-loving but beneath his exterior lay strong powers of observation and a persistence which would not let up. He believed Sera was interested in him from her response to his kisses. He was a man who had been with many women. None had affected him the way she had.

He wondered if this is how it had happened for the other Second Sons. Owen, in particular, was the biggest womanizer of their circle and, from what Win gathered, his friend had been ready to work his way through the beauties of the *ton* before he met Louisa. She was beautiful but a bit reserved, which wasn't the type of woman Owen had been drawn to in the past.

Sera was much the same, only she was even quieter than Louisa. The old Win—the dashing army officer and lover of women—would have appreciated her beauty but passed on taking her to his bed because of her reserved nature. He would have moved on, hopping from bed to bed in search of pleasure. Perhaps it had to do with his becoming an unlikely duke and being aware of his responsibilities, which included siring an heir and spare.

No, Win had already thought to make a traditional *ton* marriage and after getting children off his duchess do as he pleased. Suddenly, his entire world seemed to have shifted. He wasn't as interested in his own hedonistic pursuits as he was bringing pleasure to a woman. One woman.

Sera.

From kissing her in the carriage, he had learned that she had little experience. Yet a fire had seemed to awaken within her. He believed she had a sensual nature and had never had the opportunity to explore it. He wanted her to explore it. With him. Inside, he was a whirlwind of emotions. He liked Sera. He admitted to himself he even loved her. And he would be damned to see her wed anyone but him.

This fierce possessiveness that he hadn't known could exist within him made him want to laugh aloud. His friends had been correct. Love had struck when he least suspected it—and with a woman he never would have predicted he would consider. Yet Sera was everything Win wanted. Physically, her lush curves and fair face appealed to him. It was much more than that, however. Where he had always looked at women and judged them on their beauty, he saw far more when he looked at Sera.

He saw her heart.

Though he hadn't known her long, Win believed she was the most caring and kind person of his acquaintance. In her own way, she possessed a strength of character which would make her a perfect partner to him—and an outstanding duchess.

Now, he had to convince her.

Something told him she would not want to act upon the attraction between them. That because of her timidity around others she did not know, she would consider herself lacking, which was far from the truth. Win would have to woo her— subtly—and let her discover what she had to offer was exactly what he needed in a wife. He also wanted to tempt her so that she would be curious, even eager, to explore her passionate nature. He yearned to do so. It was funny how, in an instant, he had changed. He wanted to pledge himself to one woman.

For eternity.

Looking at her now, he saw fire in her eyes. Yes, the shy mouse was not happy about being told she would dine with him. Win suppressed a grin, which would infuriate her, even as he looked forward to verbally sparring with her.

Sera stood and his eyes were drawn to her ample bosom.

Already, he was looking forward to touching her breasts again. And tasting them. Tasting her.

"If you will excuse us, Your Grace, I need to help ready the boys for bed."

"You do?" he asked, not having considered this.

"They are but six. They need supervision." She turned and eyed them with a grin. "Else they might skip washing behind their ears and using their tooth powder."

Had he been supervised when he was that age? Win couldn't recall.

"I will help you," he said firmly, his tone not allowing refusal.

Obviously, Sera ignored it because she said, "That wouldn't be appropriate, Your Grace. I am their governess. I will handle this nightly duty. Come along, boys," she said, leaving with Freddie and Charlie even as she dismissed him.

"Wait, Miss Nicholls," he commanded in his best ducal tone.

She stopped in her tracks. "Yes, Your Grace?"

"I told you I was interested in all facets of these boys' lives. I should see where they are sleeping and what their nightly routine is." He looked to Freddie and Charlie. "You don't mind, do you?"

Freddie frowned but Charlie, who was the more open of the pair, nodded. "Come along, Your Grace. I'll show you where we sleep." His eyes lit up. "We *each* have a bed. No sharing."

He came and took Win's hand. The small gesture moved him in no small way. Charlie pulled him along, from the schoolroom and through a connecting door.

"This is our room," he announced proudly. "This is where I sleep and that bed is for Freddie."

"Why, I slept in that very bed when I was a boy," he told Charlie. "I liked it because it was by the window. I would go to bed and look out at night, watching the wind move the tree limbs and listening to the owls hoot."

"Did anyone sleep in Freddie's bed?" Charlie asked. "Did you have a brother?"

Win tamped down the loathing within him. "I did but he was

much older than I was. He had his own room by the time I came to the nursery and then was old enough to sleep in here alone without a nursery governess."

"What's that?" Freddie demanded. "A nursery governess."

He turned to the boy. "Very wealthy parents hire people to look after their children," he explained. "The Cutler children had a nursery governess when small. Someone to change our nappies and feed us and read to us. Watch over us and help us dress and play with us. Later, when I was older, I moved to this room and took lessons with a tutor in the schoolroom. I learned my letters and numbers and how to read. After that, I went away to school."

"We didn't have that," Charlie said solemnly. "We weren't wealthy."

Win knelt before the boy. "But you were loved. When I met your mama shortly before she passed, all she could talk about was you and Freddie. She spent her days caring for you. My mama and papa lived in London much of the time, while I stayed here. Even when they came to the country, I rarely saw them. They didn't love me and did not spend time with me."

He placed a hand on Charlie's shoulder. "You may not have been rich in material possessions, Charlie, but your mama showered you with love."

"Mum did love us," Charlie agreed. "She told us that all the time."

He rose. "All right. What is your routine?"

A maid appeared with hot water and Freddie took command, walking Win through what they had done for the last couple of nights while at Woodbridge. They changed into nightshirts, which had his very initials embroidered into them, and made a note to see that they each had ones of their own.

Sera took over after that because both boys wanted to climb into bed. She insisted they wash themselves and even did it for both boys, making certain they cleaned their faces and washed behind their ears. She showed them how to use the tooth powder beside the basin and both peeled with laughter as she demonstrated what to do.

"You look funny, Miss Nicholls," Freddie said.

Sera mumbled something but it was garbled because of the tooth powder. She rinsed her mouth and said, "Now, it is your turn."

Once they finished cleaning their teeth, she had them comb their hair and then she instructed them to use their chamber pots.

"I will give you privacy to do so. Come and get me in the schoolroom when you have finished."

She left and he watched both boys, cautioning them to aim carefully.

"Why?" Charlie asked, clueless.

"Because if you don't, one of the maids has to clean up after you. Yes, it is their job to clean each room but you never want to make work for someone when you can do the right thing." He paused, deciding that was the first lesson he would teach this pair. "Always strive to do the right thing."

"Why?" Freddie challenged.

"Because you want to be the best person you can be. Doing the right thing is the first step toward that. You also should treat everyone with kindness and courtesy. Most people only treat those in a position of power or authority with respect. But I say be nice to everyone. Treat them as you would want to be treated."

Freddie nodded thoughtfully and then said, "I will fetch Miss Nicholls."

When they returned, she helped them turn back their beds and climb in, covering them carefully.

"Normally, I would read a story to you but, tonight, I will merely tell you one," she said.

"The other two didn't do that," Freddie told her.

"Different people establish routines they are comfortable with. My mama and papa helped put my sister, Minta, and me to bed every night. They would always read or tell us a story and that is what I like to do with my charges."

"Were you poor like we were?" Charlie asked.

"Not poor but certainly not as wealthy as His Grace's family.

My papa works for the British government. In fact, he is in North America now, helping with the administration of Upper Canada."

Both boys looked at her blankly.

She laughed, causing tingles to ripple through Win. He loved her laugh and vowed to make her laugh every day they were together.

"I see that geography will be a lesson that will need the highest priority. Geography is all about where places are and what they are like. But that is for tomorrow."

"Tell us a story about you growing up," Charlie suggested. "About you and your sister."

"All right."

Win stood and watched as Sera talked about her household and being a twin, telling them how Minta was born first and then she came along several minutes later.

"That's like us," Freddie said. "Mum had me first and then Charlie came out. We have the same birthday, just like you and Minta. That's a funny name."

"Her given name is Araminta but she has always been Minta to me. Just like my name is Seraphina and I go by a shorter version. Sera."

"I like that name. Sera. It's pretty like you are." Charlie smiled up at her and Win thought the little boy had fallen under Sera's spell as much as he had.

"Could we call you Sera?" Freddie asked, sounding vulnerable for the first time since Win had known him. "I know you're supposed to be Miss Nicholls, but—"

"I think that is a lovely idea," she said, smoothing his hair. "But only when it is just the three of us. We should be more formal around others."

"What about the four of us?" Charlie asked, looking at Win.

He cleared his throat. "I think you could use Sera in that case. But around the servants or guests, she must be Miss Nicholls."

"Are you going to call her Sera?" Freddie asked. "I think you should. Just when it's us."

Smiling at Freddie, Win said, "I believe I will."

CHAPTER FIFTEEN

S ERA HAD MIXED emotions as she perched on the bed and kissed Charlie's forehead. He smiled up at her sleepily and then rolled to his side. She went to the other bed and brushed a kiss upon Freddie's brow. He crinkled his nose as if disgusted by the gesture. Freddie would definitely be the harder nut to crack. Unless you counted Win.

She could not for the life of her figure him out.

"Goodnight," she called softly. "Sleep well."

Turning, she reentered the schoolroom since that door was still open and the bedchamber door opening to the corridor was already closed. Win followed her and shut the door behind him.

"They are a handful," he said.

"They are charming," she countered. "I found them both quite delightful. It is hard to think they have pulled some of the pranks they have."

"Under your loving hand, I doubt they will. Or at least not very often," he amended. "They are, after all, boys. And boys will find mischief. Especially a pair such as they are."

"I agree. A little mischief can be a good thing. If they were to always obey without question and never find trouble, I would worry something might be wrong with them."

He took a step toward her and her heart sped up. "We shouldn't talk here. I don't wish to keep them awake. The sound of our voices might do so."

He smiled enigmatically. "Then we should go downstairs for dinner."

Sera opened her mouth to protest but Win added, "We both have to eat. Plus, we can talk about the boys. What you wish to teach them. Come along."

He moved through the schoolroom door to the hallway and she followed, her pulse beating rapidly. She thought about kissing him in the carriage and how that had been a mistake.

A huge mistake.

She could have stopped him. Win was gentleman enough that if she had, he wouldn't have pressed her for more. But she had reveled in his taste. His touch. She had never known people kissed like that. Or touched so intimately. The thought of his hand against her breast had her growing hot. She fought to dispel the image and the feelings it aroused within her.

He paused, waiting for her, and offered his arm.

"No, thank you. You wouldn't have escorted the two previous governesses as if they were ladies, so I don't expect you to do the same with me."

She reached the staircase and gripped the handrail firmly, trying to ground herself in reality and not fantasy.

As they moved down the stairs, Sera added, "I cannot dine with you each evening, Win. A servant—even an upper servant— would never do so. And as a single female, it wouldn't be proper."

He chuckled. "So, you would allow two little boys to address you by your first name, disregarding society's established manners, and yet you won't even dine with me."

Win stopped on the landing, blocking her way. "Sera, I beg you to change your mind. I do want to know what is going on with them. I am curious as to what you will teach them. How you will spend your time with them. They are very active children and you will be busy most of the day. Supping with me would give you a chance to relax and allow me to hear about

Freddie's and Charlie's day."

He gave her a charming smile. "Besides, we are in the country. The *ton's* rules are a little more relaxed here, outside the prying eyes of gossips. Please."

Win looked so boyish that Sera found herself weakening. "All right," she told him, knowing that nothing intimate could take place with several footmen watching and listening to every word said.

"Good." He turned and started down the stairs again and she continued holding the handrail to steady herself.

He led her to a room which was obviously not the main dining room, She knew an estate of this size would have a table that seated two to three dozen. This room was cozy, with two wingback chairs near a window and a table for four in front of a fireplace.

"This is the winter parlor," Win explained. "I have been dining in here. It seems ridiculous to eat by myself at a table where I can barely see the far end. It is also less trouble on the servants."

"I heard what you told the boys. About how to treat servants and others."

"Doing the right thing was a lesson I learned early at school," he shared. "I had done something careless in the dormitory. Left a mess. A maid took me to task. She said she was tired of thoughtless boys leaving a mess. While she did not mind cleaning up—since that was her job—she still believed that limits should be placed."

He sighed. "I had never thought of what servants actually did. To me, fires magically were laid and beds turned back with warming pans inserted at the foot. Food appeared on the table at regular intervals. I never thought of the hard work behind these tasks. That one maid scolding me left an impression which never faded. I do my best now to allow my servants to wait on me but I never want to inconvenience them."

"That is very admirable."

He pulled a cord and then gestured to seat her, taking the

place to her right instead of opposite her.

"I take pride on being the best I can be. I know I am intelligent. I view myself as brave and loyal. But I believe it truly is the little things that make a difference in life. If I can lessen the burden of others, so be it."

Sighing, he raked a hand through his hair, a gesture becoming familiar to her.

"This being a duke has me out of sorts. An army of people waiting on me. It seems wrong in so many ways. At the same time, I know I am responsible for all those people. I want to do right by them."

"You will," she told me, longing to place her hand on his but knowing that would trigger a reaction within her that she couldn't afford. It might also encourage him and that was the last thing she wished to do.

The door opened and the butler entered, followed by a maid pushing a cart. Sera noted the two plates and wondered about that, supposing the butler had anticipated she would eat with Win but not knowing why.

He set the plates before them and removed the covers.

"I hope this will be to your liking, Your Grace. When you didn't come downstairs, I thought you might wish to dine with Miss Nicholls and discuss the boys' future."

"You anticipate my every move and thought, Farmwell." Win chuckled. "Sometimes, I believe you know me better than I do myself."

"Wine, Your Grace?"

"Yes, please."

Farmwell opened the bottle and poured glasses for the both of them, as well as cut pieces of cake. Leaving the bottle, he gestured toward the maid, who rolled the cart from the room. The butler followed, closing the door behind him.

Distress filled Sera. She had supposed there would be footmen present during her meals with Win, just as when she had been at Kingwood with Minta and Percy or her aunt and uncle in

London. Instead, she found herself in a very private room, just the two of them. She reached for her wine and sipped on it, worry filling her.

By the end of the meal, however, she was laughing. It became a pleasant hour with no interruptions. No servants bringing course after course. Win told her that he enjoyed food more now than he ever did because of the scarcity of decent food during his time in the army, much of it spent on the move as they chased Bonaparte's troops.

"I think serving multiple courses, especially when it just me at the meal, is wasteful. I would rather savor what I have in front of me instead of taking a bite here and there of each course and tossing the rest."

Their single plates had included roasted chicken, two vegetables, and fresh beets, one of her favorites. Farmwell had left the bottle of wine and Win poured her a second glass, though Sera refused a third, already feeling slightly tipsy. The cart had also included a cake and he handed her the piece Farmwell had cut for her.

"Sweets were unheard of on the warfront," he shared. "To be sitting here with an entire cake is decadent."

"I have always had a bit of a sweet tooth," Sera confessed. "Minta can take or leave a sweet but I have troubling passing one up."

"Would you care for a second slice?"

"No. I already—" She stopped, already embarrassed by her curvaceous figure.

"What is it? Are you already full?"

"Yes, that it is. I couldn't eat another bite. Besides, the cake can be for tea tomorrow. The boys would like that. Due to their circumstances, I doubt they were spoiled by sweets. At least after their mother became ill and they lost their home."

As they finished their cake, Win said, "There are books in the schoolroom in the cupboards. I learned to read from them and I suppose my father, before me. Also, there are slates on which I did my sums."

She smiled. "I can imagine you as a small boy, sitting at that table. You would have been quite bright and full of mischief. Just like Freddie and Charlie."

He laughed. "I hope I wasn't quite that mischievous. Though now that I think of it, trouble did have a way of finding me."

Win told her of a few scrapes he had gotten in during his early years. "Usually, I dragged Percy into them. He was the child of propriety, even as a small boy. I was the bad influence."

They finished their dessert and wine and Sera yawned. "I'm sorry."

"You must be tired. It has been a long day. We should take you to your bedchamber." He frowned. "Or room, I should say."

"Remember, the boys believe I am a full-fledged governess. You told your butler I was one, as well. Of course, I will sleep where the governess usually does. I believe it must be close to the boys' room."

"I haven't the foggiest notion."

"I will find it."

"I will go with you," he insisted.

"Win, you would not take a governess to her room. That is not the way a duke behaves. There are rules to adhere to."

"Then what the bloody good is being a duke if I can't break a few rules? Especially in my own household."

Sera rose. "No," she said firmly. "Ring for your housekeeper. She will escort me to my room. You know I am right. Besides, I really shouldn't be here without a chaperone. Aunt Phyllis would have my hide for volunteering to come here alone. Minta told me if we keep quiet about it, no one in town will know."

He regarded her for a moment. "So that no gentleman will think you have been compromised by the Duke of Woodmont."

"Precisely. The house party is coming up and we are both expected to find a spouse among the guests. At least, Adalyn will find you one since you don't seem to care whom you wed."

Saying those words made her heart hurt but she needed to

hear them aloud and recognize that Win was meant for someone else. Not her.

His frown deepened as he rang for Mrs. Farmwell and they sat in silence. She hated ending such a lovely evening on a sour note but she didn't know what to say and retreated within herself.

When Mrs. Farmwell arrived, Win said, "Take Miss Nicholls to her room if you would. She has not seen where it is yet."

"I'd be happy to, Your Grace. Come with me, Miss Nicholls. I placed your valise in your room. Hot water will be brought to you every morning at six and every evening at eight. Also, a tray will be delivered so you may eat in your room."

Sera started to leave with the housekeeper but Win said, "Mrs. Farmwell, please make a note that the tray will be unnecessary. I wish for Miss Nicholls to dine with me each night so I may hear about the progress Freddie and Charlie are making on a daily basis."

She saw the housekeeper's bemused look, which Mrs. Farmwell quickly erased.

"Very good, Your Grace. Will you continue to eat in the winter parlor or would you prefer the small dining room?"

"Here is fine," he said brusquely. "Goodnight."

"Goodnight, Your Grace," Sera replied, following Mrs. Farmwell out the door and up the flights of stairs until they reached the top of the house.

"You know where the schoolroom is. And the boys' room. Your room is on the other side of the schoolroom. A door connects to it just as it does for the boys."

They entered and Sera saw how cramped it was. The room contained a small bed pushed against the wall and a tiny table with a basin atop it, already filled with water, and a towel next to it. No chair. No mirror. A trunk did sit at the foot.

"Farmwell told me that your trunk would arrive in a few days," the housekeeper said. "We can always remove this one and replace it with yours."

"Yes, thank you," she said.

The housekeeper looked at her beseechingly. "Let me know if you need anything, Miss Nicholls. We are ... more than grateful for your arrival. The boys ... well, they have been a handful, to say the least. We want you to be happy here. For a long time."

"I appreciate your concern, Mrs. Farmwell. I am certain the boys and I will get along splendidly. In fact, I believe we have already made a good start in that direction."

Mrs. Farmwell nodded. "Goodnight, then, Miss Nicholls."

It took Sera some time to struggle out of her clothes with no help. She realized she would need to make some adjustments to her wardrobe or ask the maid that delivered her morning water to aid her in dressing for the day.

Finally, she donned her night rail and climbed into the bed. The mattress wasn't nearly as firm as she liked and the pillow only held half the feathers hers normally did. Still, these were small concessions to make on her part. Her purpose at Woodbridge was to help Freddie and Charlie adjust to their new lives.

And avoid being around Win as much as possible.

CHAPTER SIXTEEN

S ERA AWOKE BEFORE the maid brought the hot water, eager to
start her day with the boys. She removed her night rail and
relieved herself and then placed her chemise over her head. She
laid out her corset, petticoat, and gown for the day and then
decided she could slip into her stockings and boots on her own.

She made the bed and then brushed her hair, winding it into
her usual chignon. Thank goodness, she did not go in for fussy
styles and was able to do her own hair without help.

A light tap sounded at the door and she went to it, finding a
young girl of perhaps thirteen or fourteen standing there with a
jug of water and a basin.

"Here, let me take one of those from you," she said, lifting
the heavy jug and setting it on the floor as the servant brought in
the empty basin.

"What is your name?" she asked.

"Sara," the girl replied.

Smiling, she replied, "I am Seraphina—but I have always
gone by Sera. S-E-R-A."

The servant returned her smile and removed the basin from
the table. Setting it aside, she placed the new one upon it and then
poured the hot water from the jug into it.

"Would you mind terribly if you helped me lace my corset
each morning when you bring the hot water? And if you come

again at night, might you help remove it?"

Sera saw the reluctance on the servant's part and added, "I know it is not a part of your duties but I could use the help. I'd be happy to pay you. A shilling a week?"

She knew the sum to be generous and would have to remember to borrow it from Minta when she and Percy came to visit since Sera had no coins of her own.

"I suppose I could," Sara said. "But we must be quick about it. I have lots to do."

"Thank you, Sara."

She lifted the corset and placed it on her and turned her back to the girl, who began lacing it up. It wasn't as tight as she preferred but she didn't want to seem as if she judged Sara too much.

"How long you been a governess?"

Not wanting to lie, Sera told the truth. "This is my first time to have my own charges."

Sara barked out a harsh laugh as she finished lacing the corset. "Then I'll never see that shilling. You won't last a week to pay it to me."

The girl took last night's basin and quickly left the room.

Sera sighed. The boys' exploits must have spread throughout the entire household. She supposed the Birdwells had also shared their experiences with other farmers at Kingwood. She would need to show everyone that they were good children. The sooner, the better.

She scrambled into her petticoat and gown, wishing she had a mirror to check her appearance. Not that it mattered what she looked like. Freddie and Charlie wouldn't care and she doubted she would see Win before dinner this evening. *If* she ate with him. She still hadn't decided whether that was something she was going to do or not.

Going to the connecting door, she entered the schoolroom and immediately went to the cupboards, pulling out various books in them so she could see what was available. She also found the slates Win had mentioned. She set out what she would use today and put the other things away.

Then she went to the boys' doors and knocked. "Are you awake?" she called.

Charlie answered the door in his nightshirt, rubbing his eyes sleepily. "Good morning, Sera."

He stepped back so she could enter the room. Freddie was already dressed. She had noticed initials embroidered into the nightshirts the pair wore and thought they might be from when Win was a boy. She supposed the clothes they wore were also old ones of his or his brother's.

"Have you washed up this morning?" she asked.

"Again?" Freddie complained. "They scrubbed us good when we first got here. Why do we have to be so clean all the time?"

"Because His Grace has a nice house with nice furniture and we don't want to ruin anything. Besides, I am going to be around you for most of every day, and I am not overly fond of stinky boys," she teased.

That got a smile from Freddie and a laugh from Charlie, who changed into his clothes.

Once he was ready, she had both boys wash their faces and hands and comb their hair before she led them into the schoolroom. Two maids arrived with large trays and set out breakfast for the three of them.

As they ate, she asked them questions to find out their likes and dislikes, also sharing her own. She learned their mother had taught them their alphabet and how to write their names. They had just started to learn simple words when she had grown ill and had to stop.

"Mum didn't feel like teaching us then," Charlie said mournfully.

Freddie didn't say anything but Sera saw anger burning in his eyes. Clearly, he had not come to terms with his mother's illness and death.

"It is all right to be sad that your mama has passed," she began. "It is also fine to be angry."

Freddie looked at her sharply but she spooned jam on her toast points, avoiding his gaze.

"I thought people were sad when someone died," he said.

"I'm sad. I miss Mum," Charlie said softly.

Sera wrapped her arm about his shoulder. "You may feel sad for a long time because you miss her. Gradually, your sadness will fade but you will want to remember her and the good times you shared. She is always with you—in your mind and in your heart."

She took a bite of the toast and then set it down. "While some people are sad, others are mad when a loved one dies. They are angry that person got sick and had to leave. Sometimes, they are angry at themselves because they couldn't do anything to change things."

She glanced at Freddie and he nodded. "I've been mad ever since His Grace told us Mum was gone." His mouth trembled. "I was mad at her for getting sick. We had to leave our house. She didn't talk to us hardly at all. She told us to go play."

He looked up and she saw tears brimming in his eyes. "Mum didn't feel like being with us."

She took his hand and squeezed it. "She probably hated you seeing her sick and weak. She would want you to remember her as she was before. It is hard when you are a mother and you cannot care for the children you love."

Freddie gulped loudly and then a sob broke from him. He flung himself into her arms and she held him, stroking his hair. Charlie came and patted his brother's back.

"It's gonna be all right, Freddie. We have Sera now. She'll help us."

"That's right. I am here to teach you and help you and care for you."

Freddie wiped his eyes with his sleeve and took his seat again, his face red and blotchy but the usual defiance was back in his eyes.

"What are we going to learn?" he asked.

"All kinds of things, both indoors and outdoors."

"Like what?" Charlie asked eagerly.

"Reading and writing and simple math to start. I also think history and geography. Music if you are interested."

"Music?" Freddie looked doubtful.

"His Grace has a pianoforte you can learn upon. My things will soon arrive and among them is a violin that I play."

"Like a fiddle?" Charlie asked. "We've heard someone play in the taverns and on the streets."

"Yes, that is what I refer to."

"We could play it? Your fiddle?" Freddie said.

"Yes, but only if you are interested in learning how to."

"Could we just listen to you play?" Freddie pushed.

"Of course. I would be happy to play for you anytime."

Freddie twirled his fork through his eggs. "What else do we have to learn?"

"We will explore Kingwood," she told him. "See the land and the animals on it. I told you last night we'll fish."

"And ride," Charlie reminded her.

"Yes. We can go to the stables today and talk to the head groom about mounts for you."

Fortunately, Uncle West had insisted that Minta and she learn to ride. Though he preferred town life, he loved horses and instilled a love for them in both girls. She would enjoy teaching these boys how to ride.

"Finish your breakfast. The sooner you do, we may start our indoor lessons before moving outside."

"Will His Grace come with us, Sera?" Charlie asked innocently. "To see the horses?"

"No. His Grace is a very important man and has a large estate to run. In fact, he owns several estates and has all kinds of business to attend to."

"He knew our father," Charlie told her.

"Then I suppose that is why he decided to take care of you after your mama passed," she said lightly, her throat thickening with emotion.

"He's nice," Charlie said. "Isn't he, Freddie?"

The other boy shrugged. "He did buy us meat pies."

"And he brought us here and gave us clothes and our own beds," Charlie pointed out.

"He gave us to them Birdwells—and they gave us right back. He didn't really want us," Freddie said.

"You are here now. Let us take advantage of His Grace's kindness—and always be grateful for it," Sera said.

She had them write out the alphabet and they said the letters together several times. Charlie confused B and P, saying they looked and sounded alike. They also wrote out their names. Charlie's penmanship needed a little work. Sera thought Freddie deliberately wrote messily to test her and said nothing to correct him.

They wrote out the alphabet a second time and she taught them a song, repeating the tune until they had it down. Both boys had high, clear voices and they seemed to like to sing so she taught them a few ditties, which had them laughing. She decided she would need to mix academic work with other endeavors if she were to hold their attention.

Giving them the slates and chalk, she decided to start with simple, rhyming words. On her own slate, she wrote *cat* and had them sound it out. They copied her word on theirs and she asked what else sounded like cat but started with a different letter. Soon, they were writing rat and bat and sat and fat on their slates.

She tried other words which rhymed, keeping things simple. When Charlie suggested they use *go*, she agreed.

"But English is a peculiar language," she noted. "That means odd. We take words from several other languages, which had different rules, and added them to our own. Because of that, sometimes things are spelled in an odd manner. *Go* is easy. As is *so*."

She wrote *so* on her slate.

"But there is also *sew*." She added that to the slate and told them its meaning.

Charlie frowned. "So two words sound alike but you spell them different ways?"

"Exactly!" she praised. "What else rhymes with *go*?

"*Mow*," Freddie said. "*Row. Bow. Low.*"

They added each of those words to their slates before Sera had them take parchment and make a list of the various rhyming words they had talked about. She thought writing down the words again, as well as having them practice their handwriting, would reinforce their learning.

Their attention began to wane, however, and she knew she might lose it so she said, "Let's go exploring. We'll go through the house first so you can learn all about it."

Charlie looked guilty. "We went around it some. But we got in trouble, Sera. We broke a vase in a big room and knocked a hen to the floor in the kitchens. A lady said it was supposed to be for dinner."

"Were you running either time?"

"Yes," Charlie admitted.

"Well, there's no running in a house because those kind of accidents can happen. Running is for outside and we will do lots of that."

"Can we go outside now and run?" Freddie pleaded. "We can see the house later."

"All right. Good thing I wore my boots." She stuck out her foot and hiked her skirts so the boys could see.

"They look old," Freddie said.

"I have had them a long time," she admitted. "They've been patched up three times because I am so fond of them and don't wish to give them up."

"Perhaps you'll need new ones after you've traipsed about Kingwood," a deep voice said.

Turning, Sera already knew who stood at the schoolroom door.

CHAPTER SEVENTEEN

Win's curiosity got the better of him. Or perhaps his yearning to see Sera did. Either way, he headed up the stairs. He had already breakfasted and spent time with Kepler discussing estate matters so he told himself he deserved a short break. Checking on the boys' progress seemed the thing to do.

The door was open and so he stood outside for a good half-hour, listening as she quizzed the boys on rhyming words and had them write down the words they came up with. It didn't even seem as if she were teaching. It was more a natural conversation which led to learning.

He decided Sera Nicholls was a genius.

Finally, they begin talking of exploring the house and then the estate. Little Charlie seemed quite eager to get atop a horse. Win needed to make his presence known so he could accompany them. As he stepped into the doorway, Sera raised her skirts to show the boys her boots.

All Win saw was a trim ankle and shapely calf which he wanted to run his tongue along.

Finding his voice, he said, "Perhaps you'll need new ones after you've traipsed about Kingwood."

As she turned, so did the boys. Charlie's eyes lit up and he cried, "Your Grace! We are going to run outside."

Smiling, he ventured inside the room. "I seem to recall the

days when running brought me pure pleasure. I ran everywhere, especially with my cousin. Percy and I ran all around Woodbridge and also his family's estate, Kingwood."

Charlie grew serious. "Do you want to run with us?"

Freddie snorted. "Dukes don't run."

"Unless they are chasing little boys," Win shot back. "I seem to remember running after you and Charlie."

"You weren't very fast," Freddie told him dismissively.

"Challenge me to a race and we'll see who wins," he retorted.

Freddie stood. "Let's do it."

Sera rose, laughing. "I don't think His Grace needs to be racing you, Freddie."

"Why not? He said he'd race me."

"Freddie wishes a race. I plan to give him one," Win said, causing Charlie to leap to his feet and clap. "You said you were going outside to run. We can run a bit and then go to the stables and see about mounts for the boys."

"Yes!" cried Charlie, who ran to the doorway and then skidded to a stop. He turned to look at Sera. "I know. No running in the house."

"That's right," she agreed. "Well, what are we waiting for?"

Sera and Freddie went after Charlie and Win followed them. He noticed Sera didn't stop for a parasol or bonnet. He couldn't imagine any lady of Polite Society going without one or both.

And it made him love her all the more.

As he strode down the stairs, he wondered why silly, little things seem to magnify his love for her. Then he stopped in his tracks.

Life was made up of those small moments. It wasn't always the important events he remembered clearly in his life but the little ones. Showing Percy a fish he had caught. The look on an enemy soldier's face as he bayoneted him. Galloping across the meadow. The taste of his favorite cake.

Win wanted to create a thousand of those brief moments with Sera.

The boys reached the front door and the footman looked to Sera.

"We are going for a run. Not a walk," she told the servant.

He appeared shocked by her breezy words but opened the door and the boys took off, Sera running behind them. Suddenly, Win found himself dashing down the remaining stairs and racing across the foyer and out into the open, leaving behind the footman who wore a stunned look.

The boys ran across the front lawn and then started twirling in circles. Sera did the same and he watched as they all wound up collapsing to the ground in laughter.

"I'm dizzy," Freddie said.

"I can't run," Charlie said breathlessly.

Sera merely laughed, laying back on the lawn and staring up at the sky. Then she said, "I do believe that's a cat."

"Where?" Charlie asked, looking about.

She gestured to the clouds. "Up there. Come lay with me and see for yourself."

Eagerly, the boy joined her, stretching out. Surprisingly, Freddie did the same, laying next to his brother.

"Over there. That group on the left. Do you see the cat? The pointed ears?" she asked.

"I do," Charlie told her. "I even see his tail."

"I don't," Freddie mumbled.

"You have to use your imagination, Freddie," she gently chided. "If you don't see a cat, what do you see?"

He squinted, studying the sky. "A mouse," he announced. "There."

Win looked into the sky as Freddie told where the mouse was and strolled toward the trio laying in the grass. He dropped down and unfolded his limbs until he lay next to Sera. Very close, in fact. So close that his fingers brushed hers. Though he longed to entwine his fingers with hers, he did not want to frighten her away. He turned his head and inhaled the faint scent of jasmine and then looked back to the sky.

"I see it," he told the others. "Oh, it is a fat, little mouse. He must have been feasting on the bread in the kitchens."

"Do you see anything, Your Grace?" Charlie asked him.

He concentrated and said, "I do. See that clump of clouds on the right? It looks like a dragon to me."

They lay on the ground for several minutes, finding new shapes as the clouds shifted with the wind. Win enjoyed being close to Sera—and surprisingly, listening to the boys.

Finally, Freddie tired of the game and sat up. "Ready to race?" he asked. "I'm not dizzy anymore."

"Do you see that old oak on the left?" Win counted. "The sixth one from the top of the drive? That is the end point."

He scrambled to his feet, as did Sera and Charlie.

He touched Freddie's shoulder. "Don't you dare run off before the race starts. We need an official at both the starting point and the finishing line."

"Why?" Freddie asked warily.

"To make certain no cheating goes on," he replied. "Charlie, go to the oak and stand next to it. You may judge which of us touches it first."

Charlie began running the distance to the tree.

"You, Sera, will start the race for us," he told her, sounding very businesslike. "Choose a place for us to line up and give us a mark."

She nodded, looking very serious as an official should. Glancing about, she walked to the lane and paused.

"Here. I have found your marks."

He and Freddie moved toward her and Win saw her point.

"See that rock?" She went to it and touched it. "Line your toes up evenly with it."

They did so and she raised her hand, shading her eyes. He saw the curve of her breasts and the sunlight playing upon her auburn hair and very nearly left his mark to sweep her into his arms and kiss her. That would not be wise in front of the boys.

But later?

"Are you ready, Charlie?" she called.

"Ready, Sera," he shouted.

"Then we can begin," she told them. "On your marks? Ready. Set. Go!"

Win thought Freddie leaned just a touch early and would speak to him later. For now, though, he took off after the six-year-old, who was incredibly fast for his age. The boy's shorter stride was no match for Win's long legs and he easily overtook Freddie and began to pass him. Then he thought better of it and decided the boy should claim the victory.

But Win would make him work for it.

He adjusted his pace, allowing Freddie to stay just within reach of him and then slowed slightly right before they reached the tree. Freddie reached out his hand and flung himself at the trunk, barely touching it before Win did.

"I won!" he shouted, jumping up and down, joy written on his face.

"You won!" Charlie proclaimed with glee.

Looking back, he saw Sera also jumping up and down. She stopped and ran toward them. By the time she reached them, her face was flushed, making her look more kissable than ever.

"Congratulations, Freddie," he said as Sera arrived. "You beat me. I will have to practice my running and then ask for a rematch down the road."

"Can we go to the stables now?" Charlie begged.

"First, the chickens. Then the stables," Sera declared.

The boys grumbled a bit but they each took the hand Sera offered. Win followed them, mainly to enjoy the sway of Sera's hips as she walked.

They went around the house and to its back where a door led to the kitchens. A small, fenced-in yard held a good number of clucking chickens and a coop.

Looking over her shoulder, she asked him, "Who is in charge of the chickens?"

"I haven't a clue," he admitted.

"If you are going to learn about your estate, Your Grace, you need to learn everything about it," she told him, a glint in her eyes. "I need to know who feeds the chickens and who collects their eggs."

"There is one way to find out."

He went to the back door and entered the kitchens, which buzzed with activity.

Until a scullery maid noticed he was there and dropped the pan she was drying.

"Your Grace?" an older woman asked, coming toward him. "May I help you?"

He recognized the cook. "Yes, Cook. Who feeds the chickens and gathers the eggs every morning?"

"That would be me, Your Grace."

Frowning, he asked, "Don't you have better things to do, Cook?"

"I do. But I have loved chickens since I was a girl."

"Would you come with me for a moment, Cook? I believe Miss Nicholls, the new governess, wishes to speak with you."

Cook clucked her tongue. "Oh, that poor girl. Take me to her."

Win led her outside and made the introduction between the women. He started to introduce the boys but Cook interrupted.

"Oh, I know the pair, Your Grace." She eyed them with a frown.

"We're better now," Charlie volunteered. "Miss Nicholls isn't mean to us at all. We were just being mean back to them other ones."

"And His Grace said we have to do the right thing," Freddie added. He flushed red and said, "I promise we'll stay out of your flour barrels."

He wondered what had occurred with the flour barrels and decided it was better not to ask.

"Good. Then it's a clean start with us," she declared.

"Cook here feeds the chickens and brings in the eggs every

day," Win said, wondering where this was going but pleased that the boys were making a strong effort to behave.

"I would like Charlie and Freddie to do those two tasks each morning, Cook," Sera revealed. "Routine is important. So is caring for something other than yourself. I thought they could feed the chickens and be given baskets to collect the eggs. They need to be given a bit of responsibility."

He liked the idea of having the boys contribute in a small way to the household.

"Would you mind relinquishing those tasks to the boys, Cook?" Win asked.

She looked at the pair. "I think it'd be good for 'em," she proclaimed. "But there's more to it than you might think."

Cook explained how to scatter the feed and watch so no one chicken dominated the yard.

"I won't tolerate fights between my chickens," she pronounced.

Then she said she would help the boys gather eggs tomorrow morning. "You can't rush things. You must be careful—else an egg will crack." Looking to Sera, she said, "Have them downstairs at half-past six, Miss Nicholls. The eggs must be gathered then in order for the household to be fed its breakfast."

"I will do so," Sera promised. "Thank you, Cook."

The servant returned to the kitchens.

"Why do we have to do her job?" Freddie complained.

"Because she has a far greater job," Win said. "She is feeding an entire household. That is dozens of people, both below and above stairs."

"That means both servants and those who live here or are visiting Woodbridge," Sera clarified.

"Having a small but important task allows you to contribute to the running of the household," he explained.

"That means we're a part of things here," Charlie said, pride evident in his voice and on his face.

"It is good to have some responsibility by the time you are

six," Sera said. "As you grow older, we can add to that. You might, for example, help to feed and curry your horses."

"Curry?" Freddie's nose crinkled.

"It's a word that means to brush a horse," she said.

"Then why not say that?" Freddie asked.

Sera smiled mysteriously. "Because horses are special. You are going to find that out now. Do you know where the stables are?"

The boys nodded.

"Then run to them. His Grace and I will follow at a slower pace."

Ready to release more energy, the two took off.

Win shook his head. "I have never met more energetic boys—and I was one."

Sera began following and he fell into step beside her. He longed to offer her his arm or take her hand but forced himself to keep his hands at his sides.

"You are good with them, Sera. Very good."

"I like them," she said softly. "They are sweet boys."

"I believe you are correct in thinking they were acting out because of all the things that happened so suddenly, changing their lives forever."

"Once they have stability in their lives, they will be good." She smiled up at him. "Or at least as good as they can be. I understand from what you said last night that they won't always behave as little angels. Some slips are bound to occur."

His fingers caught hers and squeezed. "Like this?"

Sera tugged on his hand. "Please, Win. Let go. Someone might see and get the wrong impression."

"What impression might that be?" he asked, though he did release her.

"I . . . I'd rather not say."

But he knew. Governesses were in a precarious position. He supposed more often than not, the master of the house took advantage of his power over them—and took advantage of them.

If his servants saw him touch Sera, they would think less of her.

And him.

He wanted the respect of his people, both tenants and servants alike.

Win also wanted to touch Sera more than anything. He would simply have to find a place to do so away from prying eyes, which included the two very curious boys now in his care.

They continued toward the stables, with him asking about the morning's lesson, though he had already heard some of it. By the time they reached the stables, the boys were talking animatedly with Harrison, his head groom.

"Ah, Your Grace," Harrison said as they arrived. "Freddie and Charlie here tell me they are going to learn to ride."

"Yes, I think they are at a perfect age to do so. You would be the best man to teach them, Harrison. After all, you taught me."

Charlie blinked. "You were here when His Grace was a little boy?"

"I was," Harrison confirmed. "A young groom wet behind the ears, I was. But I always had a way with animals. Horses, in particular. I was tasked with teaching His Grace to ride. He was a fast learner."

"We will be, too," Freddie said determinedly.

"Then let's begin," Win suggested.

Chapter Eighteen

Sera entered the stables with the others, her fingers still tingling from Win's touch. She had realized that he was a rogue. A lover—and user—of women. Else he wouldn't be toying with her feelings the way he was. He wouldn't lay down in the grass next to her, staining his breeches and coat as his fingers brushed against hers. He wouldn't take her hand out in the open where anyone could see him do so.

He was not for her. She repeated the thought several times, trying to convince herself.

She did think he was a good man. He was trying awfully hard with Charlie and Freddie. It had surprised her that he stopped by the schoolroom this morning and even more so when he agreed to race Freddie. She had been shocked when he plopped next to her and found images in the clouds and quite surprised when he allowed Freddie to win their footrace.

But for all the good in him, he had as much as told her he wasn't going to like—or love—his wife. She figured that meant he would get his heirs off whomever became his duchess and he would have a string of mistresses for the rest of his natural days. Winston Cutler was an incredibly handsome man who loved all women. Made each of them feel special in his presence. He would seek pleasure wherever and whenever he could.

But she had to be like a careful, smaller army when confronted by a larger enemy force. Set a perimeter about herself and guard it well. He had already penetrated her defenses and stolen her heart. Sera could not allow him to steal her virginity, as well.

Though she would be willing to give it to him.

No, she couldn't think such perilous thoughts. She was already in far too much trouble, over her head, with her emotions running wild within her simply from kissing this man. She couldn't let down her defenses. Even if he charmed her or she watched him charm his nephews. She was here with a specific task, that of helping the boys adjust to life at Woodbridge. Seeing that they learned to obey the rules and got off to a good start in their academics. She would leave here in six weeks' time and never return.

It made her determined to find a husband at the Danburys' house party. She would direct all of her energies to that matter and hope she never had to see Win again. A Scottish laird from the Highlands would be a perfect mate. If she could find one. And then she would insist they never set foot in England again. Minta would simply have to come and visit her.

Harrison led them down the row of horses, stopping and telling the boys each horse's name and a little about its temperament. He let them stroke the long noses, which delighted the boys to no end.

"Where are the ones we can ride?" Charlie asked.

"Let's go this way," Harrison suggested. "We've no ponies now, which would be ideal for you to learn on, but we do have a few old mares with tough mouths that will do."

"What is a tough mouth?" Freddie paused. "And why do we have to have old horses? I want a new one."

"Older ones are a bit more settled," Harrison answered. "They won't have the tendency to buck off a new rider such as you, Master Freddie." He chuckled. "Let me tell you from experience. You don't wish to be thrown by a horse."

"I will see about purchasing ponies for the boys," Win voiced. "For now, show us the older mares, Harrison."

But his words did not go unnoticed. Charlie threw his arms about Win's waist and hugged him tightly. "Thank you, Your Grace."

He ruffled Charlie's hair. "We haven't needed ponies at Woodbridge for some time. It will be a good investment for the future."

Sera swallowed the bitterness that rose within her. Of course, Win referred to the children he and his duchess would have. They would need ponies to learn to ride. The thought of him placing his child on a horse and walking beside it made her heart twist. She rapidly blinked several times, trying to keep tears from spilling down her cheeks.

"That would be kind of you, Your Grace," Freddie said. "But we know they would be your ponies and not ours." He eyed his brother steadily.

"No, they would be yours," Win said cheerfully. "Why, you could even name them if you choose to do so."

He began talking with Harrison about those in the area who might have ponies for sale. The groom thought a Mr. Jefferson would have the best selection. Even Sera caught the boys' excitement.

"Then we will go tomorrow morning to see some. I'll send a note around to let Jefferson know we are coming," Win announced.

They reached a stall and Harrison said, "This here's Marigold. She has a sweet nature. I think she would be the best choice for you to have your first lesson. You will take turns. Watching the other will do you some good and help you to learn."

"Saddle Marigold if you would, Harrison," Win said. "We'll return to the yard. I'll show the boys the paddock."

They left the dark stables and stopped at a large block, which Win explained to them was a mounting block.

"Either a groom can hand you up into the saddle or if you wish to do it on your own, you may use this."

He led them around the stables to where a paddock stood,

telling them it was fenced in to pasture or exercise animals.

"This is where I first learned to ride," he shared, a smile tugging at the corners of his mouth.

Sera knew those must be fond memories for him. She hoped the memories the boys would create would also be happy ones.

Harrison brought Marigold to them and both she and Win told them about the various parts of the saddle, as well as the bit and bridle. He had each boy feel Marigold's coat and told them when they came to the stables in the future, they would bring an apple.

"It will help you bond with your pony as you share it," he explained. "You want to be friends with your ride."

They took turns getting on and off Marigold, who stood patiently as if she hadn't a care in the world. After both boys felt comfortable sitting on her and could point out the various parts of equipment, Win told Harrison to take over. Win then led Sera to the fence and, without warning, clasped her about the waist and lifted her to sit atop it. Then he joined her.

"We'll have a perfect view from here."

"I had thought I would teach them to ride but I think it is good to allow Harrison to do so," she said, trying to make conversation so she could stop thinking about how good Win smelled.

"Yes, it is good for them to see they can learn from others. Besides, Harrison is a wonderful teacher. He couldn't have been more than sixteen when he taught me how to ride when I was young. I am glad he was named head groom at Woodbridge during my years away."

He fell silent and they watched Harrison use a leading rein to take Freddie about the paddock. The joyful look on his face made Sera's heart sing.

Charlie also got his turn and looked just as happy. Both boys were given three turns apiece on Marigold as Harrison walked the mare around the paddock.

"That's enough for today," Win called out, jumping down

from the fence and reaching up for her.

Sera held her breath as he lifted her and then placed her on the ground, his hands remaining on her waist as he stared into her eyes a moment. Then he smiled and released her.

He was far too charming for his own good.

They told Harrison goodbye and Charlie said, "I'm hungry."

"It must be close to teatime," Win proclaimed. "Sera wanted you both to have some cake today."

"Cake?" they squealed in unison.

"Yes, cake. It was quite moist and delicious last night. Be glad Sera and I saved some for the two of you and did not eat it all."

As they approached the house, he suggested, "Let us cut through the kitchens so I may speak with Cook."

The entered and the room grew quiet. Sera supposed a duke never went to his own kitchens—and Win had done so twice today.

"Cook, that cake at dinner last night was marvelous. Could we have that with our tea? And sandwiches, too. We are quite hungry. The boys and Miss Nicholls and I will take tea in the drawing room now. Milk for the boys, please."

"Yes, Your Grace. I'll see to it at once."

Sera wanted to protest but when she saw how the boys' eyes lit up at having tea with the duke, she kept silent.

Instead, she said, "We will go upstairs then to wash up and change our clothes. After all, we have been outside for several hours. I know my gown is stained from the grass and our cloud watching, plus we've touched all those horses. We need clean hands in order to take tea."

Charlie grumbled good-naturedly and Freddie nudged him. She followed them from the kitchens and had them take the back staircase.

"Why are there two stairs?" Freddie wanted to know.

"Servants usually take this back staircase, while those who live in the house take the other set. These are closer to where our rooms are and more convenient."

"There are a lot of rules," Charlie said, blowing out a breath in frustration.

She got the boys to their room and laid out clean clothes for them to put on after they had washed. They scrambled out of what they wore and came to the basin, taking turns washing up.

"Can you dress without me?" she asked. "I also need to wash and change."

"We are big boys," Freddie said proudly. "We can do it, Sera."

"All right. Go to the schoolroom and practice writing some of our rhyming words on your slates when you finish. I will be along soon."

She returned to her cramped room and as she removed her gown, she realized she would be responsible for washing her own garments. She hoped the grass stains would come out of her gown.

Quickly, she performed her ablutions and claimed a clean gown, then folded hers and dunked it into the wash basin to soak. Hopefully, that would make the stains come out more easily when she scrubbed it.

When she returned to the schoolroom, she found both boys carefully lettering on their slates. Pride filled her.

"Shall we go downstairs?"

They took her hands and the three of them went to the drawing room. Win wasn't there yet and so she walked about the room with the pair, showing them the art on the walls and telling them about it and the furniture. Win joined them and as the teacart was rolled in, the boys hurried to claim a spot near it.

"You turn everything into a teachable moment," he commented.

"They have much to learn. Things we take for granted because of the way in which we were raised are unknown to them. I don't want to preach to them. Instead, I want to incorporate as much as I can into our conversations. They are little sponges and will soak up knowledge, from academic topics to societal rules, often without even knowing they do so."

"We should join them," Win said and she moved toward the teacart.

After they sat, he asked, "Would you do the honor of pouring out, Sera?"

"I would be happy to, Your Grace."

As he passed the cups of milk to the boys, Charlie asked, "What is your name, Your Grace? What did your mum called you?"

"It is Winston."

Charlie's nose curled up.

Win chuckled. "I know. I didn't much like it myself. That is why I shortened it and always went by Win."

"That's better," Freddie said. "Can I have some cake now?"

"Cake it is," Sera said, slicing both boys a generous amount. As she handed the plates over, she reminded them, "You are to eat slowly. Chew each bite carefully. That way, you can savor the flavor and texture."

"What's savor?" Charlie asked before taking a bite.

"To thoroughly enjoy. Close your eyes as you chew," she suggested and he did so. "Move your tongue around. Taste the sweetness of the icing. The moistness of the cake."

The little boy swallowed. "Yum. That was even better than I thought."

Freddie tried doing the same and agreed. "But I don't want to eat with my eyes closed all the time."

She laughed. "You don't have to. Every now and then, though, slow down and really taste your food, especially if it is a sweet."

"Do you like sweets, Sera?" Freddie asked.

"I adore sweets. I can bake quite a few. In fact, we should make that a lesson this week. We can bake and learn all about measurements."

"That's for girls," Freddie said with disdain.

She glared at him. "Some of the best pastry chefs in the world are men. If both males and females eat, shouldn't both be allowed to cook?"

He shrugged. "I guess so."

"I think baking would be fun," Charlie said. His eyes lit up. "Especially if we can eat what we bake."

"We can have bites of some things," she agreed. "Maybe we'll bake items for tea tomorrow." She paused. "Actually, we should wait and do so the day after. Visitors are coming to Woodbridge and they'll want to meet you. Wouldn't it be fun to serve them what we baked?"

The boys agreed and they spent the rest of teatime talking about what they might serve.

Charlie sat back and rubbed his belly. "I'm stuffed. But it was all good."

"It was," Win agreed. He looked to Sera. "What is next for the boys?"

"We'll go back to the schoolroom and do some work with numbers. Then I will read to them for an hour. By then, they will eat a little something and then ready themselves for bed."

"What are we going to read, Sera?" Charlie asked.

"I have an idea of something you might enjoy," Win said. "A copy is in the library. I'll bring it up to you once I locate it."

"Very well, Your Grace," she said, rising. "Mouths and hands wiped. Napkins folded and set down."

The boys did as asked and Freddie looked at the duke. "Can we call you Win? Just when it's the four of us?"

Sera held her breath, thinking Win would bristle at Freddie's impertinence. Instead he surprised her.

"Only when it is the four of us. And only outside," he cautioned.

"Why outside?" Charlie wondered.

"Dukes are very important people. Rarely does anyone call them by their given name. Even within their families, they are referred to by their titles."

"Where is your family?" Freddie wanted to know.

"They're all dead."

Charlie took Win's hand and squeezed it. "I'm sorry, Win."

"Thank you, Charlie. Now, run along with Sera. And it's Your Grace in the house. We don't want any servants to overhear you. Save Win for our outdoor fun."

The boy nodded and Sera took both boys' hands and led them from the drawing room back upstairs to the schoolroom. She worked with them on writing numbers on their slates and taught them a few simple sums.

All the while, she thought of Win and how his attitude continued to change toward his nephews.

CHAPTER NINETEEN

W IN WENT TO the library, a room he never saw either of his parents in, much less his brother. Because of that, the room had become a refuge to Win and he had spent many happy hours within its confines. When Percy came, he would have them come here to read, play backgammon, and talk, knowing they wouldn't be disturbed.

He doubted the book he searched for had been taken from the shelf since he had placed it there years ago. Maids did come in and dust the shelves but they would have no reason to move any of the volumes.

It was just where he remembered it would be. Pulling it from the shelf, he said aloud as he looked at the cover, *"Tales of Mother Goose."*

Oh, how he had loved this book when he was a young boy. It contained stories he came to treasure. *The Sleeping Beauty. Puss in Boots. Cinderella. Little Red Riding Hood.* Eventually, he had read the fairy tales in their original French, thanks to a tutor who had loaned him a copy of it. Written by Charles Perrault—but published under the name of his last son, Pierre—the first publication was entitled *Histoires ou contes du temps passe, avec des moralites: Contes de ma mere l'Ove.*

He couldn't wait to share it with his nephews.

Win froze, suddenly feeling as if he'd been struck by a bolt of lightning. Sera's lessons were coming home to roost. He realized that he didn't want to hold these boys at arms' length. Instead, he wanted to claim them as family. The thought surprised him but it shouldn't. Sera had opened her arms to the two orphans and allowed Win to see them as not mistakes of Terrance's but unique individuals in their own right. It had been wrong on his part to visit the sins of the father upon his bastard sons. He thought to what he had told the pair only last night.

Always do the right thing. Strive to be the best person you can be.

Now, he needed to live up to his own life lessons.

Win took the book and headed to the schoolroom, both his heart and his step lighter than they had been in a long time. Outside the door, he paused as he had this morning, eavesdropping without feeling a bit of shame.

"Very good," Sera said. "You are grasping it well."

"I like reading and writing better," Charlie said.

"I like numbers," Freddie countered. "They just make more sense to me."

Ah, so he had a budding mathematician on his hands.

"Everyone has different talents," Sera explained. "I like reading and believe I have a talent for playing music and gardening. Both of you will come to know what subjects you enjoy studying and what you have a knack for. We will try different things and help you grow."

"Like a flower grows?" Charlie asked.

"Exactly," Sera replied.

He was too excited to linger in the corridor any longer. Entering, he said, "I found the book I was looking for. It is called *Tales of Mother Goose*."

"Is it about a talking goose?" Freddie asked. "That would be a fun story."

"Actually, no. A goose doesn't appear at all except inside on the title page."

"Then why is named after a goose if no goose is in it?" Charlie wondered.

"I'm not really sure," he admitted. "But the stories within are marvelous. I read them over and over as a boy. Shall we read one together now?"

He handed the collection of stories to Sera but she shook her head. "No, Your Grace, I believe you should read it to Freddie and Charlie."

"Call him Win," Freddie corrected.

"No," Charlie said, shaking his head. "He's only Win outside. The maid who brings us food could hear and His Grace wouldn't like that."

He swallowed, building courage. "I think I would like you to call me Uncle Win. All the time."

Both boys frowned at him but behind them, he saw Sera's radiant smile. Tears sparkled in her eyes.

"But you're not our uncle," Freddie pointed out. "Mum didn't have any brothers. She told us so."

"Your papa did," Win said softly. "Your father . . . was my brother."

Freddie stood quickly, knocking his chair back. "No." He backed away until he was in the corner.

He came toward the upset child and knelt, recalling how Sera had done the same to be on the boys' level. "I am your uncle, Freddie. And Charlie's uncle."

Freddie vigorously shook his head. "No. Why didn't you tell us? Back in London?"

"Because I was afraid," he admitted.

"Afraid of Charlie and me?"

He nodded. "I didn't like my brother much. We weren't close as you and Charlie are. Terrance was eight years older than I was and destined to be the Duke of Woodmont. He didn't pay a bit of attention to me. Neither did my parents. Unlike your mama, who loved you very much."

"How did he die?" Charlie asked, leaving his chair and going to where Win knelt.

He wondered how much he should tell them. A sanitized

version of the truth now, he supposed, and more of it when they matured and could understand more.

"In a fire. Last year."

"Last year?" Freddie's face scrunched. "But Mum said he was dead. That he was called Mr. Sawyer and he died before we were born."

"Your mama was trying to spare your feelings," he explained. "My brother was a selfish man. He didn't want to marry your mama and he didn't want children. He wanted to keep all his wealth for himself."

"He sounds mean," Charlie said, his bottom lip sticking out. "I don't like him."

"I didn't either," Win agreed. "Terrance always thought of himself and no one else. He wasn't a nice man and he certainly wasn't a good duke. When he died in the fire, I got a letter telling me I had to come home because I was the new duke."

"Where were you?" Freddie's mouth trembled.

"I had gone into the army and was an officer fighting in England's war against Bonaparte. I had to leave the military and return here to take care of Woodbridge and the other properties that belong to the family. I heard that my brother may have had a child and went searching. Mr. Blumer helped me find you. I am sorry I didn't know about you before. I came as soon as I knew."

"And then Mum died," Charlie said, downcast.

"I know. The doctor I brought with me told me she was very sick and there was nothing he could do to save her. She had consumption. Many people have died from it."

"Maybe I'll be a doctor and fix people who have it so they don't die," Freddie said fiercely.

Win placed a hand on the boy's shoulder. "I would like nothing better than to see a doctor in the Cutler family."

Charlie frowned. "But our name is Sawyer."

"That was your mama's last name. But you are Cutlers, as well, even though your father did not wed your mother." He paused. "I would like very much if you both would take the

Cutler name. Would you think about it?"

He glanced from Charlie to Freddie, who said, "We'll think about it."

"There is no rush," he told them. "And no pressure to do so. If you want to stay Sawyers, I will respect that choice."

"You really were afraid?" Charlie asked, his voice small.

"I was. I didn't know if you would like me, especially since it was my brother who was your father. He did not treat your mama well."

"You're not mean, Win," Charlie said, guilelessly. "It doesn't matter if our father was. I'm glad he's dead. But you love us. Don't you?"

For the first time in his life, a tear rolled down Win's cheek.

"I really do."

Suddenly, both boys were in his arms and the three of them were laughing and crying at the same time. Feeling them cling to him made his heart want to burst with pride and love in this pair. Terrance may have sired them but Sandra Sawyer had done all the hard work and produced two lovely children.

Freddie pulled away. "We can call you Uncle Win anytime? Even in front of the servants? Or anybody?"

"If you don't call me Uncle Win, I might have to tan your backside," he teased playfully.

"Can we read the storybook now?" pleaded Charlie. "Read your favorite one to us."

"All right. Come to the table."

He sat in one of the terribly tiny chairs, a nephew on each side of him, leaning close. Charlie's hand rested on Win's forearm. He placed the book on the table in front of him so they could see the illustrations. Taking a moment, he glanced up at Sera, who had taken the seat opposite all of them. Her encouraging smile helped steady him.

Opening the book, he located the story he wanted to read to them.

"This is called *Cinderella*."

"What's it about?" Freddie demanded, impatient as always.

"A beautiful, hardworking girl. An evil stepmother. And a ball held at a castle where the handsome prince falls in love with Cinderella."

His gaze met Sera's and he smiled.

Win cleared his throat and began. "Once upon a time . . ."

❯❯❯❯❮❮❮❮

SERA SAT ENTRANCED as she listened to Win's low rumble. She was so proud of the decision he had made. Telling the boys was the right thing to do. He was modeling his own philosophy and by doing so, Freddie and Charlie would know they would always have a home.

"And they all lived happily ever after," he said, finishing the fairy tale.

"I'd like to be able to turn a pumpkin into a carriage," Charlie said. "Or mice into horses. That would be fun."

"But then you would have to have a place to store both the carriage and the horses," Win said.

"And feed them," Freddie added. "Horses must eat an awful lot. They're bigger than people."

"They do," Win agreed. "Like hungry little boys," he growled and tickled Freddie, who squealed.

Charlie's fingers quickly found Win's belly and began tickling him. Then Freddie did the same.

"Attacked on both sides!" he shouted. "It's not fair."

She couldn't help but beam, seeing how happy the two boys were.

And seeing the joy on Win's face.

A maid with a tray appeared in the doorway and her jaw dropped at the sight. A second one bumped into her and almost dropped the tray she carried.

"B-b-begging your pardon, Your Grace," the first servant got out. "We've the boys' dinner."

"Thank you," he said. "Place it on the table, please."

The servants did as requested and quickly left the room. Sera knew they would be chattering—and speculating—the entire way back to the kitchens.

"Eat up," Win encouraged.

She didn't think after all Charlie and Freddie had eaten at tea that they would be hungry but she was quickly proven wrong. She supposed growing boys were always hungry.

Once they finished their meal, they went to their bedchamber. Freddie cautioned them to stay behind.

"Charlie and I can get ready ourselves," he declared. "We will tell you when we are ready."

"We'll wash behind our ears," Charlie said, smiling. "We won't forget."

After the two exited, he looked and her and sighed. "Things have changed quite a bit—and for the better."

"I knew they were good boys all along," she reminded him. "They were merely acting out because they craved attention. They have received that from you."

"And you, as well, Sera."

She studied him. "I hope you will be able to love them, Win."

His hand raked through his hair. "I already do. I was wrong to distance myself from them. I thought I was simply going to take responsibility for Terrance's bastards. See them fed and clothed and even educated. I was blaming the sin of the father upon two innocent lads. I thought I wanted nothing to do with them. I find I have changed my mind considerably."

He took her hand. "You helped me see them as my nephews. Blood relatives."

She looked down at their joined hands, his large one engulfing hers, the tingle of desire rippling through her. Why did he keep doing these things? She didn't think he was trying to seduce her. He merely wanted to share the joy he felt.

"They will be a part of the household now. I will call the

servants together and tell them the boys are family. Of course, they cannot be addressed as Lord Frederick or Lord Charles. Even though they are the sons of a duke, they are still by-blows."

"What if the servants used *Master Freddie* and *Master Charlie*?" she asked. "I noticed that is how Harrison referred to them during their riding lesson today."

"Yes, that would be appropriate. When they are older, they can be Mr. Sawyer. Or Mr. Cutler if they choose to use the family name."

"You did the right thing. Telling them you were their uncle. I noticed you did not explain fully about the father's relationship with their mothers. Or that they even have separate mothers. Will you ever share that?"

"I'm not sure if I will. Right now, they are brothers. Being half-brothers is not that important in the long run. If I did tell them, it would put Terrance in an even poorer light. Neither looks like him. Freddie is the spitting image of his mother. As they grow older, Charlie will most likely assume he favors his father."

Win sighed. "I know down the line they may have more questions. Why I inherited the dukedom over them. They will learn they are bastards by Polite Society's standards, though they certainly aren't the first. Still, I want them to know they will be loved and cherished by the Duke and Duchess of Woodmont."

Sera realized that the new duchess would have to accept the boys as members of the household. She would have no say in the matter since Win now felt so strongly about the pair. Of course, many young women would chase his title and not care about the boys because neither would inherit. She already hated the thought of being parted from Freddie and Charlie and wondered if perhaps she should ask Win if she could stay on permanently as their governess.

Then again, the thought of being in a household and watching Win with his duchess would be too hard to bear. No, she would stick with the original plan. Help the boys adjust to living at Woodbridge and then leave for the house party.

"We're ready!" called Charlie.

She rose, pulling her hand from Win's, feeling bereft at no longer being able to draw strength from his touch.

Both boys were in their separate beds, sitting up, looking clean and happy.

"Will you read us a story now, Sera?" asked Charlie. "Or you can tell us one instead."

She didn't feel like making up a story and asked Win to fetch the Mother Goose book. Once she had it, he recommended *The Master Cat*.

"Otherwise known as *Puss in Boot*," he told his nephews.

Sera read the tale of the miller's three sons, the youngest inheriting a very special cat. The cat became a lord, while the son won the love of a princess.

When she finished, she closed the book and saw Charlie's eyelids fluttering. Glancing at Freddie, she saw he also was almost asleep.

Sera kissed each boy goodnight and saw Win did the same. Freddie smiled up sleepily at his uncle and then closed his eyes.

It was too much. The emotion roiling within her threatened to erupt and cause her to break down.

They went to the schoolroom and closed that door. She took a deep breath, trying to calm herself, and looked up at Win.

"I am afraid I am as sleepy as the boys. I am also still full from that heavy tea. I think I will turn in for the night."

Disappointment crossed his face. "I understand." He gazed at her for a long moment and then said, "Goodnight, Sera."

She smiled brightly. "Goodnight, Win."

Turning, she forced her feet to move to the door to her bedchamber. She entered and closed it behind her. Sera waited, breathing shallowly, until she had given Win enough time to be gone.

Then she dissolved into tears, burying her face in the lumpy pillow, crying for a life she could never have.

CHAPTER TWENTY

S ERA SLEPT POORLY, tossing and turning most of the night. She finally got up, feeling drained.

She had decided she would have to ask Win to hire a governess for the boys. Now that the pair knew they wouldn't be shoved aside and taken from Woodbridge, they wouldn't have a need to act up. The sooner Win found a governess for them, the more quickly they could adjust.

And the better it would be for her.

She was growing too close to Freddie and Charlie. If she stayed much longer, the hurt would only grow deeper. She would take today and savor it. Tomorrow, as well, at least until Minta and Percy showed up for tea. Determination filled her. She would leave with her sister and return to Kingwood tomorrow afternoon. Her things would already be packed, making it convenient for her to go on to London. She knew if she asked, Percy would send her to Aunt Phyllis and Uncle West. Though Sera had no intention of going to any *ton* events, she would have put physical distance between her and Win.

It was the emotional distance she worried about.

She dressed, forgoing her corset. Last night, Sara had brought hot water up at eight o'clock. The servant had told Sera she was surprised she had lasted as long as she had and that she might make it until the end of the week. While the maid had helped

Sera from her corset, she didn't like the girl's attitude and had decided she would not wear a corset because it would mean asking the maid for help.

A light knock sounded at the door and she answered it, admitting Sara to the tiny room.

"Here's your water, Miss Nicholls. I see you're already dressed."

"Yes, I won't be needing your help after all," she said firmly.

"Oh." The girl looked at her. "Them boys didn't cause a bit o' trouble yesterday. Everyone's talking about it. And you. How did you make them behave?"

She didn't like to hear that she was an object of gossip. "Freddie and Charlie are pleasant children. I don't think they will be misbehaving much in the future. Thank you for the water," she said dismissively.

The servant looked put out and flounced from the room.

Sera finished getting ready and then crossed into the schoolroom and then the boys' room. They were already up and getting dressed.

"Are you excited about feeding the chickens this morning?" she asked. "And collecting the eggs? It is a big responsibility but I know the two of you will do a wonderful job each day."

"I hope I don't drop any," Charlie worried. "That would get pretty messy."

"Accidents will happen occasionally," she said. "The important thing is to take your time and be careful."

She led the boys down the back stairs and to the kitchens, where Cook awaited them. She handed each boy a basket.

"Stay here and have a cup of tea, Miss Nicholls. I'll take these two in hand."

"All right, Cook."

A maid handed her a cup and saucer and indicated a small table in the corner where she could sit.

"Want something to eat, Miss Nicholls?" she asked. "We're so happy you've come. Them boys were a handful but it only took you a day to get them straightened out."

"I will wait and eat with my charges. Thank you for the tea, though."

She sipped on the brew as she watched the workers grow busy. Soon, Cook returned with Freddie and Charlie, each boy carefully toting a full basket of eggs. They gave them over to Cook and Sera joined them.

"How did they do?"

"Right nice, Miss Nicholls. They're polite boys. The chickens scared 'em a bit but I taught them how to scatter the feed so that the birds don't gang up on 'em. They were good with the eggs, too. Took their time just as they should."

"That is high praise from Cook," she said and both boys grinned broadly.

"I'll send breakfast up to the schoolroom now," Cook promised.

"Can we eat here?" Freddie asked. "We're already in the kitchens where the food is. It's the right thing because then no one has to take it up all those stairs."

Sera nearly burst with pride, hearing Freddie talk about doing the right thing. Win's lessons were already taking root with his nephews.

"We won't be in the way," Charlie said. "We can eat over there, where Miss Nicholls was having tea."

When Cook looked doubtful, Sera added, "I don't think His Grace would mind. We promise to stay out of your way."

"Very well. Go take a seat," Cook said.

The boys scampered off and Sera thanked the older woman. "I also have a favor to ask of you, Cook. Tomorrow, I will be teaching the boys about measurements. I'd like them to help me bake a few things and put our lessons to use."

"You want to come bake? With those two?" Doubt flashed in Cook's eyes.

"Yes, I did quite a bit of baking before I came here. I would want to make an apple cake and some scones. Would that be possible? Pick a time when it would be convenient."

"After I get breakfast out to everyone would be best, I suppose."

"Very well. The items will need to be served to the guests coming for tea tomorrow afternoon, along with whatever else you were going to include."

"For the marquess and marchioness?" Cook pursed her lips. "It would have to be very, very good in order to serve to them."

"The marchioness is my sister," Sera revealed. "She has eaten my baked goods many times."

"Oh! Well, knock me over with a feather," Cook declared. "All right, Miss Nicholls. You may have time in my workplace tomorrow morning then." She narrowed her eyes. "But watch those boys like a hawk," she warned.

"I will, Cook."

She joined the boys and they ate their breakfast. Sera didn't eat as much as she usually did, conscious of being uncorseted, which usually hid her body to a degree.

"What are we learning today, Miss Nicholls?" Charlie asked.

"Thank you for addressing me properly," she said, noting he had not called her Sera since they were in the kitchens full of bustling servants.

"I want to do maths again," Freddie said.

"That is for tomorrow. Today, we will work on reading and writing all morning. Then another riding lesson, I think. Afterward, we can wander the estate and see what is here."

"We know lots about the place," Charlie said. "Freddie and I went all over when were with them Birdwells. We'll show you around."

"Very well."

They finished eating and returned to the schoolroom. They had been hard at work for a few hours, with both boys making considerable progress, when Win arrived.

"Uncle Win!" they cried, leaping to their feet and going to hug him.

"What have you been doing today?" he asked, leading them back to their seats.

They told him about the chicken duties first, which Sera thought was sweet, and then they showed him what they had been working on since returning to the schoolroom.

"Since you were literally up with the chickens, it sounds as if you have already put in a full morning despite it being only ten o'clock." Win looked at his nephews solemnly. "Do you think you could possibly tear yourselves away from your studies? I have an important errand for us to run."

"Yes!" Charlie cried.

"What?" Freddie wanted to know. "What kind of errand?"

He looked to her. "Have the boys done enough with reading and writing?"

"For now. I will pick up again later this afternoon. We were going to ask Harrison for another riding lesson, however."

His eyes twinkled. "That will work perfectly for what I have in mind. Come along, everyone. You, too, Sera. The carriage is waiting. We should go downstairs and see where it will take us."

"You aren't telling us?" Charlie asked, somewhat disappointed.

"Our errand is a surprise. And we need to stop in the foyer for something before we leave."

"Maybe it's getting a meat pie," Freddie said, his eyes lighting up.

The boys scrambled from their chairs and hurried out the door. Sera rose and she and Win followed.

"I suppose no meat pies are involved."

He chuckled. "You would be correct in that assumption."

"Then where are we going?"

Win smiled enigmatically. "Ah, you will simply have to ride along and discover where at the same time my nephews do. But first, we stop downstairs."

By the time they made the turn for the final landing, she saw Freddie and Charlie had stopped there. Both boys looked over their shoulders apprehensively. Sera glanced down to the foyer and saw a bevy of servants lined up, looking up expectantly.

Charlie wore a pained expression. "Are we in trouble?"

"Not at all. Continue down the stairs and we'll stop at the bottom."

The boys took the stairs slowly, their heads turning back and forth as they saw all those gathered. When they reached the bottom, Win placed a hand upon both their shoulders.

Sera had an inkling of what he planned to say and hung back.

"Thank you all for gathering here," he said in his commanding voice, which carried easily. "I have a brief announcement to make."

He glanced down and smiled fondly at his nephews and then back at the crowd.

"Some of you have met these two and haven't had the most favorable impression of them. This is Freddie and Charlie Sawyer. They are the sons of my brother, the late Duke of Woodmont."

A murmur rippled through the servants.

"These boys behaved terribly when they first arrived at Woodbridge. While I know they may slip in the future and get into a bit of mischief, their days of being incorrigible have passed. They were frightened. They had left the life they knew in London. They had lost their beloved mother. And they were taken away by a stranger. Me."

Win paused and looked down. Sera saw he squeezed their shoulders. "They know now that they have come home. That Woodbridge is a safe place where they will grow up and become men. They will receive all the love and attention they need and will no longer need to misbehave in order to garner attention."

Freddie spoke up. "We aim to be good. Sometimes, though, we do get into trouble. Mum always said trouble found us."

"His Grace was much the same way," Farmwell said with a smile. "And yet look how well he turned out."

Everyone chuckled at the butler's words.

Win glanced out at the crowd. "You will address them as

Master Charlie and Master Freddie."

Farmwell spoke for all. "We can certainly do so, Your Grace." He looked at the boys. "We are happy to have you at Wood-bridge."

"Thank you," Freddie said softly and Charlie echoed his brother's words.

"That will be all now," Win told the group. "Back to your tasks if you would."

The servants began dispersing, with a few coming up and saying a few words to the boys. Once everyone had gone, Win led them outside to the carriage. He assisted Sera up and she sat opposite of the forward-facing seat, not wanting to be in close proximity to him. Charlie joined her and Freddie sat opposite them.

When Win entered, he sat where she predicted and pro-claimed, "This won't do. Trade seats with Sera, Freddie."

"Why?"

"Because Sera's belly gets a bit queasy when she rides back-ward."

She was touched he remembered but was reluctant as she moved to take her place beside him.

Win tapped on the vehicle's roof and the wheels set into motion.

Charlie looked out the window. "How long until we get there?"

"Not long at all. We are headed to the village nearby."

Freddie snorted. "I hope we won't see that mean old man. The one who didn't want to touch us."

"That is exactly where we are going. You need clothes of your own. Especially night shirts with your own initials and not mine."

"But I like wearing your clothes, Uncle Win," Charlie told him.

"You may wear those old clothes for your treks outdoors with Sera," he said. "For when you roll about the grass or go fishing. You need clothes made to fit you to wear the rest of the time. In fact, we should be able to take some home with us today because we have special guests coming for tea tomorrow. I want you to meet them."

Win glanced questioningly at Sera and she shook her head, letting him know she had not shared with the boys who was coming or her relationship to them.

"We can wear your uncle's hand-me-downs when we bake tomorrow. We are going to learn about measurements in tomorrow morning's lesson and then Cook has said we could bake some for the visitors' tea."

"Do we get to sample anything?" Freddie asked, a sly look in his eyes.

"That is a very clever idea," Sera said. "We wouldn't want your guests to have something not up to Woodbridge standards. Yes, I think each of you should taste what we make to make certain we can serve it with pride."

They arrived in the village and it was obvious the tailor was expecting them, which led Sera to believe Win had sent word ahead. He fawned over Win and the boys and measured Charlie and Freddie with great care.

"I have a few adjustments to make to the garments you requested, Your Grace," the tailor said. "You can pick those up in an hour. I will begin work on the rest of the wardrobe for them after that."

"Then we will return shortly. Why don't we stop at the bakery for a sticky bun and then walk about the village?"

The boys cheered his words and, soon, they had sticky buns in hand as they walked the few streets of the hamlet. Several people greeted them, with shopkeepers coming outside in order to get a word with their duke. Finally, they made their way back to the tailor's shop and Sera insisted they try on their new clothes instead of hurrying home because Win had told them they could have their riding lesson upon their return to the estate.

The clothes fit them beautifully and she told them to change back into what they had worn to the village.

"We will save your new things for tea tomorrow. You don't want to get them dirty or sweaty as you ride today."

The tailor asked that they stop by again in a week's time and he would have everything ready by then. The boys bounced up and down inside the carriage, excited about their new things and eager to get on Marigold again.

When the carriage pulled around to the back of the house, Freddie threw open the door right as it came to a halt, jumping to the ground. Charlie followed closely behind.

"I hope Charlie won't always be the follower of the pair," she said. "Freddie is such a leader, though. It will be hard for Charlie to assert himself."

Win exited the carriage and held out a hand to her. "It is good they have such a tight bond. They will protect one another when they go off to school together, just as Percy and I looked after one another."

"Was Percy always so shy?" she asked.

"Extremely," Win confirmed. "But Minta has done wonders for him."

"Minta was always my protector. She looked after me as Freddie does Charlie."

They heard shouts and rushed to the paddock, where the boys were jumping up and down.

"Uncle Win! Sera! Sera! Uncle Win!" they heard as the boys rushed toward them.

"What is it?" she asked as Freddie almost bowled her over.

"We have ponies!" he shouted. "Our own ponies!"

They turned and ran back to the paddock and she looked at Win, arching her brows.

"I wrote to Jefferson, the local man who breeds horses, and sent the note with a footman this morning. I told him I was in need of two ponies for my nephews so that they might learn how to ride. He replied and said he would send them over. That was the true reason for our excursion into the village. I wanted the ponies to be waiting for them when we returned."

They strolled to the paddock, where Freddie and Charlie sat atop the fence as Harrison was telling them about their ponies.

"Do you like your surprise?" Win asked.

"Yes!" they said with enthusiasm.

Sera gave them a pointed look and they immediately began thanking their uncle.

"You are most welcome. The first thing you need to do is name them, I suppose. Have you decided which one you will take?"

"Harrison said to wait for you and then we could go see them," Charlie said. "He said we should pet them and talk to them and we'd just know."

The groom grinned sheepishly. "Ponies are a bit like cats, you see. They take to someone and that's their person."

"Then let's go meet them," Win said.

The ponies were approximately the same size, though one was black and the other brown. They learned both were males. After much talking and petting, Charlie said the brown had picked him and Freddie sighed, relieved because he had taken to the black.

A debate ensued on what to name each of them, with Charlie finally settling on Brownie and Freddie choosing Blackie.

"Not terribly original, I'm afraid," Win said quietly to her. "But it is what they want. Shall we watch their lesson again from the same place?"

Sera followed him to the fence and allowed him to place her on top of it. He climbed beside her and she inhaled the bergamot scent wafting from him. This might be the last time they sat so close. Tomorrow, she would stay inside during the riding lesson and decide what the boys should study for a week or so since she still planned to leave tomorrow after tea. She hoped Win would travel to London and find another governess so there wouldn't be too much of a gap in the boys' learning.

The summer sun warmed her as she watched Harrison lead

both boys around the paddock on their very own ponies. Sera thought just how rapidly their lives had changed, coming from poverty to a great ducal estate and having their own horses.

"Look at me, Sera!" cried Charlie.

"I see!" she called back to him, smiling and waving.

She would miss these little boys.

And their uncle. Very much.

CHAPTER TWENTY-ONE

WIN ROSE, EAGER that morning had finally come.

Today, he would ask Sera to marry him.

He wasn't sure exactly where or how, only that it was a burning desire within him, much as he burned for her.

Part of him wanted her all to himself when he did so in order that he could kiss her senseless, both before and after his proposal. Another thought was to make it a family affair and ask her with Freddie and Charlie present, possibly even Percy and Minta. The boys and Percy were his family. What better way to ask Sera to join his family than with that very family surrounding them?

Still, Sera was a bit shy. Oh, she hadn't been at all during her time at Woodbridge. Actually, she never had seemed so in his presence, save for when they first met on the London docks after she arrived from Upper Canada. From the minute they had gotten into his cousin's carriage, Sera and he had talked. A lot. They never seemed to stop talking and never did run out of things to say. He had been foolish to think her shyness would keep her from being a wonderful duchess. In truth, it would make her a better one. Sera would never rush to judgment. She would observe and study and always see the best in people and in any given situation. She had a wonderful sense of humor and a playfulness about her that he supposed only her family realized that she possessed.

Win knew a jewel when he saw one. And Sera would be the crown jewel in the Cutler family. She would be the glue that held them together. The voice of reason that would help him to keep a cooler head. She would be a loving aunt to Charlie and Freddie and a wonderful partner to him in every way. His tenants would adore her.

And he would light the fire he knew dwelled inside her, helping it to spiral out of control. Sera was a passionate woman and would make for a perfect lover. They would explore the ways of love together and learn to satisfy one another. He grinned, thinking of how he would tease her and tempt her and make her cry out his name again and again before he brought her to a climax. He wanted her warm, curvaceous body against his every night as he fell asleep after they'd made love—and he planned to awaken her each morning doing the very same thing. Win realized he would never be able to get enough of the lovely Sera.

His duchess.

But how to ask her to be a part of him always?

He rang for Larson to help him dress and continued to debate the best time in his mind, finding advantages to both sides of a public and private proposal. The only disadvantage he thought with a public one would be if she turned him down. He couldn't see that happening. Already, he knew she was attracted to him. Besides, she had fallen in love with his nephews and would be loath to leave them. Who would have thought that Freddie and Charlie might have been the catalyst that saw him win the woman he loved?

Larson finished shaving Win and then dressed him for the day. Win dismissed the valet and went to sit in the wing chair that overlooked the gardens. He remembered that Sera said she enjoyed gardening and wondered what her favorite flowers might be so that he could present them to her. He finally decided to offer for her this evening at dinner when the two of them were alone in the winter parlor. Farmwell would make certain they had their food and drink and then make himself scarce. Win believed Sera would appreciate a simple proposal versus one where he recruited the boys to take part.

She would make for a wonderful mother. Watching her with Freddie and Charlie told him as much. None of her habitual shyness was evident around the children and he couldn't wait until they had their own. They would get plenty of parenting practice as they raised his nephews and the rest of their brood, which he hoped would be large and contain as many girls as boys.

Win chuckled aloud, remembering how not so very long ago he had wondered about his friends and cousin and their attitude regarding female children. Win, having had no sisters, had taken the traditional point of view in that female children were not all that important. It was the male heir and other sons who mattered most.

Now, however, he longed to see tiny auburn-haired girls who would sit in his lap, calling him Papa, begging him to tell them a story. They would be like Sera, beautiful and sweet and kind. Sera also had a core of steel which ran through her and he did not think many people knew of it, especially her twin. He had seen the surprised look on Minta's face when Sera had insisted on going to Woodbridge with him immediately and not waiting. That steel would do her well as she ran their many households and helped to raise their children. Yes, he knew they would have the usual accoutrements of nannies, nursery governesses, and even governesses and tutors. He believed, however, that he and Sera—just like the Second Sons—would be actively involved in the raising of their children, unlike his parents. Win looked forward to meeting Sera's parents and might even ask her father what it was like to raise girls.

He went downstairs to the breakfast room, where Farmwell told him that his correspondence and the post awaited him in his study. Win knew many men liked to go through the post during breakfast but he was not one of them. Instead, he would enjoy, in the future, talking with his amazing duchess as they dined. He did peruse the pages of the newspaper as he ate and then went to his study. Though he longed to go to the kitchens and witness the baking lesson as it unfolded, Win believed he would be a distraction to the boys and decided to stay put.

An hour later, he had changed his mind. He simply had to see Sera. Making his way to the kitchens and entering, he supposed he had visited them more times than any of the previous dukes combined. Cook barely arched a brow as he stepped into her domain.

He stood for a moment and studied his nephews. Sera was instructing them about dividing an apple and how different parts equaled others—quarters, halves, or wholes of the entire apple. She even allowed each of them to eat a slice in reward for a series of correct answers.

Finally, Win moved closer and Charlie saw him.

"Uncle Win!" the boy exclaimed. "What are you doing here?"

"I thought I would come to see how your lesson was progressing," he told them.

Freddie grinned. "It's all about maths, Uncle Win, and measuring. I like maths."

"Then you may have a future as a steward on one of my estates," he told the small boy. "Mathematics is something used on a daily basis by a steward."

"How many estates do you have?" Freddie asked.

"Woodbridge is the main one," he explained, telling them how a duke had a country estate which served as his chief seat. "Most of my time is spent here but I also own four other country estates scattered about England and my London townhouse."

"I bet it's fancy," Charlie said. "Woodbridge is fancy."

"I have visited two of the other estates since I became the Duke of Woodmont," he shared. "I will need to see the other two at some point. Perhaps you boys would care to travel with me."

They agreed and he thought to himself that his honeymoon with Sera might consist of journeying to each of those four estates. He did not think she would mind the boys accompanying them. He would need to look into finding another governess for them soon, though. While Sera had done an outstanding job in that capacity, as his duchess, she would have many other responsibilities to attend to. Perhaps she might accompany him into London tomorrow morning in order to locate another governess. He was loath to go to the same employment agency since their two recommendations had proven to be such poor choices where his nephews were concerned. Sera might have a better idea of where to go or at least the right questions to ask of a potential employee.

She had not said a word since he arrived, allowing his nephews to do all the talking.

Wanting to include her in their conversation, he asked, "What are you making?"

"Two different items," she revealed. "The first is an apple cake and one of Minta's favorites. I had told you she is not overly fond of sweets and this one is not too sweet for her tastes. I have made it many times. The other thing we will attempt will be scones. Freddie has already told me he wishes to place raisins in them."

"Who's Minta?" Freddie asked. "I've heard that name before." He thought a moment. "Wait, that's your sister, Sera."

Win hadn't the heart to correct either boy as they used Sera's first name. If any of the kitchen staff noticed, though, none of them indicated that.

"You remembered correctly, Freddie," Sera praised. "Araminta—Minta—is my twin sister. She married your uncle Win's cousin, who is the Marquess of Kingston. They live on the estate next to Woodbridge."

"Does she have red hair like you do?" Charlie asked. "I think your hair is very pretty. Sera," he said bashfully.

"Why, thank you, Charlie. Minta does have red hair but it is a different shade than mine. Hers would be called copper. It's a warmer shade of red and brighter than mine, which is called auburn."

"Your hair looks really pretty out in the sun, Sera," Freddie complimented. "When you have babies, I bet they'll have red hair, too."

Sera's cheeks flushed with color, endearing her to Win. She was easily embarrassed, her neck and face often turning red.

Before the boys could talk about who Sera would be having those babies with, Win said, "I will be off and let you finish your lesson then. I will enjoy your handiwork at tea this afternoon. I want the two of you to be there in order to meet not only Sera's sister but her husband, my cousin. Percy and I grew up together and went away to school together, as well. He is like a brother to me."

Charlie looked thoughtful as he asked, "Was he a better brother than our father?"

Not wanting to get into his family's sordid history in front of the servants, Win merely nodded and said, "I will see you at tea this afternoon," cutting off the conversation and bidding them farewell.

As he left the kitchens and returned to his study, he doubted he would be able to concentrate on much of anything today, anticipating his proposal tonight.

Then he thought of the various pieces of jewelry his mother had possessed. She was fond of diamonds but he had seen her wear numerous other pieces, as well. Win decided he would ask Mrs. Farmwell where the jewels were and go through them, piece by piece, seeing if he could find an appropriate ring to give Sera in honor of their betrothal.

⇒⟫⟫⟪⟪⇐

SERA CUT THROUGH the kitchens with Charlie and Freddie in tow, asking for hot water to be sent up for all of them. The day had been busy, starting with a lesson in the schoolroom, which then moved to the kitchens. She was pleased at how attentive the boys had been and how well the cake had turned out. The first batch of scones was so good that not only had the boys gobbled up two apiece, but they went around the kitchens distributing them to Cook and the scullery maids, proud of their work. She could see how moved some of the servants were by the boys' thoughtfulness. They had to bake a second set of scones since none were left and, this time, she had not allowed any to be sampled. Neither boy complained, both saying they were full.

They had gone outside after that and the boys had taken their riding lesson from Harrison. Sera had slipped away for an hour and returned to the schoolroom, setting out certain books and writing out a few instructions to her successor, leaving the notes in the cupboard for the next governess to find. She returned and waved to Harrison, who ended the lesson. After the boys dismounted and the groom led their ponies back into the stables, they chattered away as they took her across the estate. They showed her the meadow and the mill, as well as the fields where many of the workers toiled in the summer sun.

Mr. Kepler, who served as the Woodbridge steward, had taken time to join them and walk a bit. At one point, the boys had run ahead to look at a pen of pigs and Kepler had turned to her, shaking his head.

"You have worked miracles with that pair, Miss Nicholls," he praised. "I was conscripted to help care for those two when they first arrived at Woodbridge. I thought they would never amount to anything and would always be wild hooligans. They are so well behaved now, it is as if they are entirely different children than before."

"I cannot take all of the credit, Mr. Kepler. I think the boys were misbehaving because they wanted a bit of attention and that was the only way they knew how to claim it. Once they got a little—especially from His Grace—they have settled down and are sweet, eager, bright boys."

After that, they had returned to the house and Sera led them upstairs.

"You will need to change into the clothing you got from the tailor yesterday. Only after you wash up," she cautioned. "We have been in the hot kitchens and traipsing about outside. All three of us need to freshen up. Can you get ready without my help?"

"We are big boys," Freddie reminded her. "We aren't babies like we used to be. We are learning the rules and how to behave."

She smoothed the boy's hair. "I know you are. I am very proud of you, as is your uncle."

Sera returned to her room and removed her boots and stockings, which were quite dusty from all their walking. She had washed one of her gowns in the basin last night and had draped it across the trunk at the foot of her bed. It was now dry, if slightly wrinkled. She wished she had time to iron it before Minta and Percy arrived but it would take too long since they were expected in the next twenty minutes or so.

A knock sounded at her door and Sara entered with hot water. The girl looked a bit contrite and said, "Are you going to change your gown, Miss Nicholls? If so, I can help lace your corset for you."

She accepted the olive branch the maid offered and said, "That would be lovely, Sara. I would appreciate your help."

The servant helped her out of her dusty gown and she washed quickly, then removed her petticoat and retrieved her corset from the trunk. Sara laced it up with just the right amount of tension and helped Sera back into her petticoat and the clean gown.

Taking the basin of used water, Sara started out the door and then turned. "I am sorry that I doubted you, Miss Nicholls. Everyone is talking about how you have worked wonders with His Grace's nephews."

"Thank you," she said simply and bowed her head in acknowledgement of the compliment. When she lifted it, the maid had gone.

Thinking she still had a bit of time to spare, Sera removed the pins from her hair and brushed it out since wisps had escaped her chignon. She twisted it up again and replaced the pins and then crossed the schoolroom to fetch the boys. They were already gone. She supposed they were eager to meet their guests and show off what they had baked.

Sera made a quick decision and returned to her room, stuffing the little clothing she had brought, along with her boots, into the valise. She had decided she should leave after tea was over and took the packed valise down the stairs. The footman at the door frowned slightly but opened it for her.

Her timing could not have been more perfect because the Kingston carriage was rolling up the drive and soon came to a stop in front of her. Percy disembarked and helped Minta down. Her twin raced over and embraced Sera.

"Oh, I have missed you so." Then Minta glanced and saw the valise sitting on the round beside Sera and her gaze met her sister's. "Has it gone that poorly?"

"There is no need to unload my trunk. I am going to come home with you and Percy." She decided further explanations could wait.

Minta merely nodded and signaled to the footman, who came and collected Sera's valise, placing it inside the carriage.

Percy stepped forward and kissed her cheek. "We have missed you, Sera."

"Come inside," she said, slipping her arm through Minta's.

Turning, Sera saw Farmwell had also joined them and he greeted Percy and Minta and asked them to accompany him to the drawing room. As they stepped into the foyer, Sera realized she was doing so for the last time.

CHAPTER TWENTY-TWO

WIN HAD GONE to the drawing room early, trying to burn off the nervous energy rippling through him. It surprised him when his nephews dashed through the door, skidding, and coming to a halt. They walked toward him at a regular pace, Charlie fidgeting a bit.

When they stopped in front of him, he said, "Let me inspect you."

He eyed them, looking up and down, and then turning his finger so they would move in a circle.

"You are more than presentable. You look quite nice in your new outfits."

"I still like wearing your clothes," Charlie muttered.

"Sera said we can keep wearing them. Just when we go outside to ride or fish or walk around," Freddie reminded his brother. "We rode our ponies today."

"Tell me about your lesson."

Win sat and indicated for the boys to do the same. They scooted onto a settee and both jabbered away. He loved hearing their enthusiasm and was happy they had enjoyed the riding lessons.

"When we can leave the paddock, Harrison said you can ride with us," Freddie told him. "If you want to," he added, looking a bit unsure of himself.

"I would like that very much. We will have to make sure Sera goes with us, too. She told me she is a good rider."

"Sera is so nice and pretty," Charlie said dreamily.

He chuckled. Though he longed to tell these boys of the future he had planned with Sera, he could not trust them to keep it to themselves. Not wanting to ruin the surprise of tonight's proposal, he decided to say nothing.

The door to the drawing room opened and Farmwell announced, "Lord and Lady Kingston, Your Grace. And Miss Nicholls."

Win stood and motioned to his nephews, who scrambled to their feet and took pains to stand tall.

Percy and Minta entered the room, followed by a bedraggled Sera. She wasn't wearing the same gown as this morning and he supposed it was covered in everything from flour from their baking to dust from their walk about the estate, which he had seen from his window. This one was clean, he supposed, but it was awfully wrinkled. Then he recognized it as the gown she had on when he had gone to tea at Kingwood. Win realized she must have washed it herself and had no way of pressing it. Guilt flooded him as he thought of her staying in the cramped room meant for the boys' governess. He would never have her do anything like this again. When tea came, he would tell Farmwell to have their best guest bedchamber made up for her. No more of this pretending she was a servant.

He smiled, greeting his cousin and wife, and then said, "Lord and Lady Kingston, may I introduce you to Frederick and Charles Sawyer?"

Sera had told him she had practiced introductions with the two and they gave a bow and offered their hands to Percy, one at a time.

"You may call me Freddie, my lord."

"And everyone calls me Charlie," his brother echoed.

The boys turned and bowed again to Minta, who smiled at them. "My, it is very nice to meet you."

"You're Sera's sister," Charlie said. "She said you had copper hair. I like it. But I like Sera's better."

Minta bit back a smile, glancing to her twin, and then returned her attention to the boys. "How are you finding Woodbridge? Do you like it?"

"We didn't like it at all at first," Charlie said blithely. "We went to live with the Birdwells. They were mean to us."

"And then Uncle Win brought us here and we had two governesses," Freddie added. "We didn't even know he was Uncle Win. They left."

"Because you helped them to decide to leave?" Percy asked, a ghost of a smile playing about his lips.

The two boys burst out laughing and Freddie admitted, "Yes. We weren't very nice to them. But we love Sera."

Charlie went and put his arm around her. "Sera is very nice. She's teaching us to read and do sums."

Win watched Sera pinken at the words.

"We also did maths today and baked a cake!" Freddie proclaimed. "You can try it. It's good. We already ate a slice. We also made scones. I wanted raisins in them because Mum liked raisins in hers."

"Why don't we sit?" Win asked. "The teacart will arrive soon."

They assembled in an area that had seating for about ten people. Charlie took Sera's hand and had her sit on a settee, placing her in the middle while he and Freddie sat on both sides of her. Win couldn't help but notice Minta's odd expression and her effort to catch Sera's eyes, which failed.

The door opened and two teacarts were rolled in, supervised by Farmwell. As the maids lined them up, Win rose and quietly said to the butler, "Please have the blue room made up for Miss Nicholls. She will be staying in it from now on. Have Mrs. Farmwell take Miss Nicholls' things down to it."

"Yes, Your Grace."

The butler motioned and the two maids followed him from

the room.

The next hour was one of the most pleasant he had spent since returning to England. The boys pressed Percy for stories about Win as a boy. His cousin was all too willing to give details of some of their more embarrassing escapades, which had the boys hooting and squealing with laughter. Percy talked a bit about his estate in very simple terms, describing the upcoming harvest and the process. Freddie asked several questions and, once again, Win thought the boy might make for a good steward down the line.

Minta praised his nephews loud and long after she sampled the apple cake.

"I believe this is the best one Sera has ever made. I am certain it is because she had such good help."

"Did she make a lot of cakes for you?" Charlie asked.

Minta smiled. "Sera is an excellent baker. Let me tell you about some of the sweets she has made for us."

The entire tea, Sera had been extremely quiet. Normally, it wouldn't concern Win, but she knew Minta and Percy well. She shouldn't be so quiet. He wondered if she had become overtired with all she had done with the boys the past few days and determined they would go into town tomorrow and hire a new governess. While they were there, he could also purchase a special license in Doctors' Commons. He saw no sense in waiting. He certainly wasn't going to let her go to the house party without marrying him. A small part of him feared he wasn't good enough for her and that she might find someone more to her liking there.

He wondered how soon she would wish to wed. Of course, all the Second Sons and their wives would need to be there. Sera would also want Lord and Lady Westlake present, as well. Since Minta had wed Percy while her parents remained in Canada, he hoped Sera would agree to do the same. Win was ready to slip a ring on her finger and have her in his bed.

"Are we going to read after tea is over?" Freddie asked. He looked at Percy and Minta. "Sera has been reading to us since we can't do it ourselves yet. Uncle Win found a really good book."

"*Tales from Mother Goose*," Charlie piped up. "Maybe Sera wants to talk to her sister some more." He looked to Win. "Would you read to us instead?"

"I can do that," he assured Charlie.

Rising, he motioned for the boys to do the same and the others followed suit.

"It was nice to meet you, my lord and lady," Charlie said, looking very serious.

"We like you," Freddie added. "I guess we'll see you lots since you live next to Uncle Win and we live with him now."

"I hope we do," Percy said, smiling. "It was also very nice to meet you two."

"If you will excuse us," Win said. "*Blackbeard* calls. Or perhaps we'll read *Little Red Riding Hood*."

"Not *Blackbeard*, Win," Percy groaned.

Freddie looked at Charlie and both shouted, "*Blackbeard!*"

Win looked helplessly at Sera, who shook her head, biting her lip to keep from laughing.

"Come here," she said, motioning for the boys, and hugging them tightly. "Be good for your uncle."

"We're always good now," Charlie said good-naturedly. "Or we're trying to be."

"Stay as long as you wish," he told his guests. "I will be an hour or so."

"We need to get back to Kingwood," Percy said. "I will talk with you soon."

He led his nephews from the room as they chanted "*Blackbeard!*" over and over.

⇥⟫⟫⟪⟪⇤

SERA WAITED FOR the door to close and then looked to Minta. "I want to leave now."

Minta frowned. "Without even saying goodbye to Win?" Then she paused, understanding dawning in her eyes. "Oh. Win is the problem. The boys never were."

She nodded, tears filling her eyes.

Her twin stood. "Come, Percy. We need to return to Kingwood immediately."

Sera glanced at her brother-in-law and saw disapproval in his eyes. Still, he was wise enough not to comment as they left the drawing room and made their way downstairs.

The footman on duty opened the door for them and they stepped outside, the door closing behind them. Percy motioned and the stairs were placed down. He helped Minta into the carriage and then held out a hand to Sera. She took it.

"Is this the way you want to end things?" he asked softly.

She nodded and he handed her up, following behind her. The door to the carriage closed and, moments later, the wheels began to turn.

As they drove down the lane, her tears began to flow freely. Minta moved next to Sera and wrapped her arms around her, saying nothing, just letting her cry.

She knew she didn't have long and so wiped at her tears. Looking to Percy, Sera said, "I know I haven't long. When we reach Kingwood, Percy, might I have the use of your carriage to take me back to London?"

"Of course, Sera. I will go with you if you wish."

"No, that isn't necessary. I want to go to Aunt Phyllis and Uncle West."

"That can be arranged. This time of year it remains light for a long time. Once the carriage drops you at the Westlakes, I will see that it stops overnight at my townhouse in order for the horses to rest."

Minta squeezed her hand. "Will you tell us why you want to leave, Sera?"

She sighed. "I have fallen in love with Win," she told them, swallowing down the thick emotion causing her throat to tighten.

"I would think that would be marvelous," her twin said. "Apparently, it isn't. Tell me why. Please." She tightened her hold on Sera's hand. "Is it because he does not return your feelings?"

"He doesn't know how I feel because I haven't told him." Sera sniffed. "Oh, Minta, you must understand. He is a duke, for goodness' sake. A leading member of the *ton*. I am bashful. I clam up around anyone I do not know. You know how reticent and private I am. Going to *ton* events will make me feel as if I am a lamb led to the slaughter. Win is genial and gregarious. He possesses a conviviality which is the complete opposite of my nature. I know the Duchess of Woodmont must be an equal to him in order for her to be a leader in Polite Society."

Tears poured down her cheeks. "I could never be what he needs—or wants. And I want him desperately."

She burst into heaving sobs and pressed her face against Minta's shoulder. Her sister stroked her back and murmured soothing words.

The carriage began to slow and Sera realized they had already reached Kingwood. She pulled away from Minta and met her twin's gaze.

"If I am going to survive, I need to cut all ties with him. With those precious boys. I cannot be around him anymore without making a fool of myself."

"Opposites do attract, Sera," Percy said quietly. "Look at Minta and me. Win might have feelings for you."

She shook her head. "Even if he did, I am all wrong for him, Percy. If I stayed at Woodbridge, I would start hoping for things I can never have. Attending the house party and seeing the vivacious, elegant woman Adalyn decides will be Win's perfect match would push me over the edge."

Sera turned back to her sister. "I cannot go to the house party. I cannot be around Win. He needs to find his duchess and wed her."

"But—"

"I know you hoped to help me find a match at this house

party, Minta. I simply cannot attend. I would be miserable. I will wait and my make my come-out next Season. Hopefully, I will gain some confidence by then. I know how our aunt and uncle prefer town to the country so I should be able to meet a few people and practice opening up and getting to know others."

"What about the baby?" Minta said, her face showing her distress. "I wanted you here for the birth."

"I will think about it," she said. "But I need time and distance away from Win. I don't want him right next door to me. It was bad enough when I used to constantly run into Mrs. Marsh and all she wanted to do was cling to me and talk about Edward."

Resolve filled her. "I am doing the right thing for me, Minta. I have never put myself first."

"All right," her twin said, giving in. "But you are to write to me three times a week."

"I will," she promised, dabbing her eyes with a handkerchief Percy handed to her.

Minta kissed Sera's cheek. "Tell Aunt Phyllis and Uncle West hello for me. I may try and come to town in a couple of weeks to see how you are and spend some time with you."

"I'd like that," Sera said. "Goodbye."

Minta kissed her again and then allowed Percy, who had exited the carriage in order to give them a more private goodbye, to hand her down.

The door closed and she moved to the window. Pasting on a smile, she waved as the carriage started up again, knowing Percy must have given the coachman his instructions.

Settling back into the cushion, Sera allowed herself to weep for the next hour.

CHAPTER TWENTY-THREE

W IN ACCOMPANIED HIS nephews upstairs to the schoolroom and Charlie ran to a cupboard, opening it and removing *Tales from Mother Goose*. He brought it to Win and said, "I want to read *Blackbeard*."

"You don't even know what *Blackbeard* is about," Win countered. "You might enjoy *Little Red Riding Hood* even more."

Freddie said, "I think we should read both stories. Then Charlie and I can make up our minds which one we like best."

He chuckled, thinking Freddie was already skilled in the art of negotiation.

"All right," he agreed. "We shall read both stories."

Charlie looked at him. "Do you think we can sit in bed to read them instead of here at the table?" He smiled shyly at Win and added, "I like when we sit close."

He wrapped his arm around the boy's shoulder and nodded. "I think that is an excellent idea."

The boys hurried through the door and jumped on the bed, leaving a place for him. Win settled against the pillows between them as the boys snuggled close to him. He opened the book and found the story of *Blackbeard* and began to read.

As he did so, a deep contentment filled him. He was thrilled the boys had taken to him so and even more surprised how much they had become such an important part of his life in a short amount of time. The same held true for Sera. Though they had not known each other for very long, he wanted to spend the rest of his life with her, knowing it would be a good one.

When they finished *Blackbeard*, Charlie shivered. "That was scary," he said.

"Well, I liked it," Freddie proclaimed.

It amazed him how different the two boys were, both having come from Terrance, but he and his older brother had been very different, as well.

"Shall we read *Little Red Riding Hood* now?" he asked.

He received an enthusiastic yes from both nephews. Locating the story, he read it to them, having fun voicing the Big Bad Wolf, who pretended to be Little Red Riding Hood's grandmother.

At the end of the fairy tale, Charlie clapped. "I liked that one much better," he told them. "It was still a little scary but Little Red Riding Hood was smart, wasn't she, Uncle Win?"

"She was indeed, Charlie. Just as you and Freddie are."

"Do you really think we are smart?"

Win looked at Freddie, who probably would always be the Doubting Thomas of the pair. "Yes, I do. I don't think there is anything you won't be able to do."

Freddie nodded. "I told you I liked to do maths. I also like reading and hearing stories, too."

"I am glad you do. Reading is the foundation of everything. There are many things to learn through reading but we will also teach you other ways of learning."

"You mean like Harrison is teaching us how to ride?" Charlie asked eagerly.

"Exactly, Charlie."

He heard movement in the schoolroom and thought it must be a maid delivering dinner to the boys. He had them climb off the bed and the three of them entered the room. The servant placed the covered plates and cups of milk upon the table and then bobbed a curtsey before she left.

Win joined his nephews at the table, figuring Sera was still visiting with Percy and Minta, else she would already be here. The boys chattered happily throughout the meal, mostly talking about Blackie and Brownie and how they couldn't wait to ride again tomorrow. He recalled how horse-mad he and Percy were at that age and smiled.

After they finished eating, Win accompanied them back to their shared bedchamber and watched them get ready for bed. They did not want his help so he merely served as their supervisor, reminding Freddie to wash the back of his neck and getting Charlie out of bed because he had yet to use his tooth powder. He got the boys settled and told them goodnight, first brushing a kiss on Charlie's brow and then going to Freddie's bed to do the same.

His nephew looked up at him, his face quite serious.

"Is something wrong, Freddie"? he asked.

Freddie sat up and looked across to Charlie, who nodded at his brother. Then Freddie said, "Today, you introduced us as Freddie and Charlie Sawyer."

"Yes, I recall I did so." Win's heart began beating faster, already knowing what the boy would say.

"You also told us we are really a part of your family." Freddie looked at him pleadingly and asked, "Could we have your same name, Uncle Win? Charlie and I talked about it and we agreed. Can we change it?"

Love swelled within him. "I would like nothing better than for you to share the Cutler name with me," he told the pair. "It does not mean you will forget your mother. She loved you with everything she had but I am honored you wish to take on the family surname."

Freddie hugged him and then eased back onto the pillows.

Win stood. "Goodnight," he said, his throat thick with emotion.

He exited the bedchamber and made his way back to the drawing room, thinking he would find Sera there with Percy and

Minta. No one was present, however, and he decided his cousin and wife had already left. Eagerness filled him at what would come next. He reached into his pocket and pulled out the pearl ring he had found among his mother's jewels. He intended to give Sera this ring tonight when he asked for her hand in marriage. It would be the first symbol—of many—of his love for her.

Win entered the winter parlor and also found it empty. He sat at the table, waiting for Sera to appear, his heartbeat quickening in anticipation.

When the door opened several minutes later, he rose. Instead of Sera, Farmwell came through the door, followed by a maid rolling a cart.

The butler himself placed the two covered dishes onto the table as Win took his seat.

"Shall I open and pour the wine, Your Grace?"

"You may do so and then please summon Miss Nicholls to dinner if you would. She was not in the drawing room and may have gone to her room to freshen up and lost track of time."

"Of course, Your Grace," Farmwell said as he handled the wine before exiting the room with the maid.

Win sat, a bundle of nerves now. He couldn't remember the last time he was nervous. Possibly going into his last battle but that seemed a lifetime ago.

After a quarter-hour, his anxiety building, Farmwell entered the room again.

"Your Grace, I have not been able to locate Miss Nicholls. I went to her previous room, as well as the bedchamber Mrs. Farmwell had prepared for her." The butler paused, swallowing hard, and Win knew something was wrong.

"Continue," he said brusquely.

"Miss Nicholls' things . . . are gone, Your Grace."

"What do you mean? Gone?"

"One of the maids told us Miss Nicholls had a small valise. It was in neither room."

Panic began to fill Win. "What about her trunk? Her sister was supposed to bring it today."

"I know nothing about a trunk, Your Grace. Nothing was brought into the house this afternoon when Lord and Lady Kingston visited."

Win sprang to his feet, a thousand thoughts swirling through him. But the one thought that stood above all others was that Sera was gone.

Gone . . .

Without a word, he hurried from the room, going to the foyer where a footman was on duty.

"Did you see Lord and Lady Kingston leave?" he demanded harshly, causing the footman to wince.

"Yes, Your Grace. Miss Nicholls went outside to tell them goodbye."

"When was this?"

"A little after five o'clock, Your Grace."

"And did Miss Nicholls return after the marquess and marchioness left?" he asked, his heart pounding, the blood whooshing in his ears.

The footman frowned. "I don't remember her coming back inside. She might have gone to the gardens."

The footman's words confirmed his worst thoughts. Sera had left with her sister without a word to him.

The question was why she had done so.

He wheeled and saw Farmwell standing nearby. "Ready my carriage at once. I am going to Kingwood."

"Yes, Your Grace," his butler replied and hurried off.

Win left the foyer, throwing the front door open himself. He paced in front of the house as he waited for his carriage to appear. Questions filled him and yet he had no answers to them. Something was terribly wrong. Something he had done to force Sera to flee Woodbridge.

But what?

He racked his brain, going over the entire day. All he could think was that Sera had been unusually quiet during tea. He had thought it was to allow the boys to shine but now he wasn't certain at all. In fact, he wasn't certain of anything. Had she worried about their growing feelings and wished to put distance between them? He would soon find out.

The carriage rounded the corner of the house and paused in front of it. Win did not wait for the stairs to be placed down, yanking open the vehicle's door and jumping inside it. He rapped loudly on its roof and the carriage started into motion.

It did not take long to reach Kingwood. When he arrived, he threw open the door before the carriage had even come to a complete halt. Win raced to the door and threw it open without knocking. A startled footman seated in the foyer leaped to his feet.

"Your Grace!" he called.

"Where is she?" he demanded.

By now, Bailey had appeared in the foyer. "How may I help you, Your Grace?" he asked calmly.

Win got control of his emotions and said, "I need to see Miss Nicholls at once."

Bailey shook his head. "Miss Nicholls is not here, Your Grace."

She had to be. Instead, he said, "Take me to my cousin then."

"Lord and Lady Kingwood have retired for the evening, Your Grace. Perhaps you would care to call upon them tomorrow."

Clenching his fists, he closed the gap between himself and Bailey and said, "I want to see my cousin. Now," his tone deadly.

Win stepped away.

"If you will wait in the drawing room, Your Grace, I will see if Lord Kingwood wishes to see you."

He did not wait for an escort and took the stairs two at a time. He entered the drawing room and paced the length of it numerous times until Percy appeared in his banyan.

Striding toward his cousin, he asked, "Where is she?"

Sympathy filled Percy's eyes. "She is not here, Win."

"Then where the bloody hell is she?"

"She is gone," a voice said.

Turning, he saw Minta approaching, wearing her dressing gown.

"I'll ask again. Where is Sera?"

Minta bit her lip. "Win, you need to allow Sera some time and space. She has some very important things to think about."

Anguish filled him. "What things?"

"Things regarding her future."

"Her future is with me," he hissed.

Minta looked startled. "What do you mean?"

"I meant to offer marriage to her this evening," he revealed, his voice breaking. "I don't need any house party full of eligible young ladies. I don't want Adalyn choosing my bride for me. I have found the woman I love. The one I wish to spend eternity with. It is Sera."

Minta burst into tears and Percy hurried to comfort her. Win chomped at the bit, waiting for her to get her feelings under control.

Finally, her tears subsided and she said, "Sera does not think you want her as your duchess. She believes you are complete opposites. She understands the lofty position a duchess holds in Polite Society and doesn't feel she could fulfill that."

Minta's eyes flooded with tears again. "She does love you, Win. Of that, I am certain. But she doesn't feel she is good enough for you. That is why she had to leave."

"I don't give a bloody fig what the *ton* wants from my duchess," he roared. "All I know is that I am incomplete without Sera in my life." He took Minta's hands in his. "Please. Tell me where she has gone. I must find her and make things right between us."

She looked to Percy, who nodded.

"She went to Aunt Phyllis and Uncle West."

Win knew the hour was growing late and it would take a long time to reach London in the darkness. By the time he reached her, Sera would be exhausted and in bed. Instead, he would go first thing in the morning.

Looking at the pair, he said, "I will go to town first thing in the morning. I had planned to do so anyway, taking Sera with me. I was going to purchase a special license at Doctors' Commons and get her help in hiring a new governess for the boys. I still plan to do both of those things—and return with Sera sometime tomorrow afternoon. There will be a wedding. It will be as soon as possible. You might as well send word for the Second Sons to come so they might witness our vows."

"I will send messengers to all three first thing tomorrow morning," Percy promised. "I will ask that they come immediately to Woodbridge."

"I will also make certain Lord and Lady Westlake come, as well. Sera will want them there. Thank you for sharing with me where she is." He looked to Minta. "I promise you this—I will make Sera happy. Always."

Chapter Twenty-Four

S ERA AWOKE, HER eyes gritty from lack of sleep. She had lain awake most of the night, images of Win flitting through her head.

It was done, though. She had walked away. The only thing she could do. She regretted not telling Freddie and Charlie goodbye but if she had, they would have let the cat out of the bag and told Win. He would have tried to convince her to stay until the house party.

By then, her heart would have been in shreds.

No, she had done what needed to be done in order to protect her heart. Still, she was utterly miserable right now—and knew she would be for some time. Eventually, she would return to Minta at Kingwood. After all, she was going to be an aunt. She wanted to be present for the birth and hold her sweet niece or nephew in her arms.

A soft knock sounded at the door and then her aunt pushed it open, concern written on her brow. She came in and closed the door behind her, coming to the bed and perching on the edge.

Taking Sera's hand, she said, "I don't need to ask how you are this morning. Your eyes are practically swollen shut."

Sera had arrived just as her aunt and uncle were leaving for a ball. Immediately, Uncle West had told the coachman to return the carriage to the mews and they had taken Sera inside, where she had bawled like a newborn. Gently, Aunt Phyllis coaxed the story out of her. She had said they would be happy for Sera to remain in town with them for as long as she wished.

Then Uncle West had asked if she might like to go to West-field instead. It was his country estate in Essex. Although it was located close to Woodbridge, Sera decided she would prefer being in the country and told him she would like to go there in a few days, after she had spent time catching up with them.

"I have been better," she admitted. "I got myself into this mess. I know it will take time for my heart to mend."

"There's nothing like a strong cup of tea and a hot bath. Would you like both now?"

She nodded. She had not had a full bath since she'd left King-wood. The thought of that small luxury perked her up a bit.

Aunt Phyllis rose and bent, kissing Sera's cheek. "I will see to it, then. I can also send some breakfast up for you after you bathe."

Sera started to protest, not feeling the least bit hungry, but she might change her mind after her bath.

Her aunt left and she brought the bedclothes up to her chin, burying herself until the hot water arrived. She let her mind go blank.

Half an hour later, servants began arriving with a tub and buckets of hot and cold water. Her aunt instructed a maid to begin unpacking Sera's trunk and asked that she see to her clothes being ironed.

"Iron this sea green gown first," Aunt Phyllis instructed. "Miss Nicholls will wear it today." To Sera, she said, "I do love how when you wear green, the color of your eyes stand out."

Her aunt also discovered the vial of jasmine that Sera liked to add to her bath water and did so, swirling her hand through the water to stir it in.

"Would you like me to stay and help you bathe and wash your hair? Or I can have one of the maids assist you."

"Actually, I would rather do so myself. I . . . need a little time to myself if you don't mind."

"I understand," her aunt said, her eyes glimmering with tears. She took Sera's hand in hers. "I know this has been difficult. Giving your heart to someone always is."

"What is worse is knowing that Win never could have returned my affections," she said, blinking away fresh tears.

Aunt Phyllis cradled Sera's cheek. "Time will help heal you."

Everyone left and Sera shed her night rail. She stepped into the bath and sank into the hot water, leaning back and submerging herself before quickly springing up. She washed her hair first and rinsed it, lifting it and setting it outside the tub before taking up the soap and lathering it. Her aunt was right. The bath felt wonderful. She reached for the hot tea which had been brought and sipped it, allowing it to soothe her.

A maid came in carrying the green gown. "All nice and ready for you, Miss Nicholls," she said brightly. "I'll place it on the bed. I already have your undergarments laid out for you. Just ring when you are ready and I'll return to help you dress and then I'll unpack for you."

"Thank you."

The servant left and Sera luxuriated in the water a bit longer. It finally began to cool and she stood, taking a bucket of warm water and sluicing it over her body to rinse away the last of the soap. She reached for the bath sheet and wrapped herself in it before stepping from the tub. Feeling the breeze of the door opening, she assumed another maid had returned, probably sent by Aunt Phyllis to help Sera in combing out her hair, which had a tendency to tangle when wet.

"I don't need any help just yet," she called out. "I will ring when I do."

"Are you certain you don't need any help?" a deep, familiar voice said.

Sera wheeled, shock pouring through her. "You . . . you can't be here," she sputtered, tightening the bath sheet around her. "Get out!"

"I don't believe I choose to do so," Win said, slowly moving toward her. "I am a duke, Sera. I do whatever I want."

"No, no, no," she moaned. "I will be ruined."

He reached her, the back of his fingers grazing her cheek. "That is the point."

Her eyes nearly popped from their sockets. "You *want* to ruin me?"

"Absolutely."

His arms went about her, pulling her to him. She felt his warmth. Smelled the bergamot's spice. Then Sera began wriggling, trying to keep the bath sheet around her while she tried to escape.

"No," Win said firmly. "You aren't going anywhere." His arms tightened about her.

Fat tears rolled down her cheeks.

"No, my darling. Please, don't cry." He brushed away her tears with his lips. "I never want to make you cry unless they are tears of happiness."

Her mouth trembled. "How can I be happy? I am standing here naked, a duke in my bedchamber! That is a recipe for disaster. I will never be able to hold my head up in Polite Society."

He grinned. "You overthink things, Sera Nicholls. I find the idea of you naked and in my arms utterly divine."

She began weeping. Her head fell to his broad, muscular chest. She gulped for air, feeling as if she were suffocating.

One hand came up and tilted her chin until her watery gaze met his. "I never took you for a coward."

"I am not!" she protested.

"You left Woodbridge without saying goodbye to the boys. Without saying goodbye to me."

"Oh, Win." More tears streamed down her cheeks. "Don't you see? You are a duke. From the highest echelons of society. I am barely on the lowest rung of the *ton*. You are magnetic, drawing people to you, where I wish to hide in a corner and keep from being seen. You want to wed a woman without giving her your heart. I want the heart—and the love—of the man I hope to wed. Yes, I do love you. Desperately. But I know you could never love me. I won't settle for a marriage of the kind you wish to have. I may be meek but I am not a woman who would look the other way while her husband had a parade of mistresses."

His dark eyes penetrated her, seeing to her soul.

"Don't you understand, Sera?" he asked softly. "You don't have to change a bit. I am the one who has changed—for the better—because of your influence. I convinced myself I wanted a typical *ton* marriage because I didn't feel worthy of love."

Win smiled. "And then I found you. You were nothing that I thought I wanted. Yet everything I needed and desired. I love you for who you are and who I am when I am with you. I want no other woman to be my duchess. My lover. My best friend. My partner in life."

His thumb stroked her bottom lip. "You are the woman I will spend the rest of my life with. I was going to ask you to marry me last night at dinner. I had thought to do so at tea and have the boys be a part of the proposal. Then I thought you and I would prefer a more private moment." He paused. "When I found you gone, Sera, I went mad. I am lost without you. You complete me in a way I never knew existed."

She sucked in a quick breath.

"I love you, Sera Nicholls. I may have from the time we rode in the carriage together to Percy's townhouse. You have rattled the cage I imprisoned myself in long ago. I never knew I was in jail—or that a beautiful, kindhearted, auburn-haired beauty possessed the key to set me free."

Her tears flowed freely now.

"So, what will it be, Sera? Will you marry me? Spend the rest of your life with me? Build a family and grow old together?"

"Yes!" she cried. "Yes to all of those things. Oh, Win, I do love you."

He smiled ruefully. "Dare I hope you love me and are not

merely agreeing to wed me because you love those rascal nephews of mine?"

Sera laughed. "Oh, I love them, too. But I absolutely, totally adore and love *you*, Your Grace."

"It's about time you said so."

Win's lips met hers in a searing kiss. His hands pushed into her damp, tangled hair as he held her still, ravishing her mouth. Desire filled her as she longed for this man. For all of him. For all time. Sera answered his kiss, pouring every ounce of love into it.

They kissed for what seemed like forever. At some point, her bath sheet slipped to her waist. Win broke the kiss, staring down at her breasts.

"Oh, how I have wanted to taste your breasts," he murmured. "I have dreamed of them, so full and delicious."

His lips traveled slowly down her throat until he reached one, his tongue tracing its curve and then flicking playfully across her nipple. She gasped at the sensation, feeling it swell. He took it into his mouth then, laving, sucking, nipping. Sensations shot through her like never before. Want. Need. Desire.

He feasted upon one and then the other, until her body felt it had been lit on fire. Her mouth sought his again and their tongues tangled with fierce need.

Finally, Win broke the kiss. "We should get you dressed."

"Win!" she cried, pulling the sheet up. "You cannot do that."

He shrugged. "I am already here, love. Though I hate to admit it, I do know a thing or two about women's undergarments. I have been a man of voracious appetites where women were concerned." He cradled her cheek. "Now, there is but one woman who satisfies my hunger."

Taking her hand, he led her to the bed. "I will fight every instinct I possess not to take you here and now. I will save that for our wedding night. Which will be very soon. In fact, Percy is sending letters today to the Second Sons, asking them to move with haste to reach Woodbridge in time for our wedding. I also told your aunt and uncle to pack because they need to leave today to journey down to Woodbridge, too.

"I had decided today that you and I would come into town and collect our special license and hire a governess for the little monsters. I also have thought about our honeymoon. I want to take you on a tour of my other estates, bringing the boys with us, of course. I didn't think you would mind."

Sera smiled. "They would be heartbroken if we left them alone at home."

Win beamed. "Did you hear yourself? You said *home*."

"I did, didn't I?"

"I hope you always think of Woodbridge as home, my love. Do you agree to everything? A quick marriage and honeymoon to follow? It would mean we wouldn't be able to attend the house party Owen and Louisa are holding." He stroked her cheek. "Then again, we don't need to go and find our spouse there when we've already found each other."

She laughed. "You have everything planned out. I might as well go along with it. Oh!"

"What is it?"

"I won't have to worry about making my come-out next Season. There will be no awkward moments as I meet strangers and assess them as future husband material."

Win growled and kissed her hard. "No, you will step into Polite Society as my duchess. And you are all mine, Sera. All mine." He kissed her again, making her knees go weak.

"Turn around," she instructed. "At least let me slip into my chemise."

Win sighed. "If I must." Then he gave her a lascivious look. "But I will soon be taking it off you and loving every inch of your delectable body."

He faced the opposite direction and Sera dropped the bath sheet, quickly slipping her chemise over her head. Win then laced her into her corset and placed her petticoat and gown over her head. He insisted she sit and he slid her feet into her stockings, carefully stretching them up her calves and thighs, the movement so sensual that her insides flipped over.

With great patience, he worked the tangles from her hair. It was still damp but Sera twisted it into her usual chignon as he watched, fascinated, and then kissed her nape now that it was uncovered.

"Oh, I am going to love introducing you into the ways of love, my sweet Sera," he proclaimed.

Then he pulled something from his pocket and quickly took her hand, slipping on a ring that featured a large pearl, with a pair of diamonds on each side of it.

"This is a sign of our betrothal," he explained. "You will have a different ring for when we wed."

"But I love this one. It is from you."

He kissed her brow. "There will be many more jewels to come—for my favorite jewel of all."

They left her bedchamber, the one she had always stayed in when sleeping over, and went to the drawing room, fingers entwined. Aunt Phyllis and Uncle West waited for them. Her aunt rushed to her and embraced her.

"Oh, Sera, I hope it was all right to let His Grace come to you," she whispered. "Actually, I don't think anything would have stopped him. You do realize you are compromised and will have to wed him now?"

She beamed. "I do. And I will. With great happiness, I might add."

"We are packed, Your Grace," Uncle West said. "Just as you instructed."

"Then you may leave for Woodbridge whenever you see fit," Win declared. "My staff knows you are coming."

Sera looked at him mischievously. "You were that certain I would say yes to you?"

Win lifted their joined hands and kissed her fingers. "More than certain, my love. We were meant to be. I was up with the boys as they fed the chickens at the crack of dawn, telling them that you and I were heading into town to get our license and find them a governess since you would now fill the role of wife and duchess."

"So, you didn't tell them that I ran away?"

"No. I merely told them you had left earlier than I had to see about the governess. That means we really need to hire one today."

She went and hugged her aunt and then her uncle, who said, "The marriage settlements just arrived before you came downstairs. His Grace said he stopped at his solicitor's before he came here and asked that they be drawn up."

"Win, you must have gotten the poor man out of bed!" she scolded.

"I did. He is paid well enough that he should be available at all hours to me. Look over the contracts, Lord Westlake, but I believe you will find them generous to Sera."

"I will do so, Your Grace. And thank you," Uncle West said.

Win looked puzzled. "For what?"

"For recognizing the worth of our niece. I think the two of you will have a wonderful life together."

Win slipped an arm about her waist. "I think so, too."

CHAPTER TWENTY-FIVE

WIN ESCORTED SERA to his carriage, having told the Westlake butler to see that Sera's things were packed and her trunk brought to Woodbridge with Lord and Lady Westlake.

The moment the carriage door closed, Win pulled her close for a thrilling kiss, a kiss she didn't think would ever happen again between them. He broke it and stroked her cheek.

"We are off to Doctors' Commons first for our special license," he told her. "It will allow us to wed anywhere and at the time of our choosing." He brushed his lips softly against hers a moment. "Do you have any preferences?"

"You said the Second Sons were all coming to Woodbridge, along with my aunt and uncle, so I suppose the ceremony should be held there," she told him.

"We can have it take place inside the house if you'd like. In the gardens. Or there's a small chapel on the estate. Anywhere will suffice for me."

"I have a fondness for gardens. I would like it to be outdoors."

"Then so it shall be." He took her hands and kissed them. "Tomorrow may be too soon. Not everyone may be able to drop what they are doing and come today but I would think the day after tomorrow would be good."

"Do all your friends live that close to one another?" she asked.

"We are fortunate to be within a few hours' carriage ride

away from each other. Percy and I are in Essex and the other three are located in Kent. Spence has the greatest distance to travel but he can be at Woodbridge in three to four hours from Stoneridge."

"Shall I confess something to you?"

He eyed her appreciatively. "That you adore me?"

"No. I was hoping I could find a husband who lived somewhere far off. Scotland. Cornwall. It didn't matter. I simply didn't think I could be around you and see you with another woman as your wife."

Win pressed kisses along her knuckles again. "I was worried about the house party and watching you flirt with all the eligible bachelors." He gazed at her lovingly. "We don't have to worry about that anymore. Instead of a house party, we will be on our extended honeymoon."

This time, it was Sera who pressed her mouth softly to his. "I still have a feeling that I will wake up and find this has all been a dream."

"It is no dream, my love. We are together, as we should be, and will be from this day forth." He kissed her again. "I was even thinking that although the wedding would be scheduled for two days from now, we might actually move up the wedding night. To tonight."

A thrill rippled through her. "You mean . . . you want us to couple tonight? Before we are wed?"

"Yes. It would be scandalous if word got out—but we will be buried in the country. Who would ever know?"

"Yes," she said, surprised at her quick answer because she had never been a spontaneous person, much less about something so important.

He kissed her again. "Oh, I knew I had chosen the right woman to be my duchess."

They arrived at Doctors' Commons and she asked, "How do we go about this?"

"A special license is dispensed by the Archbishop of Canterbury. Or rather, his representative. We will have to have our names placed upon the license and our eligibility to wed will be ascertained. The Archbishop of Canterbury does not grant these frequently—or lightly. However, I am a duke. That should come in handy. I don't think anyone has the audacity to say no to a duke about anything."

Sera laughed and he helped her alight from the carriage. "I think it was your laugh that truly caused me to fall in love with you. I promised myself that I would make you laugh every day of our marriage so that I might hear it."

"Then you better be funny," she warned, laughing again. She had never felt so free as she did now, the weight of her problems lifted, her engagement to Win now official.

Inside, they were directed to an office and when the clerk asked how they might be helped, he merely said, "I am the Duke of Woodmont and wish to purchase a special license."

Several people came to help and within a quarter-hour, they were already back inside the carriage and headed to their next destination.

"That went remarkably well," she said.

He gave her a knowing look. "I told you being a duke helped. You will know the advantages available once you become the Duchess of Woodmont."

Sera bit her lip. "Win, I don't know if I will make for a very good duchess."

He looked at her sternly. "You will be *my* duchess. Anyone that does not afford you everything that goes with that title will answer to me."

His tone let her understand how serious he was.

"Besides, we might even forgo the Season," he shared. "After all, we have each other."

She relaxed and then realized because she would be wed to Win, she had no reason to be nervous. It would a *fait accompli* by the time the *ton* gathered next spring.

"I think I might actually enjoy going. At least for a few weeks and to some events. Minta seemed to enjoy this past spring immensely."

"If you wish to, we can. I know the Second Sons go for two months or so and then retire to the country when the heat of London becomes too much. They enjoy seeing each other."

"I hope the others I have yet to meet will like me."

"They will adore you," Win assured her. "Because I chose you. They will trust my judgment." He smiled. "Besides, they are all love matches. So are we. Who can argue with love?"

They went to the same employment agency he had used twice before in his search for a governess. This time, Sera had said she would do all the talking. Her assertiveness with the agency head surprised him until he realized she advocated for two small boys she loved very much. She looked over several files, studying various candidates' qualifications and previous posts, and settled upon a Miss Birmingham.

"Can we meet with her?" Sera asked. "As soon as possible."

"Miss Birmingham is completing an assignment at this time," the agency's owner revealed. "Her two charges are boys aged seven and eight and they will be going off to school in the autumn. She would not be free for another six weeks or more."

"Please give me her address so that I may write to her regarding the position," Sera said. "I will know from her response if she will do or not. We will be taking the boys with us on a trip to visit His Grace's various estates and will not need a governess until after we return."

"No governess on a lengthy trip?" the man asked, clearly shocked.

"The address?" Sera said, her brows arching slightly.

"Of course." He scribbled it down and handed the page over to her.

"Thank you. I will be in touch if Miss Birmingham suits."

As they left, Win said, "My, I knew you had a core of steel but it was entertaining seeing you assert yourself."

"I know what Freddie and Charlie need. That's all."

The clerk who sat just outside the office rose.

"Your Grace? I couldn't help but overhear you discussing Miss Birmingham. My family is friendly with the one who employs her. They are now in town because of the Season and I know Miss Birmingham enjoys taking her charges to Hyde Park around this time of day. The boys like to walk along the Serpentine and feed the ducks and sail their little boats."

The clerk handed Win a folded note. "If you are able to actually find Miss Birmingham, you may give her this. It informs her that you are who you say you are and that I have sent you to her."

"How might we recognize her?" Win asked.

"Well, she will have the two boys with her. She is of medium height with blond hair that is almost silver. Besides, there will be few others in the park at this time of day, I believe."

"Thank you," Win said to the clerk. "We will go now and see if we might happen upon her."

They returned to the carriage and Win gave the coachman his instructions. Soon, they were in Hyde Park, both of them carefully peering out the window as they tried to spy Miss Birmingham.

"That could be her!" called Win and the coachman hollered back, "I agree, Your Grace."

He drove the vehicle as close as he could and then Win and Sera disembarked. As they moved toward the woman, who looked to be in her mid-twenties and had the distinctive hair color, they could hear her calling out to the boys.

"She is the one," Sera said. "I can feel it in my bones. Besides, she has worked with these two the last three years."

They approached her and Win called out, "Miss Birmingham."

She turned and Sera saw her countenance to be kind.

Win handed over the note and explained who he was and that they were in need of a governess for his nephews.

"Tell me about them," Miss Birmingham said.

He held back nothing, sharing they were his brother's by-blows and that Terrance had abandoned all duty to them. He explained how he had recently found them and they had acted out because of their lives being in turmoil, not knowing their place in the world.

"I agree, Your Grace. They misbehaved for attention. Bad behavior was the only way they thought they could gain it."

Sera then talked about the boys and the good she had seen in them, sharing what she had been doing with them in their studies.

"They also are very active little boys and need a good deal of time outdoors," she concluded. "I think lessons in botany and geography should be woven into their more formal learning. They are also learning to ride and His Grace has purchased two ponies for them, which is the highlight of their day."

The governess nodded, seeming to have come to a decision. "I very much would like to meet them and serve in your household, Your Grace. I suppose I would do so at least for two years. By then, they should be caught up enough to their peers so that they might go away to school."

"Exactly what I had envisioned, Miss Birmingham," Win replied. "What do you say?"

"I am committed to my current position until the end of August. I am close to my charges and will not shirk my duty to them."

Win explained about their upcoming nuptials and how the boys would go on the honeymoon.

"So you see Miss Birmingham, we wouldn't need you until the time when your current position concludes." He looked to Sera and she nodded. "We would like to have you come to Woodbridge."

"I look forward to meeting Freddie and Charlie. Yes, I will accept."

Win quickly discussed salary with her and said he would contact her employment agency to let them know things were set.

"I can do so for you, Your Grace," Miss Birmingham said. "It sounds as if you will be plenty busy in the near future."

They thanked her and returned to the carriage, where Win told the driver to take them back to Woodbridge.

They hadn't gotten out of the park when he pulled her into his lap and spent the next hour kissing her thoroughly. Sera held nothing back, trying to show Win through her kisses how much she truly loved him.

They reached Woodbridge and as they came up the drive, Sera felt she had come home.

"I've spotted the boys," Win said and she saw them jumping up and down in excitement.

"I cannot wait to hug them," she admitted. "I have missed them so much."

He laughed. "It has only been a day since you last saw them."

"Sometimes, a day can fly by, while other times it passes as slow as molasses," she said.

Win kissed her. "Every day with you will be the perfect length," he predicted.

Farmwell himself opened the carriage door and a footman placed the stairs in front of the open door. Win climbed from the vehicle first and reached out his hand to Sera, who took it and squeezed as she descended the stairs.

"Sera!" the boys cried, running to greet her and then Win.

She thought how she had almost given up on ever seeing them again and counted her blessings.

"Your guests have just finished having tea in the drawing room, Your Grace," the butler informed them. "I gather there is to be a wedding." He smiled broadly.

"Yes, I think the day after tomorrow. Miss Nicholls will need to meet with Cook to discuss the wedding breakfast. Who has already arrived?"

"Your cousin and his wife were the first here, followed shortly by Lord and Lady Middlefield. Then the Duke and Duchess of

Camden arrived about two hours ago. Lord and Lady Danbury turned up just as tea began."

"They are all here then," Win said, smiling down at her. "Shall we go meet everyone, my love?"

Sera slipped her hand through the crook of his arm. "I am ready." She glanced over her shoulder. "Come along, boys."

Farmwell called out that he would have more tea sent up.

Charlie came and took her hand as Freddie took Win's and the four of them went upstairs to the drawing room. She was glad she was already acquainted with Tessa and Spencer or it truly would have been overwhelming.

Still, she had been eager to meet Minta's other friends and their Second Sons' husbands. Owen proved incredibly charming and Louisa a bit quiet but friendly. Everett was very reserved but had a sparkle in his eyes, while his wife, Adalyn, was quite large for a woman who still had several months to go before she gave birth. Still, she was a whirlwind, as Minta had described her, and she immediately took charge of the upcoming events.

"Have you decided where to hold the ceremony?" Adalyn asked.

When she learned it was to take place in the gardens, she breathed a sigh of relief. "Ah, that will keep decorating to a minimum since the lush beauty of the gardens speak for themselves."

Soon, Adalyn had coaxed out of Sera things she would like to see incorporated into the ceremony and Adalyn promised her they all would happen. The women began talking about what gown Sera should wear and decided to split from the men, who had contributed nothing to the wedding talk.

Upstairs, they decided upon which gown she should wear after Sera told Aunt Phyllis that she would take her recommendation, noting her aunt's keen sense of fashion. Sera also showed off the pearl ring Win had given her. The four women exclaimed over it and they returned to the drawing room, seating themselves away from the men and Freddie and Charlie, who seemed to continue to eat as if they had a bottomless pit in their bellies which would never be filled.

Win excused himself to go read to the boys, telling Sera to remain behind and get to know her new friends better. By the time he returned over an hour later, she was feeling quite relaxed in their company and glad that her aunt and uncle had made the trip from London so that they could see her wed.

Farmwell announced that dinner was served and Win claimed her, escorting her to what he said was the smaller of two dining rooms. He seated her on his right.

"I know the next time we have guests for dinner that you will take your place at the other end of the table. For now, though, I am being selfish and want you close by."

Dinner was a lovely affair, with much laughter and witty conversation. They started to retire to the drawing room but Adalyn, cradling her swollen belly with both hands, said she was exhausted after such a full day. Others admitted the same and every couple headed off to their guest chambers, leaving Win alone with Sera.

"I will send a maid to you to help ready you for bed. I will come to you in an hour," he promised.

As Sera waited during the final minutes of that hour, she eagerly anticipated what would soon occur between them.

CHAPTER TWENTY-SIX

WIN DISMISSED HIS valet and shrugged into his banyan, anticipation filling him at what was to come. He had been with a good many women. At one point during their university days, Owen and he had tried to outdo one another in the number of women they could couple with during a month's time. All these years later, he couldn't remember a single one of them—or who had even won their silly contest.

Tonight would be different from all those other times. Because he would be with Sera.

He regretted not having her placed in the duchess' quarters although events had moved swiftly. To think he would be a married man two nights from now simply astounded him.

Leaving his room, Win padded barefoot down the carpeted corridor, past the rooms of his friends and their wives. He thought of Minta and Adalyn, who both carried children, and longed for the day when Sera would bear him a child. Perhaps they might even make that child tonight.

He reached the blue room and tapped lightly on the door. It opened immediately and Sera admitted him, swiftly closing it.

"No one saw you?" she asked, looking a bit worried.

"No one," he assured her, though if one of his friends had it wouldn't have made a difference. In fact, they would have been pleased that Win had found what they had all discovered.

Love.

He stepped to Sera and wrapped his arms about her, drawing her close. Kissing the top of her head, breathing in the jasmine scent, he said, "I love you. I never thought I would say those words to anyone."

She gazed up at him. "Least of all a shy wallflower?" Her smiled teased him.

"You have never been shy around me. I hope that will continue as we explore one another tonight."

A hot blush immediately splashed across her cheeks. He saw tears form in her eyes.

"What's wrong?" he asked, gently cradling her cheek.

"I do love you, Win. So much that it hurts. But I still think I am wrong for you. You . . . have been with many women, I assume. You have done what we are about to do many times." She swallowed. "I have no experience. I fear I will not be able to satisfy you."

"My Sera," he said, bending and kissing her lush mouth softly. "Don't you understand? All those other times. All those other women. It meant nothing to me. But tonight, here with you, means the world to me. I want to love you, my darling. Please you. Satisfy you. Think back on how you felt when we kissed in the carriage most of the way home today. Do you believe I was not happy?"

"You seemed to enjoy it," she said, biting her lip. "I didn't know how to kiss and you've certainly taught me that."

"Then trust me to teach you the rest. We will explore one another. Find what pleases the other. Every time we couple will be different. Sometimes our passion will blaze out of control. Other times, it will be gentle and loving. But what we do together is for us. The bonds will strengthen between us a thousandfold each time we come together."

Win tucked a stray curl behind her ear. "I am selfish and actually happy I will be the first and only man you will make love with. Tonight starts our journey of a lifetime in love."

She trembled slightly. "Well, you better get started. I suppose we kiss to begin?"

He chuckled. "We will most certainly kiss. I plan to kiss you in places you never dreamed of being kissed."

Her puzzled look was priceless.

He dipped his head and took her mouth in a slow, tantalizing kiss. Inside him, something uncoiled. He couldn't put a name to it but it made him relax.

Win knew he had come home. For Sera would always be his home.

Their kisses heated and his fingers found the knot on her dressing gown, slowly untying it. His hands ran up the length of her arms to her shoulders and then he tugged on the dressing gown, slipping it from her shoulders, removing it and tossing it aside.

She stood in her night rail now and he wanted that gone, as well. He wanted to see every bit of her beautiful flesh. Knowing she might be a little shy, though, he continued kissing her, deepening those kisses until she was as needy as he was. He bent and caught the hem of the gown and pulled it up, over her head, and letting it flutter to the ground.

Win studied her naked body a moment. "You are magnificent."

"You don't think I have . . . too many curves?" she asked, uncertainty in her voice.

His hands moved up and down the curve of her hips. "You are perfect in every way, Sera. Perfect for me."

Sweeping her up, he carried her to the bed and placed her upon it. He threw off his banyan and saw her eyes widen. Win stood a moment, allowing her to take him in, including his cock, which now stood at attention. Seeking attention. From her.

But that would have to wait. For now, he wanted to give her exquisite pleasure.

"You are . . ." Her voice trailed off and she shook her head in wonder. "You are simply perfect, Win."

He joined her on the bed. "Then we are well matched."

He kissed her long and hard, one hand roaming her back, the other kneading her breast. Breaking the kiss, he trailed his lips down the long column of her throat, finding her pulse beating out of control. He licked the spot and then nipped at it, hearing her sigh. Continuing down to her breasts, his tongue traced the curve of one, then the other. By now, Sera's fingers had pushed into his hair and tightened as he toyed with her nipple, first with his fingers and then his teeth. He might never get enough of her full breasts, so very tempting, and he spent a good while touching and sucking and kissing them.

Her body had grown hot under his touch and he placed a hand on her thigh, slowly dragging it up until it reached her core. Gliding his thumb along the seam of her sex, Sera whimpered.

"Do you like that?" he asked, his voice a low rumble.

"Yes," she whispered.

"Should I keep doing this?" He stroked her.

"Yes," she replied, more urgency in her voice.

"How about this?"

Win dipped a finger inside her and she gasped. He stroked deeply into her, plunging another finger inside and she shuddered.

"Oh, Win!"

He smiled and kissed her, allowing his tongue to mimic his fingers, teasing her until she panted breathlessly.

"What's happening?" she asked, a slight panic in her voice. "I feel . . . as if . . . oh, I don't know what! It's something building."

"Abandon yourself to the feeling, my love," he urged. "Fly high."

He continued caressing her and suddenly she cried out. "Win! Win! Oh, my goodness! Win!"

He watched her face as she rode the waves of pleasure for the first time, promising himself he would always touch her thus and move her to feel such wonders. Her body trembled, her nails digging into his shoulders, marking him as hers, always hers, forever and together one.

"Win . . ." Her voice was a sigh as she came back to earth.

But he wasn't through with her yet.

He dragged his tongue down her body, lower, lower, as she shivered. Then he reached her belly's button and swirled his tongue around it before dipping inside, hearing her giggle. He moved lower and she stiffened.

"Win, whatever are you doing now?"

"You liked it before with my fingers so I thought I would try my tongue."

"Win!" she protested. "That's indecent."

He lifted his head, his gaze penetrating hers. "Anything we do together is for us. For our pleasure. For two people who love one another. Nothing is sacrosanct. Your body is the temple I worship, Sera. Always."

Then she smiled at him and warmth filled Win. It permeated him, this tremendous happiness which Sera had brought into his life.

"All right," she agreed saucily. "Do with me as you see fit." Then her eyes lit with mischief. "But remember that I intend to also have my way with you."

By God, he loved this woman.

And he showed her how much he did.

His tongue found her core and teased it with quick strokes, then longer ones, before he dipped into the nectar. She tasted of Sera, his Sera, the joy and light of his life. His lips and teeth and tongue combined to bring her to a violent orgasm, rocking her body as she called out his name.

She went limp. He kissed his way back up her body and to her mouth and positioned himself at her entrance. He doubted she knew anything about what would occur next. He could talk to her and prepare her.

Or he could act.

He chose the latter and pushed into her. She squeaked, her nails digging into his shoulders a moment. He stilled.

"It hurt. I know it did. But it never does again. Of that, I promise you." Win kissed her brow.

"Everything was lovely until then," she said. "Are you certain . . ."

"More than certain. If you give me permission to move, I will show you."

Sera smiled up at him, love shining in her eyes. "You have permission to do whatever. I am yours, Win. In every way possible. Make me yours and you will be mine."

He moved and she said, "Oh! Do that again, please."

He did and she grinned. "I believe this is going to prove most interesting. Even entertaining."

Withdrawing, he plunged into her again and heard her sigh. They began a dance as old as time, yet one which seemed made just for them. By its end, Sera had picked up on the steps and moved as one with him, meeting each thrust, crying out in pleasure as they both reached their climax.

Win collapsed atop her a moment, driving her into the mattress, and then rolling to his side, bringing her along. He kissed her over and over, not ever thinking he could get enough of her.

"Do you think I was too loud?" she asked out of the blue. "I would hate if someone had overheard us."

He chuckled and kissed her hard. "If they did, they would be happy for us. We have found each other, Sera, and love has found us. I think our friends and family are delighted for us."

She snuggled close to him. "Will it always be this way? Will you want me as much as you did this night?"

He smoothed her hair and then lovingly stroked her back. "I will want you more each time we come together."

"Am I really enough for you, Win?" she asked, a bit of doubt in her voice.

"You are more than enough for me, Sera. Tonight, I shared with the love of my life the most important thing that can occur between a man and a woman. Have I coupled with other women before? Yes. But have I ever made love before tonight? No."

He framed her face with his hands. "You are the one who has made a difference in my life, Sera Nicholls. You are the woman I love. And I will love you more and more and more with the passing of each day."

"Good. Because I love you, Win. With all my heart. And I will never let you go."

He basked in the afterglow of their love and they talked of things to come. Their hopes and dreams. Where they would be in a year. Five years. Ten. A lifetime from now.

"Go to sleep," he whispered.

Her fingers, which stroked his chest, finally stilled and she began breathing evenly. Win slipped from the bed and kissed her brow, covering her glorious, naked form with the bedclothes. He would leave her now—but it would be the last time he did so. Yes, she would have her own rooms and store her wardrobe and jewels within them. She would even dress each day in them. But her nights would always be spent with him. She would be the last thing he felt before he dropped into slumber and the first thing he would feel upon awakening.

He gazed down at her sleeping form, reluctant to leave her. He said a quick prayer, though he had never been much of a praying man, thanking God for Sera coming into his life and for bringing love into his heart.

Win now understood what the Second Sons had. A lasting love with a woman who was their entire life. He had been a fool to think so little of love. Now, he saw it was the most powerful thing in the world. He could conquer mountains for Sera, all because she loved him.

Bending, he pressed his lips against her cheek and she sighed.

"Goodnight, my love, my dearest, sweetest love."

Win retreated to his own bedchamber. As he placed his head on his pillow, he caught the scent of jasmine—and smiled.

He dreamed of Sera.

CHAPTER TWENTY-SEVEN

A FLURRY OF activity consumed Sera's bedchamber, with the four wives of the Second Sons preparing her for her wedding as Aunt Phyllis watched in approval.

Adalyn touched Sera's shoulder. "I am going downstairs to make certain everything is prepared in the garden for the ceremony."

"Thank you for organizing everything in regard to this wedding," she said as Adalyn kissed her cheek.

Though she had only known Adalyn and Louisa for a short while, Sera already felt close to them. She knew in the years to come she would be celebrating many occasions with them, along with Minta and Tessa, as their families grew.

Adalyn waddled away and once the door closed, Tessa said, "I believe she is carrying twins. She wasn't nearly so large when she was carrying Edwin. And she still has until November."

"Do twins run in her family? Or Everett's?" asked Louisa.

"Not that I know of," Minta said. "That would be more likely with Sera or me since we are twins." Minta rubbed her belly, which was just starting to protrude. "I had not given a thought to having more than one babe. I suppose I should have thought it is a possibility."

Aunt Phyllis put her arm about Minta's shoulders. "One day at a time, my darling. I remember when your mother had the two of you. It became obvious in those last few months that there would be more than one of you. Try not to worry."

Tessa smoothed a stray lock of Sera's hair, securing it with a pin. "Well, what do you think?"

Sera gazed at her image and saw not only how well Tessa had dressed her hair—but that she glowed with happiness.

"You did an excellent job, Tessa," she praised and stood, smoothing her gown.

"We should all go downstairs and give Sera a few moments to collect herself," Louisa advised.

They each came and embraced her, wishing her the best, and then Sera found herself alone. She savored the quiet, knowing the rest of the afternoon would be busy.

But what she looked forward to was tonight and being with Win.

He hadn't come to her bed last night. He had told her she needed to get her rest—because he was going to keep her awake until dawn, making love to her in every way she could imagine.

A knock sounded on the door and Sera went to answer it. Uncle West stood there, beaming at her.

"Ah, Sera. You look lovely," he praised. "And so very happy."

"I am happy, Uncle. More than I could have ever imagined possible."

"Are you ready to be escorted to your groom?" He offered his arm to her.

"I most certainly am," she said with enthusiasm.

As they made their way down the corridor, he said, "I am pleased His Grace will become your husband. I like him, Sera. He is a good man."

"He is, Uncle West. The very best."

"Your parents will like him, as they will Lord Kingston. I am sorry they had to miss both their daughters' weddings."

"They will return to England next spring. Mama's last letter guaranteed they would be here no later than May."

"Then they will meet their first grandchild," he said. "Who

knows? You may have one of your own by then."

It was her greatest hope. She had wondered if she and Win had already made a babe.

They descended the stairs and several of the servants were lined up to see her. She smiled at them and thanked them for preparing everything today. Then Uncle West led her from the house and toward the Woodbridge gardens. Sera spied an arch and they walked through it, down a path strewn with petals. When they reached a gazebo, she saw a group gathered.

Her eyes went straight to Win. He was so tall and broad and so very handsome that it made her teeth ache, as if she'd eaten too many sweets. Freddie and Charlie stood on either side of him, both grinning from ear to ear. Charlie even waved to her as she floated down the path. He had lost a tooth the previous evening and as he smiled at her, she saw the gap.

Uncle West handed her over and Win clasped her hand in his, warm and reassuring. They spoke their vows before the clergy-man as their friends and family looked on. The minister pronounced them man and wife and Win framed her face in his hands and kissed her for a long moment.

"Do we get cake now?" Freddie asked, causing Win to break the kiss as he laughed heartily.

"Yes to cake—but the other food comes first. Cake is last. You always save the best for last," Win pronounced.

He took Freddie's hand in his and Sera's in his other. She clasped Charlie's hand and they went back up the garden path, the scent of roses hanging in the air. The others followed and, soon, they made merry at the wedding breakfast. Win had a few locals come and play for them. A short time later, there was dancing and toasts. Sera had never felt so alive.

Win claimed everyone's attention. "I want to thank Lord Westlake for not throwing me out when I followed Sera to London. I wish to thank the four wives of the Second Sons for accepting me and offering their friendship to Sera. I give thanks to the Second Sons for, in them, I have found the family I never had."

He turned and looked at her with a love so powerful, it almost drove Sera to her knees.

"Most of all, I want to thank Sera for coming into my life and bringing love and laughter. My future is bright because it is tied to this woman."

He pulled her to him for a long, lovely kiss as the others cheered.

Sera knew complete happiness in that moment.

EPILOGUE

Three months later

T HE CARRIAGE NEARED Woodbridge and Win thought how different coming home this time was than any before. He was returning with his wife and two nephews after their honeymoon, which had taken them to his other estates. It had been good see them and meet the staff who managed each place. Sera had particularly grown fond of his estate near Bristol and he decided they would have to visit it more often in the future.

He glanced down at his sleeping wife, whose head was pillowed in his lap. She was with child now. It was very early but she already awoke nauseated and emptied her belly every morning. He brushed back a lock of hair from her face as love swelled in his heart.

Win glanced across at the two young boys, also sleep. The weeks away from Woodbridge with them had been good ones. They truly believed they were a part of his family now. Charlie had confessed when they were alone one day that he and his brother had feared Win might give them up, as the Birdwells had. Win dispelled that notion and told him that he and Sera loved them tremendously and would never be parted from them.

Freddie continued to show signs of being skilled with numbers, while Charlie had an affinity with animals. He could see them in contributing roles to his estates as the years passed.

His eyes went to where his hand rested on Sera's belly. To think a life grew within her was a bit astonishing. He wondered if it would be a boy or girl and his heart told him it didn't matter. The child would be loved, as would all the ones which followed.

Sera stirred, her eyelids fluttering and then opening. He helped her to sit up.

"We are almost home," he told her, pressing a kiss to her brow.

"I am ready to be home after traveling so much. It was good to see all your estates, though, Win."

"Our estates, love. Everything I have is yours."

She tugged on his cravat, bringing him down for a tender kiss.

He broke it. "There will be plenty more of that when we arrive. I believe you will need to get some rest after so long a journey. Naturally, I will rest with you."

She giggled. "Something tells me there won't be much rest, Your Grace."

"Ah, I married such a clever girl." He kissed her again.

"We should wake the boys," she said. "They can be a bit cranky when they first awaken. I want them to make a good impression upon Miss Birmingham."

The governess had written to them, saying she would be at Woodbridge by the time they arrived. Sera had written back, telling her they would probably not arrive until mid-October but that Miss Birmingham was welcome to come as soon as she wished and become acquainted with the estate.

Win helped Sera sit up and then reached across, waking each boy. They yawned sleepily and then grew excited as they realized their long trip had almost come to an end.

"Remember, Miss Birmingham will be here," Sera reminded. "You want to be on your best behavior for her."

"I like you being our governess, Sera," Freddie whined.

"I will still read with you. We can also go out on the estate for a few lessons," she promised.

"I've missed Brownie," Charlie said. "I can't wait to ride him again."

They had continued with riding lessons for the boys and Win had also taught them to fish during their trip. Sera had continued working with them on their letters and numbers and both boys were reading simple books now.

The carriage made its final turn and went up the drive toward the main house. The boys began jumping excitedly on the seats. Win didn't have the heart to make them be still. Their exuberance was part of their charm.

As the vehicle came to a halt, he saw a good portion of servants gathered in two lines, waiting to greet them after their long sojourn. The door opened and Freddie bounded down the stairs, followed by Charlie. Win went next and handed Sera down.

"Greetings!" he called to those assembled. "Thank you for welcoming us upon our return."

Farmwell stepped forward. "It is good to have you home again, Your Graces."

"It is very good to be home, Farmwell," Win told the butler.

He led Sera and his nephews to Miss Birmingham and made the introductions. The boys made him proud with their bows and offering of hands to their new governess.

"Have you been in residence long, Miss Birmingham?" he asked.

"Just two days, Your Grace." The governess looked to her charges. "I was hoping Charlie and Freddie would be able to show me about the estate now. After all, they have been in a cramped carriage for a long time. It would do them good to stretch their legs a bit."

"Can we?" Freddie asked. "Show Miss Birmingham around?"

"Of course," he said.

The three started off and Win led Sera inside.

She paused, looking around. "Once, I thought I would never set foot inside this foyer again." She turned to him. "I am sorry I was a coward and ran from you, Win. I am grateful you chased

230

after me."

He put his arms about her, bringing her close. "I would chase you to the ends of the earth, Your Grace. Even further if I had to."

Her radiant smile caused his heart to sing. "And I would let you catch me every single time."

Win bent and kissed his wife, his reason for living, the woman who had brought every true and good thing to him.

Breaking the kiss, he waggled his brows at her and said, "Are you ready for a rest, my love?"

Before she could reply, Win swept Sera into his arms and carried her up the staircase. To their bed. Where he would make love to her the entire afternoon.

And for a lifetime to come.

About the Author

Award-winning and internationally bestselling author Alexa Aston's historical romances use history as a backdrop to place her characters in extraordinary circumstances, where their intense desire for one another grows into the treasured gift of love.

She is the author of Regency and Medieval romance, including: Dukes of Distinction; Soldiers & Soulmates; The St. Clairs; The King's Cousins; and The Knights of Honor.

A native Texan, Alexa lives with her husband in a Dallas suburb, where she eats her fair share of dark chocolate and plots out stories while she walks every morning. She enjoys a good Netflix binge; travel; seafood; and can't get enough of *Survivor* or *The Crown*.

Lightning Source UK Ltd.
Milton Keynes UK
UKHW020850230822
407709UK00010B/782